Experiment X-One-Six

Experiment X-One-Six

Avril Sabine

Cracked Acorn Productions
Australia

Experiment X-One-Six

Published by

Cracked Acorn Productions

PO Box 1365

Gympie, Queensland 4570

Australia

email: office@crackedacornproductions.com

978-1-925131-46-8 (Kindle)

978-1-925617-53-5 (EPUB)

978-1-925131-47-5 (Print)

Genre: Urban Sci-Fi/Superheroes

For my Dad, who told me he believed in my writing by giving me a desktop computer when I was twenty-three, saying that if I was serious about my writing I needed it. Thank you. Not only for the computer, but for all you taught me when I was a child. Including how to wire up my dollhouse for lights, use power tools, find answers in books and especially for listening to me.

I miss you.

When Douglas bursts into the bookstore, Gina is meant to be on the beach enjoying the end of the school holidays before she starts her final year of high school, not working an extra shift. Along with two teenage boys, she's kidnapped by a crazy gunman talking about human experimentation and a highly contagious virus that was meant to create a super army. Instead it brings death. If the virus doesn't kill you, those that want it kept secret will.

*

This story was written by an Australian author using Australian spelling.

Chapter One

Gina stared through her reflection in the front window of the bookstore to the people outside. People who had more sense than to be stuck inside when it was a summer day made for a trip to the beach. She sighed. She'd been ready to head to the beach with friends. Then her sister had rung. The girl rostered to work today had called in sick.

Yeah, right. Probably sick of being inside and dying for a day at the beach. Too bad she'd made plans. According to her parents, family stuck together. So she was stuck working in the bookstore instead of going to the beach.

"Gina? You going to daydream all day or are you actually going to earn the money I'm paying you?"

Gina turned to face her oldest sister. Leona was twenty-six and had the same olive skin as Gina and her twenty-two-year-old sister Renata. The straight black hair, which all three sisters had inherited, was worn short to bob around Leona's face. Gina, like Renata, preferred hers long, all one length and pulled back into a ponytail, leaving her forehead visible. She stared into the dark brown eyes of her sister, identical to her own, and sighed again. It was the last week of the school holidays. Could they blame her for being annoyed she had to work? Didn't they care she had plans of her own?

"It's not like we've got any customers in here at the moment. Or anything that needs doing." Gina's gesture swept the store. The aisles were empty of people, the books on the timber shelves neatly arranged and the beige carpet was clean.

"Then you won't find it too taxing to take care of things while I dash out to the loo."

Gina shrugged. "Whatever."

Leona stared at her for a moment, eyes narrowed. "I can't wait until you're past these drama years."

Gina managed not to fling a reply at her sister's back. Only because she was looking forward to a few minutes by herself. She clearly remembered what her sister had been like as a teenager and she certainly hadn't been mellow.

Leaning her elbows on the counter near the cash register, she went back to gazing wistfully outside.

Less than one week and she'd be in year twelve. There wouldn't be much time for going to the beach then. Her last year of school and she didn't have a clue what she was going to do with the rest of her life. All she knew was that she wasn't going to take Nonna's advice. She wasn't about to find a nice Italian boy and settle down. No way. Nonna was so last century. She wouldn't be seventeen for another three days. Weddings were a long way off, if ever. Look what had happened to Leona. She used to be fun, now she sounded like their mum.

She straightened as the door swung open and a boy walked in. He blinked as his eyes became accustomed to the dimness of the store. He was tall and slim and his brown hair had been tossed carelessly about by the breeze outside. When his gaze landed on her he smiled, losing the slightly lost look he'd worn.

Gina couldn't help admiring his smile as he strode towards the counter and his smile became a grin. "Hi. Can I help you?" Her own lips curved into a smile. That wasn't all that was worth admiring. Maybe the day wouldn't be a waste after all. She wondered if Leona would go mad at her if she asked him for his number.

"I hope so." He pulled a crumpled piece of paper from his jeans' pocket. "One of my mates swears I have to read this book." He glanced down as his fingers smoothed the creases from the paper.

Gina opened her mouth to comment on how blue his eyes were then quickly closed it as she reminded herself she wasn't amongst her large, noisy and vocal family right now. She reached for the piece of paper instead. "Let me see."

Before she had a chance to look, the door burst open again and another boy strode in. Gina nearly groaned as she recognised him. All round athlete, overly sure of himself, in your face and didn't know the meaning of the word no, Connor Davis. Dark brown hair always perfectly styled, square jaw line and a body that most of the girls at school obsessed about. You'd think someone who was kept back in primary school would have been tormented, but not Connor. Everybody loved him. Which was part of the reason she avoided him. People like that expected others to fawn over them and she wasn't very good at hero worship. She tended to say the wrong thing and often struggled to be tactful. Like right now. She was pretty certain her sister would get mad if she told Connor to come back later.

"Gina." Connor leaned on the counter, ignoring the other boy already there.

"I'll be with you in just a moment." Gina made her

voice as frosty as possible and turned pointedly back to her first customer.

"Come on, Gina. I'm running late. I need to pick up a book for Mum. It's her birthday tomorrow." Connor reached out, resting his hand on her arm.

Gina looked pointedly at where his hand continued to rest on her. "I will be with you in a minute, Connor." She made her words slower and more precise.

Connor chuckled and, removing his hand, turned to the other boy. "You don't mind do you, mate? I'm in a bit of a hurry." He turned back to Gina before the boy had a chance to speak. "I don't care what you pick out for Mum. She's into true crime. Something not long out so she's less likely to have read it."

Gina opened her mouth to tell Connor to wait, but the front door swung open and her gaze was drawn to a man in a crumpled suit. As if she didn't have enough customers already in the store. Knowing her sister, she'd probably run into one of her friends and was chatting away instead of hurrying back, thinking the day had remained quiet.

Both boys turned to see who had entered the store and the three of them stared at the man who staggered in. His hair was thinning and his forehead was beaded with sweat, his face flushed. He glanced around the store and took several steps towards them. The door swung shut behind him and he drew a gun from the pocket of his jacket.

"Stay calm. I don't want to hurt anyone. You, girl. Is there another way out of here?"

Gina's mouth remained open and she could only nod. The piece of paper slipped from her fingers and drifted to the counter as she struggled to grasp what was happening. It was all too surreal.

"Lead the way then. All of you. And put your hands on your heads. No sudden movements." The man gestured to each of them with the gun.

They put their hands on their heads and Gina led the way to the storeroom in a daze. She was surprised at how hard her body trembled. Each step an effort. She couldn't believe this was happening. Things like this didn't happen to ordinary people like her. Her family had lived in Brisbane for decades. Ever since Nonna and Nonno had come out from Italy. And nothing like this had ever happened to any of them.

"Hurry up, girl. If another person comes into the shop, I'm shooting them."

Gina went light headed and stumbled forward quickly. Don't come back. Don't come back. Stay away, Leona. She chanted the words over and over in her mind as her trembling fingers opened the door at the back of the store and she stepped inside the book-strewn room. She slid through the towers of books and boxes and opened the rear door.

"Outside. All of you. Put your hands down first. But keep them in sight. And remember, even if you can't see it, I've got my gun pointed at you." The man slid the gun into his jacket pocket.

Gina blinked rapidly as she stepped outside. She looked at the short shadow she cast on the bitumen of the car park and wondered what her sister would think when she returned to find her missing.

"Any of you have a car here?"

"I do." Connor's voice was almost a squeak. He cleared his throat and shot a hasty look towards Gina.

She almost shook her head, unable to believe he was worrying about his image at a time like this. Then her gaze returned to the gunman and she swallowed hard. She wasn't seventeen yet. Three more days. She wanted to live to see her seventeenth birthday. This wasn't right. Nothing about this day had been right. It should have been someone else here today. Not her.

"Where is it? Which car?" The man pulled a handkerchief from his pocket and mopped his forehead. A shudder went through him and he started coughing.

Maybe he'd shoot himself. Gina sent quick looks in his direction. No such luck. The coughing fit subsided along with her hopes.

"Lead the way, boy. No time to waste. Come on. They're getting closer. I can hear them."

Gina glanced around. Hear them! The man was a lunatic. She couldn't hear anyone. But she wasn't going to argue with him. Instead, she forced herself to follow Connor, who now led the way. She glanced towards the other boy. His skin had lost what little colour it had and he looked as ill as she felt.

Connor pulled keys from his pocket as they approached a four-wheel-drive parked crookedly in two parking bays. He unlocked the doors with a push of a button and looked towards the gunman.

"Get in the car, boy. You're driving. You can get in the front too." He pointed towards the other boy before he turned to Gina. "You're in the back seat with me."

Gina's mouth dried at the thought of sitting next to him. Instead she focused on the vehicle. She opened the door, the new car smell hitting her. Nothing like the worn sedan her parents drove. She wondered if it was Connor's or if it belonged to his parents. She pulled on the seat belt as soon as she was in and stared ahead as the man climbed in beside her. The seam along the edge of the seat took all her attention. It was better to focus on absolutely anything else rather than the man sitting beside her. She didn't want to think about what he planned to do with them. If she didn't think of more than one second ahead, she might actually make it through the day.

"Well? Get moving. We can't sit here all day." He took the gun from his pocket and rested it on his lap. He shrugged out of a small backpack, which Gina noticed for the first time, before buckling up.

Connor started the vehicle. "Wh… Where to?"

"Drive. I'll tell you when I want you to change directions."

Gina stared at the back door of the bookstore, her breath catching in her throat when her sister appeared in it, running a hand through her hair as she glanced around. Her mouth became a circle of surprise when she spotted Gina in the vehicle. Gina could only stare helplessly, wishing there was some way she could tell her sister what was happening. Then it was too late and they were out of the car park and turning left on the road. She closed her eyes and leaned back against the headrest. Please let me live. Let all of us live. Even Connor.

She felt moisture form behind her eyelids and squeezed them closed tighter. A single tear ran down her cheek, but she couldn't bring herself to wipe it away. Instead she turned her head a little more so the man wouldn't see the tear. He swore and she turned in time to see him clutch at his head, swearing again.

Still holding his head, he demanded, "Find a chemist, boy."

"I… I don't know wh… where one is." Connor glanced in the rear view mirror.

"Take the second right." The other boy spoke softly. "Halfway along the street on the left. They've got their own car park."

When Connor pulled into the car park of the pharmacy and turned off the engine, they all sat silently. Gina stared out her window at the people only a couple of metres from her, laughing and talking. Free people. People without a worry. People without a gun right next to them.

"You boy, what's your name?" They all turned to face the gunman as he gestured towards the front passenger, no longer clutching his head.

"Seth Lilly. What's yours?"

The man stared at him for a moment, startled. "Douglas. Douglas Finney." He sounded as if he was surprised to hear his own name. His expression hardened and he glared at Seth. "You will go in there and get me the strongest painkiller you can buy over the counter. Tell them your father is sick with a cold and has a headache. And…" he turned his gaze on Connor and Gina before he looked back at Seth. "If you don't return within ten minutes I kill the girl first. Another ten, the boy dies. Think you can live with them on your conscience?"

Seth shook his head. "It often takes ten minutes just to get served. I'll need twenty."

"Fifteen. Not a second longer." Douglas reached into his pocket and pulled out his wallet. He flipped it open and slid a hundred dollar note out. "Here. Now get out."

Chapter Two

Seth took the money and hopped out of the car with a glance at his watch. Douglas also looked at his own watch. Gina's gaze followed Seth until he disappeared inside the pharmacy. Would he be back? He owed them nothing. And he didn't know them well enough to risk his life for them. He could run. Call the police. Anything other than return to them.

Douglas glanced at his watch again before he looked pointedly at Gina. A fit of coughing had him doubling over. Gina watched as the gun slid off his lap and landed on the floor. She tensed, her gaze drawn to the weapon. Her breath stopped as Douglas reached out and picked up the gun. Her gaze followed it as he returned it to his lap. Slowly she looked up to find his gaze on her. She breathed in jerkily.

"What's your name, girl?"

"Gina Lancione." Her voice was a whisper.

"Don't even think about trying to touch my gun. Got it?"

Gina could only nod and was relieved when Douglas turned his feverish eyes on Connor.

"And you, boy. What's your name?"

"C… C… Connor Davis."

Douglas glanced at his watch. "Two minutes left." He turned to Gina. "Any preferences to where you want the bullet?"

Gina stared at him. Fear twisted in her stomach. The fear that had sat in her stomach like a lead weight ever since Douglas had pulled his gun on them. She spotted Seth running towards the car, a coloured paper bag in one hand, the logo of the pharmacy splashed across it. Relief rushed through her. She was glad she was sitting. Her entire body felt like wet spaghetti. It took every bit of effort to stay upright and not slide to the floor in a boneless puddle.

Seth opened the door and handed the paper bag through before he hopped in. "Your change is in the bag. There's all sorts of stuff in there. Vitamin C, something to dry your nose up, cough suppressant, painkillers, whatever the woman thought you'd need. I wasn't about to argue with her. I didn't think you'd want me to take any longer than necessary."

Douglas ignored Seth's words to rip the bag open. He pulled out a box and fumbled with the plastic wrap. "What are you waiting for, Connor? The end of the world? Start driving or I'll show you what it looks like." He finally opened the packet and pressed two capsules out of the card. He swallowed them dry, running the back of his hand across his forehead.

Connor pulled out onto the street and narrowly missed another car. His knuckles showed white from how hard he gripped the steering wheel. "Where do you want me to take you?" He managed to speak the words without stuttering, but there was still a wobble in his voice.

"West. Pick a town. Any town. I don't give a shit. Just go west." Douglas closed his eyes as another coughing fit wracked his body. He kept his eyes closed and pressed his head against the headrest once he'd stopped coughing. His right hand covered the gun that lay in his lap.

Seth turned on the navigator that was installed above the stereo and keyed in Roma.

"What if he doesn't want to go there?" Connor asked softly.

Seth shrugged. "At least it'll get us out of the city and headed west. It was the first town that came to mind."

Silence fell in the car. Thoughts rushed through Gina's head. Of her family. Friends. The plans she had for the year. She alternated between hoping she'd get through the day and believing it was only a matter of time before Douglas shot them. She jumped as he jerked up straight beside her.

He glared warily at each of them, his hand tightening around the gun. After a few seconds he relaxed his grip and his eyes became unfocused again. Silence filled the car until Seth turned in his seat to face Douglas. He was instantly alert, gun aimed at Seth.

"Think we could call into a McDonald's or something and get lunch? You certainly look like you need to get some food into you."

"I wouldn't choose that place if I wanted to eat." Douglas lowered the gun.

Seth shrugged. "Thought it'd be easiest. We can use the drive-through and you won't have to risk letting us out in public. Doesn't have to be Macca's. Could be KFC or Red." He shrugged again. "Any fast food place with a drive through would do. You also need something to drink. You don't want to become dehydrated."

Douglas pulled his wallet out again. He handed a fifty dollar note over this time. "First place we come to. But you try and pull any stunts and I will shoot. All of you. Understand?"

Seth nodded as he took the money. "Perfectly."

Within minutes they were at a McDonald's drive through. Connor ordered a burger and coke and Seth ordered more food than Gina thought necessary. He turned to her. "What about you?"

Gina shook her head. "I couldn't eat." She still couldn't manage more than a whisper. "My parents must be worried sick by now. They've probably called the cops." She glanced nervously at Douglas when he snarled.

"Four boxes of cookies," Seth called out as he leaned across Connor to be heard clearer.

"Will that… all?" a voice crackled over the speaker.

"Yeah. Thanks."

"That will… please… the… window." The crackle distorted the words, leaving only a few understandable.

Connor slowly drove forward, pulling up at the open window to be greeted by a smiling girl. She took the money he handed her and leaned against the windowsill once she'd given him his change and drinks. "You planning on a party? I love parties."

Connor smiled weakly. "Not really. Just big eaters."

The girl pouted theatrically, the smile still in her eyes. "If you want help getting a party together–"

Seth leaned in front of Connor. An easy smile flashed across his lips. "We've got other plans for tonight. We're going on holiday with our father." He gestured into the back seat with another easy grin. Douglas had his backpack on his lap to hide the gun.

"Oh, that's too bad." The girl turned and took the three paper bags she was handed and held them out one at a time for Connor to take. "Maybe you'll call back in here on your way home." Her gaze lingered on Connor.

Connor forced another smile and slowly drove forward. He pressed the button to put his window up and glanced up the road before he pulled onto it.

Seth held a burger out to Douglas who shook his head. "What about fries?"

Douglas waved him away, doubling over with another coughing fit.

Seth frowned. "Maybe you should have some of that cough suppressant. You sound like you're about to lose a lung."

Douglas only grunted, but he did rummage around in the bag from the pharmacy and pulled out a bottle. He gave it a shake before he broke the seal, opened it and had a mouthful. He grimaced and replaced the cap.

Seth held a packet of fries out to Gina. "You want some?"

Gina shook her head, the smell of food making her stomach heave. She pressed the window button in her door until it was down a few centimetres. "Maybe later." She didn't think so. Her stomach was already crowded with fear. There wasn't room for food too.

"Pull up at the next public phone. You kids can ring home. I don't care what you tell your parents. Make something up. I don't want anyone looking for you yet." Douglas eyed each of them. "And I'll be standing beside you while you ring. One wrong word and it's all over."

Gina's mind whirled. How was she meant to explain this to her parents? She was never allowed anywhere unless her parents had thoroughly checked out every aspect of it. Even new friends were subjected to major questioning before she could hang out with them. She shuddered as she recalled the last time she'd brought a new friend home.

Her parents, her grandparents, one of her uncles, two older cousins and both her sisters had been there. Michelle, the girl she'd taken home, had been peppered with so many questions she'd avoided Gina ever since. Gina often wondered what Michelle had told her other friends about the afternoon, but guessed she was probably better off not knowing.

They reached a public phone before Gina could think of a plausible reason for having run out on her sister. There was none. How could she even think of ringing her parents when she didn't know what to tell them?

"Get out. All of you. Seth. You ring home first." Douglas shoved the gun in his pocket and held his hand out to Connor. "The car keys."

Connor's hand shook as he handed them over. He lurched out of the car and stood by the phone as Seth pushed the coin Douglas had given him, into the slot.

"Hey Dad… nah, haven't been home all day… not very observant are you?" Seth laughed softly. "Anyway, just wanted to let you know I'd be away for a few days… yeah…. Giving a mate a hand to move… I know… sure… okay, I'll see you when I'm home… take care of yourself and say hello to Lucy for me…yeah… bye." He hung up the phone and turned to face Douglas, his smile gone. "Happy?"

"No. Now Gina, you ring home. Then Connor." Douglas held out a coin to Gina.

She reluctantly took it and turned to use the phone when a voice had her whirling around. Her fingers closed tightly on the coin, her heart speeding up. It was a girl with blond hair and green eyes. Gina took a deep breath and hoped the girl would say nothing to upset Douglas.

"Excuse me. I seem to be a bit lost. Even though it's been less than a year since I was last here. Are any of you locals?" The girl smiled, glancing around the circle they formed.

Seth grinned. "We're not from here, but we happen to have a navigator. Hey, Dad." He turned towards Douglas. "Let's give her a hand to find where she needs to go." His gaze clashed with Douglas'. "We'd be happy to do it."

With a pointed look at Gina, Douglas opened up the front passenger door of the car and slid in. Seth turned towards Gina and mouthed the word 'ring' before he ushered the girl over to the vehicle.

Gina needed no more urging. She dropped the coin into the slot and rang home.

"Hello?"

"Mama." Her voice broke on the word.

"Gina! Where are you? What's going on? Your sister rang here, hysterical. What's happening, bambina?"

"He has a gun. I can't talk long. He forced us to go with him. From the shop."

"Gun!"

"Shh. I don't know where he's taking us. Connor Davis from school is with me. And Seth Lilly. I don't know him."

"Talk up, Gina. I can barely hear you."

"I can't." Tears started to track down her cheeks, cold against her warm skin as soon as the breeze touched them.

"Where is he? Where are you?"

"I don't know. But you can't call the police. His name is Douglas Finney. If he was to find out… I don't… oh Mama, I don't know what to do."

"Gina."

Connor whispered in her ear. "Tell her my car can be tracked."

"Connor's car can be tracked. Get a hold of his parents. They're doctors."

A touch on Gina's shoulder made her turn to face Connor. He glanced back to where Douglas was getting out of the car. A shudder went through Gina and she turned her back on him. "I'm sorry I took off like that, Mum. I'm staying with friends."

"He's there?"

"I'm not sure when I'll be home. I love you, Mama." Gina hung up the phone, spun away and ran into Seth. He steadied her as she wiped the back of her hand across her eyes. Pulling away from him, she blinked her eyes until her vision was no longer blurred. A glance around told her the girl was gone.

"You better not have told them anything," Douglas warned.

Gina shook her head. She sniffed, wishing she had a tissue.

Douglas turned to Connor. "Your turn."

Connor took the coin Douglas held out and picked up the phone. He tapped his fingers on the top of the phone as he waited. "Mum, I know I said I'd be home tomorrow night for your birthday, but something came up. It's the last week of the school holidays so I didn't think you'd mind. Anyway, I won't be home for a few days. Have a good birthday tomorrow." He hung up the phone and turned to face Douglas. "Answering machine."

"Get back in the car. All of you." Douglas waited until they were seated before he hopped in the back and handed the keys to Connor. "Now drive."

Silence filled the vehicle and Gina stared out the window, the scene a blur as she fought back tears. Her family laughed and cried easily. But she wasn't going to give Douglas the satisfaction of seeing her tears. Not when he'd know they were from fear. As they were leaving the city behind, a noise made

Gina turn towards Douglas. She watched as he took another swig of the medicine. She looked away, hoping he overdosed on it. Her jaw tightened, anger and fear filling her. Why did she have to be at the shop today? She wasn't meant to have been there. Right this moment she should have been lying on the beach, half asleep after a morning spent in the water. It should have been someone else. For a moment she thought it would have been the girl who'd rung in sick. But what if it hadn't been? What if it had been her sister instead? No. Absolutely not. She couldn't even think it. Emptying her mind, she stared out the window.

Chapter Three

No one in the car spoke. The day slowly turned into night and Connor was forced to stop for petrol, parking near a brightly lit petrol bowser. It was Seth who was sent inside to pay for it. And Seth who suggested a bathroom stop so they didn't need to take another break until the next time the car needed filling.

Douglas sent Gina into the disabled toilet and stood outside the door. She quickly used the toilet, her gaze continually drawn to the door. She glanced in the mirror as she washed her hands and was surprised at the underlying pallor of her olive skin. There was an impatient rap on the door. Forcing herself to unlock it, she swung the door open to meet Douglas' glare. He turned from her and with a look at the boys gestured towards the men's toilet. He followed behind them. Just before the door closed, Douglas glanced back at her. "Remember." He patted his right pocket with his left hand. His right hand he kept in his pocket with the gun.

Gina had no doubt about what he was telling her. He had two hostages and their lives were now in her hands. She forced herself to stay still. Her legs ached with the need to run. But Seth hadn't when he'd had the chance. Twice now he'd returned instead of saving himself. She had to do the same. She couldn't repay him like that. It was nearly impossible. Several times her body jerked towards the car park and she had to make herself stop. She wrapped her arms around herself. Then the opportunity was gone. Douglas pushed the boys out the door in front of him. He froze in mid-step before running to the vehicle.

Douglas swung open the driver's door and pried at the dash. "You think you can use a tracking device to be rescued?" He bent by the rear tyre and placed the object in front of it. "Get in the car."

How had he known it had been activated? Gina hadn't heard anything.

When no one moved, Douglas spoke again. "Now! All of you in the back."

They hurried to obey and Douglas got in the front seat, holding the gun. He tore out of the car park before they were barely seated. Several minutes down the road, he pulled over, hopped out of the car and opened the back door. The interior light dispelled the darkness as Douglas pulled four pairs of handcuffs from his backpack, a couple of pairs still left in the bag.

"Hands out."

Sitting between the two boys Gina stared at the handcuffs, wishing they'd tried to overpower Douglas while they'd all been sitting together in the back. It hadn't occurred to her. The sight of the gun tended to make her mind go blank. She was fairly certain Connor had the same problem, but she wasn't sure about Seth who seemed too calm considering the situation.

"We didn't activate it. Only my parents can. I guess they were checking up on me." Connor held his hands out in front of him. "They do that sometimes."

Gina held her hands out too and bit her lip when the handcuffs snapped closed on her wrists. Douglas linked them together then chained the boy's wrists to the door handles. He slammed the doors closed and clambered back in the driver's seat, coughing and gasping for breath. The cold metal sent a shiver through her. What kind of person carried not only a gun but also handcuffs? And more than a single pair.

"Why did you kidnap us? Why don't you let us go

now?" Seth's voice was quiet and even. "Surely you don't need us."

"Insurance. Maybe they'll think twice about killing kids. They probably won't, but if nothing else, I might be able to use you to slow them down. They're not going to exterminate me like the rest of the program. I'm too smart for them." Douglas nodded vehemently. "Too smart." He fell silent again, his head dropped forward slightly, only to jerk back again. He started the vehicle and pulled out onto the road.

Gina shuddered every time she saw Douglas appear to drift off. Seth linked his fingers in hers and she looked over at him. She couldn't make out his expression in the dim light from the dash, but when he squeezed her hand, she didn't feel so alone. There were three of them. And only one of him. They were handcuffed to each other and the doors and Douglas had a gun. But it was still three to one. Surely those odds must count for something.

It was well after midnight when Douglas pulled up at a rest area. He parked as far from the road as possible, under the deep shadows of a broad tree. He turned off the engine, the headlights next. Gina tensed as the car was plunged into darkness. Seth's fingers tightened on hers. She forced herself to relax. All she could hear was the sound of their breathing.

Hers was a little fast so she forced herself to slow it down, matching Seth's even pace. Connor's was a touch ragged, but Douglas sounded the worst of them all. His breath came in gasps, like each one was a struggle. It was punctuated by coughs that seemed to involve his entire body, almost ripping it apart.

As the darkness continued and nothing happened Gina relaxed even more, eventually falling asleep. It wasn't until the sky began to lighten that she slowly woke. She tried to reach up and rub the sleep from her eyes and was jolted fully awake by a weight dragging at her wrist. She stared at the handcuff that joined her to Connor. When Seth's fingers brushed across hers, she turned her head to look at him. He pursed his lips as if to shush her, no sound escaping. He glanced towards Douglas.

Gina turned her head and was shocked to find Douglas huddled in the front passenger seat, a picnic blanket over him as he shivered uncontrollably. His eyes were closed tight and his breathing seemed worse. She hadn't thought that possible. She turned back to Seth and placed her lips against his ear.

"Do you think he's dying?" She pulled back to meet Seth's clear blue eyes.

He shrugged and grinned before pressing his lips to her ear. "I hope so. Then we can search him for the key and get out of here."

Gina couldn't resist returning his grin. She turned with a frown when Connor tugged on her wrist. When he opened his mouth to talk, she pressed her hand against his lips, dragging his arm up with hers. She shook her head.

Connor pulled away from her hand to whisper in her ear. "What's going on?"

"I don't know." Gina grinned when Connor squirmed as she whispered in his ear. He glared at her and she forced down the laughter that threatened to bubble up. She sobered and glanced towards Douglas. He muttered under his breath as he tossed and turned in the confined space, still shivering.

Seth tugged on her arm. As soon as she turned to him, he pointed to the backpack lying on the driver's seat. Next he pointed to her and Connor, who sat behind it. Gina nodded. She turned to Connor who also nodded and they both eased forward on the seat. It was a stretch and Gina held her breath the entire time. Her gaze travelled between the backpack and Douglas. When she had it, she handed it to Seth.

He grinned at her before he bent his head over the bag. He pulled out a change of clothes, an envelope of money, a leather notebook, a small laptop, two pairs of handcuffs and a toiletries bag. Returning everything carefully, he left only the notebook out. He made a quick search of the three pockets on the outside of the backpack. Waving the little key he found, he shook his head when Connor held up his hand.

Seth slipped the key into a front pocket of his jeans, straightening out a little so he could. He handed the bag back to Gina and pointed to the front seat. Holding her breath, she and Connor returned it to the same position. Next, Seth delved into the paper bags on the floor and handed out boxes of cookies and bottles of water.

Gina was surprised to find she was hungry. Within minutes she'd eaten the cookies and drunk half the water. She bit back a groan as her bladder protested. Peering out the window, she spotted a toilet block. She turned helplessly to Seth. He stared at Douglas for a moment before he nodded.

As soon as the handcuffs were off, Gina rubbed at her wrists. She pointed to Douglas, a questioning look on her face as she stared at Seth. He looked thoughtful for a moment before he nodded. He pressed at Gina's shoulder so she moved close to

Connor. She pushed Connor's arm away when he draped it around her shoulders to pull her against him.

Seth leaned into the front seat and slowly moved the picnic blanket aside. His hand shot out and grabbed the gun. He gave it to Gina. Next he snapped a handcuff to the door and onto Douglas' wrist. Douglas woke instantly, swinging his fist at Seth who tried to get out of the way, but was clipped on the jaw.

Seth swore and grabbed the gun off Gina to train it on Douglas. "Don't move. You're not the only one who knows how to use a gun."

Douglas froze instantly, staring at them a moment before he started to laugh. "You know, we're all dead. None of them survived. I thought I could make it. I injected myself with the drug they decided not to test. I thought I had a chance. But I don't. None of us do. We're all walking corpses. The moment that first major headache hits, you'll know I'm right. That's when you're contagious and that's when it hits you the hardest." He started to laugh again, but it turned into another coughing fit. "Shoot me. It'll be quicker than dying of this virus."

Gina pushed against Connor. "Let me out of here. I need to use the toilet." More importantly she needed to get away from the words Douglas hurled at them.

She ran towards the building and pushed the door open hard. She winced when the timber hit the block wall. It seemed ridiculously loud and she frowned at the brief ache it caused in her ears. She hurriedly used the toilet then washed her hands at the rust stained sink. The dingy mirror hanging on the wall made her look dreadful. She only hoped she didn't really look that bad. Not that it mattered. She'd spent a day in the dubious care of a mad gunman and had slept the night sitting up in a car. Who'd look presentable after that? She sighed. Connor did of course, but he wasn't normal. That was her theory and it wasn't like anyone was going to be able to disagree with her.

She shook her head and smiled wryly, still staring at herself in the mirror. "Who cares how he looks," she muttered under her breath.

Gina straightened her shoulders and pulled her hair band out. She ran her fingers through her hair before she pulled it into a ponytail. It looked slightly better. There was nothing she could do about her slept in clothes and the smell of fear that clung to her. She just wanted to go home. To her parents. Wanted to crawl onto her mum's generous lap and have her rock her like she had when she was a child. Rock all the fears, all the hurts and all the worries away.

"Gina? You okay?"

Seth's voice came from outside, but sounded much closer. Obviously limited sleep didn't agree with her. She took a steadying breath before she answered him. "I'm not so sure about that." She stepped outside. "Did he mean it? About the virus?"

Seth shrugged. "I don't know. But should we chance going home if we're carrying some disease that could wipe out mankind? Do you want to kill your family? Your friends?"

Gina's eyes closed. Seth's words rang in her mind like a line from a horror movie. "No." The word was a whisper.

"We should give it a day. See what develops. I want to read through the notebook. It's about something called Experiment X-One-Six."

"You think that's what this virus is?"

"I don't know. But we should get back to the vehicle before Connor accidentally shoots Douglas. He was shaking so hard when I gave him the gun I was worried he'd shoot himself too."

Gina smiled weakly. "Why haven't you been as scared as me and Connor?"

"I'll save that story for later."

"If we're still alive later."

Seth patted her on the shoulder. "We will be. We'll

have some vitamin C tablets. Don't they say you should have mega doses of them when you're sick?"

Gina allowed Seth to guide her back to the vehicle. She hid the smile that wanted to break free when she saw Connor with the gun aimed at Douglas. He willingly relinquished it to Seth and covered his face with his hands. He dropped his hands when Seth held five vitamin C tablets out to him.

Connor stared at the orange disks. "What're these for?"

Douglas laughed. "We even tried vitamin B injections. You're wasting your time. There's no cure. They thought it was the answer to everything. A super army. Instead it was a dead army."

"Enough with the crap." Connor tossed the tablets into his mouth as he glared at Douglas.

"What do you mean by super army?" Seth held the gun loosely in his hands.

"Genetic manipulation using viruses. Stronger and faster humans. Except the body can't handle the changes. It rejects them. Brings on flu type symptoms and you pass the mutating virus on. We didn't realise that to start with. Not until the scientists on the team started dropping like flies. Now I'm the last of the team. We thought we were so clever. Gods. We could manipulate the human body and design it to fit our specifications." Douglas laughed bitterly. "Guess the joke's on us. Nature won after all."

"Super powers? Like the incredible hulk or something?" Connor stared at Douglas.

"Grow up, kid. There's no such things as super powers. Didn't you listen?" Douglas' laugh was filled with hysteria. "Grow up. Guess that's not likely now. You better enjoy your last few days. This virus hits hard and fast."

"How easy is it to catch?" Seth demanded.

"You worried about Blondie? What was your plan? You used her as a distraction, didn't you? Doesn't seem to have done you much good. And it's signed her death warrant too."

Seth swore. "We've got to find her. Keep her away from other people so she doesn't infect them." He turned on the navigator and brought up the address she'd been looking for. "What about anyone else?"

Gina held her breath as she waited for the answer. Was everyone doomed? Had Douglas passed the virus on to others? Didn't he care that his actions could kill?

"Only her. I didn't become contagious until we first got in the car. When I needed painkillers. But it won't make any difference. She'll infect her family and they'll infect others. The first thing they'll do is rush her off to the hospital. Humans never learn. It's too late. Too, too, too late." Douglas started to laugh and ended up coughing again.

"He's getting worse." The dread that had momentarily left Gina's stomach when they'd retrieved the gun was back with a vengeance. The day hadn't looked so bad when they'd handcuffed Douglas to the door. Now. Well, now it was taking a rapid descent towards the day from hell.

"Shut the doors. We need to get back to the city. We have to find the girl." Seth gestured towards the address on the navigator. "If this is as bad as Douglas says, we might have wiped out most of the population by letting her near him." He sneezed.

Gina stared at him, her mouth hanging open. She finally managed to close it. "Please tell me you get hay fever or something."

Seth shook his head. "I'm rarely sick a day in my life."

The fear twisted in Gina's stomach and her breakfast threatened to return. She pressed her fingers to her mouth and tried to think of something else. Anything else. Her family. Thinking of them always cheered her, but not this time. She started picturing them as sick as Douglas. She squeezed her eyes shut and tried to see only blackness. Emptiness. Nothingness. Not my family. Please, not my family.

They had to find the girl in time. Before she infected anyone else. She ran her hand across her forehead and was surprised to find beads of sweat there. She groaned. Hadn't that been one of Douglas' symptoms yesterday? She was going to die. It wasn't going to be a bullet after all. No, it was going to be some stupid virus there was no cure for. And she didn't even know if she'd last the two days until her birthday. What would be the point anyway? See her seventeenth birthday only to die after she cut the cake? Not that she had any hopes of a birthday cake.

Gina buried her head in her hands and forced her breathing to slow. No point in hyperventilating and blacking out. Or was there? At least that would give her a few minutes where she wouldn't have to face the mess her life had become. No, it wasn't worth the headache. Gina's breath caught on a ragged gasp. Headache! Too late. There was already one starting. How bad did it have to be before she was contagious? She remembered how Douglas had grabbed at his head yesterday. She gently rubbed her temples. It didn't help.

Chapter Four

Late afternoon they pulled up in front of a lowset brick house with well tended gardens edging a low chain wire fence, having followed the directions to the address the girl had put in the navigator yesterday. Douglas had stopped talking hours ago, now only able to moan from his feverish nightmares. And the three of them were sick with classic flu symptoms.

Seth rested his head on the steering wheel. He'd taken turns with Connor to drive. Gina hadn't offered to take a turn as she didn't have her provisional license yet. Seth slowly lifted his head from the wheel. "Think someone can get the gate? I want to park in front of the garage. If we're lucky we'll be able to fit the four-wheel-drive in there."

Gina staggered out and grabbed the door when she nearly collapsed on the ground. She pushed the door closed, barely finding enough energy to make it move. Then she had the slow, agonising walk to the gate. It was only a couple of metres, but felt like a kilometre. She pulled the gate open wide and leaned against the fence as Seth drove in. She didn't even have the energy to shut the gate and hoped there were no dogs that would escape if she left it open.

As Gina reached the vehicle, Seth and Connor staggered out. The three of them supported each other to the front door and Seth pressed the buzzer. There was silence. Not a single sound. Although Gina would have been surprised to be able to hear anything over the intermittent buzzing in her ears. Seth knocked.

"I'm coming," a voice called irritably from inside.

"It's the girl." Seth's voice was filled with relief.

She swung the door open, a dressing gown wrapped tightly around her, eyes red and a tissue held at her nose. "Not you. Your dad gave this to me. I should have known better than to stand near someone with a cold. I always get them."

"Yeah, that's why we're here. We just found out it's highly contagious and deadly," Seth said.

The girl stared at him, her expression filled with disbelief. "You're joking, right?"

"You need to take mega doses of vitamin C." Seth took a step forward. "Can we come in?"

She shook her head, still gripping the door. "No. I don't know you. Besides, I can take care of myself. Gran has millions of bottles of vitamins and a huge one of vitamin C. I'll be right. Thanks for letting me know what to do."

Gina guessed from the tone of the girl's voice she didn't believe them.

"Is your gran here with you?" Seth placed his foot in the doorway.

The girl sneezed into the tissue and shook her head again. "Nah. Had a fall. That's why I'm here. She gets out of hospital next week. But someone had to come and look after her plants. Although if I feel like this for too long they'll probably all die."

"Did you come into contact with anyone else after you spoke to us yesterday?" Seth took a half step forward, his shoulder now past the doorframe.

From what Gina knew, after Douglas' limited explanation, the girl shouldn't be contagious yet. But she didn't blame Seth for being cautious. She didn't want anyone else catching it and risk them spreading it. She had too many family members to lose.

The girl shook her head. "Nah. I was exhausted. I'd been on a bus for nearly a day. I just wanted to come here and go straight to sleep. I didn't even bother with my bags. I left them in a locker at the bus terminal. I needed to walk after being on the bus for so long. Look, it was nice of you all to come check on me, but I've got to lie down. I'm so dizzy I'll probably crash soon." She moved the door a centimetre towards Seth, who stood in the way.

Seth held out his hand. "I'm Seth. This is Gina and Connor. Douglas is in the car. He's not really our father. In fact, you're probably going to think our entire first meeting with him is fabricated when we tell you about it."

Gina barely managed not to smile at Seth's patience in the face of the girl's polite efforts to get rid of him.

"Yeah, nice to meet you and all that. I'm Ashley and I've really got to lie down." She swayed in the doorway, one hand holding the door, the other hand shooting out to try and grab the doorframe. Missing it, she started to topple forward.

Connor and Seth tried to catch her, both managing to grab an arm. Ashley's limp body hung between them.

Seth glanced at Gina. "See if you can figure out where to stash the car. We'll get Ashley sorted."

She stood in the doorway a moment longer before she managed to follow them inside. She was half envious of Ashley. Collapsing sounded very tempting right now.

* * *

Gina clamped her hands over her ears as the kitchen timer went off again. At least this time the headache that had made her feel like her head was about to explode didn't seem as bad. She struggled to sit up in the armchair and glanced around the lounge room. Connor was sprawled on the floor with a pillow and several blankets. Seth was in the other armchair hunched over Douglas' laptop, a pile of loose pages spread around him and a pencil tucked behind his ear. The couch had blankets piled up on one end, but Ashley was nowhere in sight. She guessed Douglas was still chained up in the bathroom. Or at least she hoped he was.

She wondered where Ashley was. Hopefully she wasn't hysterical again like she had been when they'd finally convinced her earlier that they were all highly contagious and there was a good chance they'd die. That had been followed by Ashley wanting to punch Douglas, her anger fading when he'd remained unconscious while she'd yelled at him.

Gina reached down for the box of tissues on the floor near the armchair and pulled one out, wondering if she should look for Ashley. After gingerly blowing her nose, she dropped it in the nearly full wastepaper bin beside the chair. She was sick of blowing her nose. The tablets didn't seem to be doing much at all. Glaring at the large bottle of vitamin C sitting on the coffee table, she staggered over to it and tipped tablets into the lid. She popped five in her mouth and nudged Connor with her foot.

He rolled over to squint up at her. "Not again. They're not helping. I just want to sleep."

Gina ignored his complaints and held the lid out to him. "It's better than doing nothing."

Connor picked out five tablets. "You think Lilly," he sneered the name, "knows what he's talking about? He isn't a scientist. He's wasting his time reading all that crap."

Seth glanced up from the paper he scribbled on. "You wouldn't have a clue what you're talking about, Connie."

"If this is going to be the last day of my life, I don't want it filled with arguments." Gina glared at each of them in turn.

"I still think he's wasting his time," Connor muttered as he leaned back on the pillow, his hands behind his head.

"My time to waste." Seth glanced at the bottle Gina held. "Do I get any of them?" He smiled slightly.

Gina forced her aching body to walk the short distance and held out the lid. "I feel like I've been beaten up by a professional boxer."

Ashley stepped into the room. "Thought I heard the timer. I'm going to be peeing orange by tonight." She crossed the room, took her tablets and put them in her mouth one at a time. She held up the bottle she carried, condensation sliding down the glass. "Gran swears by this. Olive leaf extract. Thought it wouldn't hurt to try it."

Seth held out his hand for the bottle and read the information on the label. He shrugged. "I guess it won't hurt. Grab some glasses?"

Ashley pulled a tube of ointment from her dressing gown pocket. "Vitamin K cream. To help with the bruise on your jaw. Gran says it helps them disappear quicker."

"Your gran seems to have more crap than a chemist," Connor grumbled.

Ashley laughed. "You should see her bathroom cupboards. Enough stuff in them to heal half the city." Her smile vanished when she started to cough.

"I'll get some glasses." Gina forced her body to take her to the kitchen. Every step made her ache, but she'd had to leave the room. Ashley's cough had sounded exactly like the one Douglas had started with. And it terrified her. She didn't want to be sick. She automatically glanced up at the clock on the wall. Nearly another day over. She forced herself to stop thinking and opened cupboards instead. The glasses were behind the third door she tried. Grabbing four she returned to the lounge room.

Ashley tried to get off the couch she was slumped in, but her struggle seemed to have no effect. Gina took the glasses to Ashley who held out a trembling hand to take one.

"Thanks. I can't believe how weak I feel. Everything I catch always hits me so hard." Ashley smiled feebly, her small nose red and her green eyes watery. She poured a small amount of the greenish brown liquid into the glass she held and returned it to Gina.

Connor eyed the glass Gina handed him. "You don't expect me to drink that, do you?"

"It doesn't taste as bad as it looks." Ashley took another glass from Gina and poured a second dose of olive leaf extract.

"If I had access to the internet I could check out a couple of other theories I have. But I can't risk spreading this virus to the public." Seth put the laptop aside and stood up to stretch. He rubbed the back of his neck.

"Sorry about that," Ashley said. "Gran doesn't even own a mobile phone. She reckons modern technology is too confusing."

Connor downed the contents of his glass before taking a mobile phone from his pocket and holding it towards Seth. "Here. Try this. I've set it for calls to go directly to the message bank now so you shouldn't be interrupted. You can either use the phone to access the Internet or use it as a wireless hotspot for the laptop."

"You had a phone the whole time and you didn't use it?" Gina took the glass Ashley handed her and drank it. She made a face and quickly reached for the bottle of water near the armchair she'd been using.

"There was never a chance. I kept thinking it'd ring and he'd shoot me. It took me ages to get it turned off." Connor grimaced. "I hope that crap helps." He placed the glass on the floor, as far from him as possible.

Seth eyed the olive leaf extract in his glass before he drank it. He shrugged. "It wasn't that bad." He grinned. "I've certainly tasted worse."

"Haven't we all?" Ashley grinned as she drank hers. "My cooking for instance." She reached out and placed the glass and bottle on the coffee table that was in front of the couch.

Gina considered returning the bottle to the fridge, but it seemed like too much effort. Instead, she reset the kitchen timer and sat it near the two bottles and empty glass. She was barely settled in the armchair when Seth startled her.

"Yes. Excellent. An email from Dad." He started scribbling on another piece of paper.

"What?" Gina struggled out of the chair and staggered over to stand behind Seth. She frowned as she stared at Douglas' laptop he was using. "Who's Lucy?"

Seth shook his head as he continued to write.

"And why are you reading her email?" She leaned forward. "Her unexciting email. Who cares what colour a kitten is and how many the cat had?"

Seth laughed. "Code."

"Huh? That doesn't make any sense at all. What's a litter of cats code for?"

Connor sat up. "Didn't you say something about Lucy to your dad?"

"Who is Lou? Is that your dad's name?" Gina perched on the left arm of the chair. It made her feel light headed to stand up too long.

Seth shook his head. "No, his name is Anthony. Shush. It's hard enough to focus without everyone trying to distract me."

"Didn't you say it was an email from your dad? Why would he sign his name as Lou? And you still haven't told me who Lucy is." Gina started to tilt the screen back on the laptop so she could read it easier. She quickly pulled her fingers away when Seth hit them with his pencil.

As soon as he finished writing, Seth read over the page and shook his head. He looked around at the three faces turned to him. "Dad's a chemist."

"As in the man who fills prescriptions?" Ashley asked.

Seth smiled slightly and shook his head. "As in research and development. There've been times when he's been isolated at a research centre and all his correspondence has been read before it's been allowed out. He devised a code we could use so we could share things important to us without having to share them with anyone else."

"Why would he use a code to send you an email?" Gina asked.

"Yeah, that doesn't make sense," Ashley said.

"What did he say?" Connor grabbed a tissue from the box sitting near him. Boxes of tissues had been something else Ashley's gran had plenty of, along with toilet paper, cotton wool balls and ear buds.

"What mess have you got yourself into? Bugs

everywhere. Tail. Look to be the kind to kill first, ask questions later. How can I help?" Seth put the page on the keyboard. "Looks like they've connected us with Douglas. Whoever they are."

Ashley frowned. "What's he mean by bugs and tail? Makes me think of seafood."

Seth played with the pencil he still held. "Listening devices and people following his every move. I've got to send him a message. We have to figure out what to do. If this virus is as bad as Douglas said, they're going to be expecting one of two things. And when Douglas said army, I've got a feeling he wasn't talking defence forces. What I've read over sounds more like a foreign group using Australia as their base."

"Like terrorists?" Connor demanded.

Seth shrugged. "Possibly."

"So even if we live, we're going to have this group after us." Gina pressed her hand against her stomach. "I don't feel so good." She shakily stood up and rushed to the bathroom. She paused in the doorway to stare at Douglas who was slumped between the toilet and the wall, his hand chained to the handrail. It hadn't been the most ideal place to chain him, but with how weak he was, they'd hoped it would be enough to hold him. Seeing him there was enough to take her mind off wanting to throw up.

Chapter Five

It took Gina a moment to realise he was completely still and silent. Douglas no longer suffered from laboured breathing, but only because it looked like he no longer needed to breathe. She wasn't about to go any closer to check, but it seemed like it only took a day and a half to die once you became contagious. She wasn't ready to die. When a hand rested on her shoulder, she shrieked, spinning to face Seth.

"Are you okay?"

She shook her head and pointed towards Douglas.

Seth stepped into the bathroom and squatted beside the slumped body, pressing his fingers against Douglas' neck. He dropped his hand and looked up at her. "He's gone."

Gina winced and clapped her hands over her ears. "No need to shout."

Seth rose to his feet and crossed the room to stand

in front of her. "I didn't." When Gina opened her mouth to argue, Seth held up his hand. "It's a symptom. Some of the subjects complained of increased hearing. Others better sight, thermal imaging, x-ray vision, improved smell, perfect balance, jump long distances, better taste or control of body temperature. The symptoms were intermittent, but the scientists believed the subjects would eventually gain control over the abilities."

Gina shook her head. "I don't want this. The only thought on my mind yesterday was going to the beach and having a great seventeenth birthday. The last thing I need to think about is death or special abilities."

"When's your birthday?"

She stared at Seth for a moment. "Saturday." Two days away. She wasn't going to make it. Not if how quickly Douglas had died was any indication of the amount of time she had left.

Seth linked his fingers through hers. "You will see it and I will make sure you get to celebrate."

"You can't promise me that. Look what the virus does." She glanced at Douglas, unable to look at him for more than a second.

"You ready to come back to the lounge room and discuss a plan of action?"

"How old are you, Seth?"

"Seventeen. Eighteen in June."

"How do you know all this stuff? How can you make sense of those scientific notes?"

Seth grinned. "Ask my dad. He'll tell you I teethed on scientific notes. He had to do the experiments all over again since they were a sodden mess and couldn't be rescued."

Gina reluctantly returned his grin. "Fine. So you ingested scientific data when you were a baby and now you're Einstein and know everything about that sort of stuff."

Seth chuckled. "Not everything. Otherwise I wouldn't need to start uni this year. Come on then. Lounge room?"

Gina sighed. "I guess." She glanced at Douglas again. "But what are we going to do about him? Once it's the middle of the day even the air-con won't stop him from starting to stink."

"We'll put Douglas on our list of things to discuss. Coming?"

Gina slowly returned to the lounge room and paused in the doorway when she saw Connor with his arm around Ashley. She bit back the comment that came to mind as she stepped into the room. Flirting with girls was as natural as breathing for

Connor. And she couldn't exactly blame him. Ashley was striking with her petite features, slim body and long blond hair. She looked like she belonged in some beach movie. Well, she had before Douglas had infected her.

Seth took hold of Gina's hand and led her to the couch. He sat quietly for a moment before he spoke. "Douglas is dead."

"What? No! Not in Gran's bathroom." Ashley struggled to rise.

Connor pulled her back against him. "It's okay. We'll get him out of there."

Seth's voice remained quiet and steady. "I think we should fake our deaths until we have a better idea of what's going on and who we're up against."

"No!" Gina pulled back from Seth until she was prevented from moving further by the arm of the couch. "That'd kill my parents."

Seth met her gaze, his solemn. "Have you considered that you going home might kill them? These people have no conscience. They killed people to end this experiment. Donned their hazard suits and gave them lethal injections, burning the building down afterwards. Why do you think Douglas ran as soon as he realised he was sick? The experiment has been deemed a failure. All evidence of it is to be destroyed. We're now evidence."

"Not if we end up like Douglas we aren't," Connor muttered.

Ashley dropped her head in her hands. "I'm never going to do a favour for another person in my life. Look what happens to you. Why didn't I tell them to find a gardening service to take care of the place for the week? Then I'd be safe at home and never have met Douglas."

"Considering how short your life's likely to be, that won't be too hard a promise to keep," Connor muttered.

"Enough," Seth said sharply. "We're not going to die. We're going to survive this."

"What crap, Lilly. You want to lie to yourself, go right ahead. But I'm not going to believe it. I say we ditch the body and make ourselves comfortable and enjoy the last few days of our lives as best we can." He grinned. "I've got alcohol in the car. Should make the end more bearable."

"Forget it, Connie." Seth turned to face Gina. "We have a lot of things in our favour. The rest of the test subjects were between the ages of twenty-five and forty. The one that lasted the longest was the twenty-five-year-old. One of the things this virus does is affect the growth plates. The scientists couldn't understand why, but they had no choice other than to believe the findings of the autopsies. Our growth plates haven't hardened yet. I believe that's a positive. We're also healthy and I don't think we've got it as bad as Douglas and the ones they experimented on. Douglas made some notes about his own symptoms before he kidnapped us as shields. We're not as badly affected." Seth gestured towards the notebook near the laptop. "It's all in there if you want to read it. He was part of the experiment almost from the beginning."

Ashley looked towards the notebook. "I do. Science has always been my strongest subject. If I could have afforded to do uni this year I would have chosen something science based."

"How about you sum it up for those of us who aren't scientifically minded?" Gina asked.

"They used one of the complex viruses as a vector for the DNA they wanted to introduce into the body. It was changed and enhanced to rapidly attack and alter all cells. I think that was part of their problem. The process is too fast for most adult bodies to survive. Teens have an advantage. Our bodies are going through rapid changes already. That's another reason I think we'll be able to cope with it."

"How about next explanation you use normal English, Lilly?"

Seth ignored Connor. "Anyway, we still need to come to a decision on what to do."

"If it's terrorists, why don't we go to our army? That's if we live. Isn't that why we have them? To protect us?" Connor turned to Ashley. "Not that you have this problem. No one knows about you."

Seth shook his head. "Just because they're meant to protect us, doesn't mean they will. Who's to say they won't see the opportunity to use us as a weapon. Instant super army."

"We can't just disappear. I cannot spend the rest of my life never having anything to do with my family again. You can't expect it of me." Gina glared at Seth.

Seth stared at her quietly before nodding briefly. "Ring your parents. Tell them Douglas dumped us out in the middle of nowhere. That we're sick with a flu he had and Connor's phone is nearly out of charge. We'll find somewhere to ditch Douglas and leave everyone to wonder what happened to us. That'll give us time to figure out what to do without making any definite statements."

Gina hesitated. Her parents would be sick with worry. "I guess. It's better than letting them think I'm dead. And I seriously don't know how you'd arrange that scenario."

"My dad would help," Seth said.

"Unfair. Why would your dad get to know what's going on and not my parents? And what about Connor's parents? They must be frantic."

Connor laughed sharply. "Now that I'd love to see." He raised his head and straightened his shoulders, peering down his nose. "One must act with decorum at all times."

Ashley hit him lightly on the arm. "Oh they would not say that."

Connor nodded. "All the time. Although I can probably understand why they said that the last time. I was completely and utterly trashed and couldn't even figure out how to open the front door. Not to mention I stunk worse than a pub and was singing at the top of my lungs." He grinned unrepentantly.

Ashley giggled. "If it was my mum, she would have dumped a bucket of cold water over me, took my key and slammed the door shut."

"Certainly not. You mustn't make a spectacle of yourself in front of the neighbours." Connor made his haughty pose again.

"They sound like they're a hundred years old," Ashley said.

"Nearly. Connor Senior is sixty-two, but I think he was born a century too late."

Gina rose from the couch. "If we're going to do this, let's get it over and done with before I rethink it."

Seth walked to the armchair he'd been using and picked up the phone. "One minute and then hang up. I'm timing you."

Gina held out her hand for the phone. "They get longer than that on the movies."

"One minute." Seth held onto the phone until Gina nodded before he let her take it.

Her fingers trembled as she dialled her home number. She listened to it ring once.

"Hello?"

The fear and uncertainty in her mum's voice made her want to burst into tears. "Mama-"

"Gina. Where are you? Are you okay? All the family is here. We're praying for you, bambina."

"I can't talk for long. The battery on Connor's phone is nearly flat. I don't know where we are. Douglas ditched us and drove away. Some dirt road with no civilisation in sight. And I'm sick. We all are."

"What kind of sick, Gina?"

"Give me the phone, Ariana."

Gina smiled when she heard Nonna argue at her mum's refusal to hand it over. Some things never changed. "I guess it's the flu. I don't know. We all feel miserable. Just going to sit on the side of the road until someone comes along. Too sick to do anything else."

"Bambina, you have to move. As soon as it's daylight. Dirt roads aren't always used regularly."

"Mama, I-" she broke off when Seth made a slashing motion across his throat. "Mama-"

Seth took the phone from her and disconnected the call. "One minute. Not one minute and ten seconds."

Gina couldn't answer him. Her hands curled into fists and her throat ached. She turned away and headed for the bathroom. Halfway there, she remembered Douglas and froze. There was nowhere for her to go. She spun at a noise behind her. Seth stopped an arm's length away.

"I'm sorry. But we don't want them to find us."

Gina looked away. "You're going to think I'm a baby, but I'm homesick."

"I am too."

Gina's gaze was drawn back to him. "Really?"

"You think guys don't get homesick?" He grinned wryly at her.

Gina reluctantly smiled. "I wouldn't have a clue. I

only have sisters. And I don't think many boys would admit to it even if they were. At least not the ones I know."

Seth shrugged then his expression sobered. "Can you help Ashley get everything out of the back of the four-wheel-drive? We're going to put Douglas in there. If we leave it much longer rigor mortis will make it difficult to move him. Anyway, it's best that livor mortis looks accurate. We want people to believe he crawled in the back of the vehicle before he died. Not have them think someone put him in there."

"Liver what?"

"Livor. Where the blood pools when it stops pumping through the system."

Gina shuddered. "Too much info. I'm going to help Ashley." She forced herself to move as quickly as possible towards the laundry that had a door opening directly into the garage, not wanting to hear any more. Ashley was already in the back of the vehicle, removing Conner's camping gear. Not that they were the things she was likely to take camping, other than the sleeping bag, a bag of clothes and a battery powered lantern. Connor had packed mostly junk food and alcohol for the party he'd missed out on attending.

They stacked everything in front of the vehicle and Gina collapsed on a carton of beer once they were finished. "I feel half dead." She closed her eyes with a groan.

"The world keeps swimming out of focus and I want to sleep for a week." Ashley dropped down beside her on a second carton. She frowned. "He wasn't planning to drink all this by himself, was he? I saw three bottles of spirits in one of those boxes."

Connor stepped backwards into the garage, holding Douglas' feet. "Nah, I get to buy it since I'm the only one who's eighteen."

"Oh!" Ashley clapped a hand over her mouth and closed her eyes. "Tell me when he's gone."

"Death is a natural part of life." Seth had his arms wrapped under Douglas so his hands linked together on the still chest.

"Then I naturally don't want to see it." Ashley's eyes remained tightly closed.

Gina turned her head away. "I don't blame you. It seems so undignified. I mean, what are we going to do? Just ditch him somewhere? Push him out the back of the four-wheel-drive?" As soon as she asked the question, she remembered Seth had said he planned for Douglas to be found in the vehicle. She frowned. It hurt her head to think.

Chapter Six

Seth finished arranging Douglas in the back and pushed the rear door closed. "Nope. We've got to ditch the vehicle too."

"What? You never said anything about that." Connor grabbed Seth by the shoulder and forced him to turn and face him. "We're not ditching my car. I haven't even had it for a month. It was my eighteenth birthday present."

Seth shrugged Connor's hand off him. "Get whatever you want out of it. We'll be having a change in transport. Hurry up. We need to deal with this before daylight arrives."

"Lilly–"

"Your vehicle has to go. The police will be watching for it." Seth turned away and headed inside.

Gina held out her hand when Connor was about to follow Seth. "Help me up? I don't think I could move even if there was a red bellied black snake headed for me."

Ashley shuddered. "Let's not talk about snakes either."

Connor stepped closer and helped each of them up, sliding an arm around their waists. "Good. You can help me inside. Douglas weighed a tonne."

"Yuck." Ashley pulled away from him. "You've been touching a dead body."

"What about the rest of the stuff you need from your car?" Gina asked.

"My phone charger and iPod. The rest is only crap. I'll get them later. I've got to sit down first." Connor started forward, tugging Gina with him, leaning against her.

She didn't bother to draw away. Exhaustion washed over her and they weaved down the hallway together, Ashley on their heels. She ignored the strange look Seth gave her when they entered the lounge room. Letting go of Connor, she took the last few steps on her own and collapsed onto the armchair. Connor returned to the floor with a groan.

Ashley huddled on the couch. "I can't help you get rid of the car. I've got no energy left. I need to sleep. I was doing okay up until a few minutes ago. Now I can't get warm."

"You want me to stay with you?" Connor pushed a pillow under his head and yawned.

Ashley looked over to Seth who was back at the computer. "Can he? Do you need him with you?"

Seth looked at each of them. "You want me to do this by myself?"

Gina hesitated. She longed to say yes, but that didn't seem fair. "I'll come with you." She made a face. "As long as I don't have to touch Douglas."

Seth laughed softly. "Deal." He glanced at the laptop. "We'll leave in about fifteen minutes."

Gina groaned. "I should probably have a shower to try and wake up. I feel half asleep."

Ashley looked Gina over. "I'd offer to lend you some of the clothes I left here last time, but you've got more curves than me. And you're a bit taller. I'm not even sure if they'll still fit me. Although I've barely grown in the past year."

Gina forced herself to her feet. "That's okay. But a towel would be good."

"Bathroom cupboard. I'm not moving from this spot unless the house is on fire. And even then I'd probably have to think about it." Ashley pulled a blanket over herself as she closed her eyes. "Wake me when all this is over."

Gina had a quick shower, feeling a little better even

though she was forced to put her stale clothes back on. She found Seth still in the lounge room at the laptop. He glanced up and gestured towards the table before he turned back to what he was doing. Gina watched him for a moment, his fingers flying over the keys, before she looked at the coffee table. Five tablets and olive leaf extract in a glass, waited for her. She sighed, hardly believing how quickly the time had passed.

She swallowed the liquid and chewed up the tablets, washing them down with bottled water. She nearly jumped when Seth closed the laptop with a snap and got to his feet, taking it and the phone with him. He looked from Ashley to Connor, both fast asleep.

"He only wanted two more things out of the car," Gina said.

Seth nodded. "Okay. See if you can find them. And anything else you think might be of use. I'll get the garage door."

Within minutes, they were on the road. Gina looked out the window. "Where are we headed?"

Seth kept glancing at the road as he set the navigator. "Twenty-three minutes away."

"I guess you've got a licence?"

Seth laughed. "Yeah. Although considering we've

got a dead body in the back, I'm not about to stop if a police car wants to pull me over."

Gina crossed her fingers. "God no. I hope not."

"I doubt it. The roads seem fairly quiet at this hour."

"I must be the only one out of the four of us who doesn't have a licence. I was booked in to do my test next week. I suppose I'm going to miss it."

Seth reached out and patted the back of her hand where it rested on her lap. "We'll sort this out. Don't worry."

"I can't help but worry. As you said, we've got a dead body in the back. And we've got the same illness he had. Anyone would worry in those circumstances."

"Think about something else instead. It helps."

"Is that how you've managed to stay so calm?"

Seth glanced at her. "I've had more practice at this."

"That's right. You were going to tell me about it."

Seth nodded, but remained silent for several minutes. "My Pop was a prisoner of war. Most of the time he was great. Better than a best friend. Dad, Pop and I. Mum bailed when I was little and Dad talked her into letting him have me. She couldn't cope with Pop. Actually, she couldn't cope with the slightest bit of stress. But that's another story. I was going to tell you about Pop."

Gina frowned. "How can your grandfather being a POW have anything to do with how calm you are when someone has a gun pointed at you?"

"Most of the time Pop managed to put his experiences behind him, but then something would set him off. Might be a phrase, the sound of a car backfiring, anything that reminded him of those times. He'd become a different man. Desperate. Aggressive. Determined to escape and take out as many of the enemy as he could. Usually I was one of his mates. And he'd be trying to protect me. A couple of times, he thought I was the enemy, but that wasn't until I was about thirteen."

"How did you cope?"

"We had regular counselling sessions and were taught how to deal with him when he was like that. Guess I never expected to use the skills again." Seth smiled fondly. "We lost him almost a year ago. But the weapons he managed to get hold of. Gun, knife, axe…" Seth laughed wryly. "Anything. Didn't matter. Shit! The old bugger probably could have turned a toothpick into a weapon."

"You loved him? Even when he threatened you?"

"It wasn't me he was threatening. He was tortured,

Gina. We loved him and had to accept he was a little broken." He tapped the side of his head. "And no matter what they did, they couldn't put him back together again. As he used to say after an episode, Humpty Dumpty had been turned into scrambled eggs."

"So Douglas holding a gun on you didn't bother you?"

"Of course it bothered me. But I've learned to stay calm in that type of situation. You never want to stress the gunman. You don't know what he'll do in the heat of the moment." Seth pulled up on the side of the road.

"What are we doing?"

"We've arrived."

Gina glanced outside. "But there's nothing here."

"Exactly." He cleared the details from the inbuilt navigator before taking a cloth from his pocket and wiping over the steering wheel, indicator and door handle. "Anything else we need out of here?" He grabbed the laptop and phone.

Gina shook her head. She'd removed everything back at the house.

"Come on then." As soon as they were out of the vehicle he locked the doors, wiped over the key and slid it through the slightly open front window so it landed on the driver's seat.

Gina followed Seth across the road, surprised to see a sedan parked in the shadows of a tree. "What are you doing?" She watched as Seth knelt at the back of the vehicle and put his hand underneath near the tow bar.

He held up a key. "Our new transportation."

"How'd you know the key was there?"

"Dad organised the car for me and told me where the key was. I also asked him to get several changes of clothes for you and me." He unlocked the car.

"You probably didn't even get the right size." Gina glanced away when she felt her cheeks heat. When had he checked her out well enough to be able to guess her size? She'd thought he'd spent every spare minute focused on the laptop and notebook.

"Guess we'll find out when we get back to the house." He waited until Gina was in the car before he started it.

Gina glanced around. "Where's your dad?"

"Avoiding getting sick."

"Did he stay in the area?"

Seth nodded. "Yeah, I saw him."

Gina looked at him sceptically. "Really? In the dark."

"I can see in the dark right now. It comes and goes. Every now and then my vision is completely blurry. I've also been getting bursts of energy and strength. Have you?"

Gina shook her head. "No. I still feel half dead. Only my hearing seems to be going haywire. I could do with a burst of energy. Or a good sleep." She sneezed and groaned as she fumbled in her pocket for a tissue. "My nose feels like someone took sandpaper to it."

Seth chuckled. "I'll be smart and avoid commenting on that statement."

"I know. I always look terrible when I'm sick. Not like Ashley. Slightly flushed cheeks and a pink nose don't make her look like something the cat dragged in. Actually, something the cat dragged in probably looks healthier than I do."

"We should have a turning point around lunch time."

"Which means what exactly?" When Seth didn't answer her, she turned to face him. "What's that mean, Seth?"

"That if we haven't started getting better by then our chances of recovery drop dramatically."

"Why don't you just come out and say we're going to die?"

Seth reached out and laced his fingers through hers. "I've read all the information and I've taken pics with Connor's phone and sent a lot of it through to Dad. Between the two of us, we've come up with a few ideas. We will get through this. I promise."

"What sort of ideas?"

"How are you with needles?"

"Why?" Suspicion filled her voice.

"Dad packed some vials and sharps. We need to take an injection every two hours."

"What will it do?"

"Hopefully slow the process down so our bodies can cope more easily with the changes." He squeezed her fingers. "And at five a.m. we have to keep our sleeping to less than half an hour at a time. We don't want to risk going into a coma."

Gina closed her eyes. "Any other good news to tell me?"

"Yeah. I've got a birthday present for you."

Gina's eyes popped open and she stared at Seth. She wished she could see him clearer. "Really?"

"Nothing major. I don't even know exactly what it looks like. I asked Dad to get it for me."

"Thank you." She smiled, surprised he'd gone to the trouble.

Seth swore, let go of her hand and turned off the headlights at the same moment as he sped up.

Gina braced herself as they took a corner fast. "What do you think you're doing?" She glanced around, wishing she'd been paying more attention to what was happening outside instead of staring at Seth.

"Remember when you asked me if I had a licence and we talked about it not being a good idea to be pulled over by the police?"

"Don't tell me you lied about the licence."

"No. But the cops just tried to get me to pull over. Random breath test. We can't come into contact with anyone, Gina. We're contagious."

"Oh." She turned in her seat to see flashing lights behind them. The sirens began a moment later and she winced as her hearing improved dramatically.

"Hold on." Seth took a sharp right and parked the car in a shadowy driveway. He turned the car off and, pressing her head down, ducked down too.

"I can hear them calling for backup," Gina whispered, trying to figure out how to ignore the sirens and still listen in. They made her head ache.

"What else?"

She frowned. "It's hard to focus on the direction. They keep moving. They're trying to work out where we've gone."

"We'll stay here a bit longer. Anything else?"

"They didn't get the number plate."

"That's good. I wouldn't want to have to dump this car so soon after getting it." Seth sat up and moved his hand off her head.

"Who's it registered to?"

"Some non-existent person. Don't worry. No one will be questioned over the whereabouts of this car."

Gina scanned outside with a frown. "They're checking some of the streets off this one. There's another two cars on the way."

"I guess it's time for us to get out of here." Seth started the car and reversed onto the road.

Gina couldn't sit still. The rest of the drive she listened in every direction for sounds of pursuit. She heard snippets of private conversations, someone yelling at their dog and a few conversations that made her blush, but no police. When they were still ten minutes from Ashley's place, buzzing filled her ears and the rush of energy she hadn't noticed arriving was suddenly replaced with exhaustion. She slumped back in the seat.

Seth glanced towards her, the headlights on again. "You okay?"

"I don't know. I thought I was exhausted before. Now I'm totally wiped."

"We're nearly there and you can sleep until five."

Gina checked the time. "Like that's such a bonus. I need more than an hour and a bit."

"When we've beaten the virus."

"If we beat the virus," Gina muttered.

Seth drove into the garage that was still open and staggered out of the car to close and lock the roller door. He used a key to unlock the laundry door and turned back towards the car. "You coming?"

Gina forced her body to move. "Where'd you get the key?"

"Ashley gave it to me while you were in the shower."

Gina leaned against the doorframe and eyed the lino. "You know, the floor looks pretty comfy right there."

Seth wrapped an arm around her waist. "Come on then. At least use the armchair."

"I'm dying to crawl into a bed." She clapped her hand over her mouth and groaned. "Forget I said that." Dying was the last thing she wanted to do.

"You can have the sewing room. There's a bed in there. I won't complain if you use it. If Connor complains, he can have Ashley's grandmother's room."

"What about Ashley?"

"She's got the guest room."

Gina reached up to run a finger lightly across the shadow under Seth's left eye. The one under the right was equally dark. "What about you?"

"I've still got things to do. But there's always the couch if I need sleep. Come on then. Five will be here before you know it." Seth guided her down the hall and to the sewing room. "Sleep well. First needle is at five."

Gina glared at his retreating back, too exhausted to argue. She dropped onto the bed. Her last thought was to wonder if the clothes Seth had for her would fit. She was desperate to get out of the ones she wore.

Chapter Seven

"Gina. Wake up."

She stirred as a hand ran across her forehead. She smiled at the coolness of it against the heat of her skin. "So hot. And tired."

"I know. But you've got to wake up."

Gina struggled to open her eyes, staring up at Seth who sat beside her on the single bed. She watched as his lips curved into a smile. Her eyes closed again and she started to roll over and snuggle back into the pillow.

"Do you want to be awake for this needle or would you rather sleep through it?"

Gina sat up quickly, her eyes wide as she looked around for the needle. She glared at Seth when he laughed and flopped back onto the bed. "Bastard."

"A couple of minutes before I need to give it to

you. Do you need to use the bathroom or anything first?" He rose to his feet.

"Yeah, I guess." Anything to postpone the needle. Gina swung her legs over the edge of the bed.

"Don't be long. We'll be waiting in the lounge room for you." Seth paused at the doorway to watch her for a few seconds before he left the bedroom.

Gina remained sitting on the edge of the bed for a moment while she tried to force her body to obey. All she wanted to do was curl up and go back to sleep. She sneezed and pulled a tissue from her pocket. With a sigh, she blew her nose before staggering to the bathroom. Once she used the toilet, she splashed water on her face, but it didn't help. She still felt half dead. She stared at the corner where Douglas had died before hurrying to the lounge room. She didn't even want to think about him.

"About time. Just because you're last doesn't mean you're going to miss out." Connor rubbed his arm.

Ashley was curled up on the couch. "Oh don't be a baby, Connor. It didn't hurt that much."

"It was probably deliberate." Connor glared at Seth.

Gina reluctantly walked over to Seth. She closed her eyes the moment he turned away. Nothing happened. She waited, tempted to open her eyes. "Hurry up."

"Don't be impatient. I'm going to wipe a cotton wool ball across your arm. It'll be cold."

Gina was glad of the warning or she might have opened her eyes. There was no way she wanted to see how big the needle was.

"Now just a little sting." Seth held her arm.

"Ow. That wasn't little. Who taught you how to give needles? A two-year-old?"

"See. I told you," Connor said.

"Stay still." Seth's hand tightened on her arm. "Not long now."

Gina drew her breath in sharply as fire trickled through her arm. "That's burning."

"Okay. All done." He removed the needle and let go of her arm.

She kept her eyes closed. "Tell me when all the needles are away so I can open my eyes."

"You and Connor are as bad as each other," Ashley said. "Next you'll be wanting someone to kiss it better."

"Here," Connor said. "Since you offered."

Gina wanted to open her eyes and see what was happening. Instead she squeezed them tighter.

"You can open your eyes now." Seth sounded right in front of her.

She opened her eyes to find he was. A slight smile

curved his lips. "Don't laugh at me. You don't know how bad you are at giving needles."

His smile turned into a chuckle. "Actually, I didn't think I was that bad."

Gina's mouth dropped open. "You gave yourself a needle?"

Seth shrugged. "It wasn't like there was anyone else to do it."

Gina opened her mouth to speak, shook her head then closed it again. "What about the clothes? Think I can see if any of them fit?"

Seth nodded. "I'll get them for you."

"Can you leave them in the sewing room? I'm going to take a cold shower. I'm burning."

Gina half expected the water to turn to steam the moment it touched her body. It didn't, but it also wasn't much help cooling her down so she didn't bother staying in for long. Wrapped in her towel, she returned to the sewing room, her clothes in a bundle. She dropped them inside the door and, seeing the room was empty, locked it. Two plastic bags sat on the bed. She tipped the freshly laundered clothes out and grabbed a pair of knickers and a cotton dress. She was surprised to find they fit.

She found Seth in the lounge room, wearing a fresh pair of jeans and a grey shirt that looked like it had been washed a hundred times. He was once again at the laptop, not even pausing in his typing when she entered. It wasn't until she was nearly at his side that he glanced up and smiled when his gaze met hers.

"I guess they were the right size after all."

"Makes me wonder how many girls you've shopped for that you know the sizes so well."

Seth laughed. "Absolutely none. I'm just observant and make a good sounding board."

"Huh?"

"One of my friends was overweight and your size was the one she aimed for. You've got a similar build to what she has now. We all counted down the sizes with her."

"Oh." Gina glanced around the room. "Where's the other two?"

"Crashed in the bedrooms. I've set the timer to do the wake-up rounds if you want to go to sleep."

"Well…" she wanted to say yes, but wondered if it was fair to leave Seth to stay up by himself.

Seth gestured towards the laptop. "I've still got at least an hour here. You can spell me then and I'll have a nap."

"Okay." She smiled in relief. "See you in half an hour." She wandered back to the sewing room and pushed all the clothes into the plastic bags. Dropping them at the foot of the bed, she willingly lay down. Her eyes immediately closed. It seemed like only seconds before Seth woke her.

"You're not much for waking up, are you?" Seth smiled down at her.

"I'm tired."

"Go back to sleep. I'll see you in another half an hour."

Gina let her eyes close and was asleep again in a heartbeat. She groaned when she was shaken moments later. "You've already woken me."

"That was half an hour ago."

Gina peered up at Seth, trying to open her eyes properly. "Really?"

He nodded. "Think you can stay up for a bit?"

She reluctantly sat up. "Yeah." She yawned, covering her mouth with her hand.

"You sure?"

Gina nodded as she stumbled out of the bed and grabbed Seth's shoulder for support. "Yeah. You need sleep too." She took a wobbly step away from him.

"Okay. Make sure you wake everyone when the timer goes and see that they speak to you." He handed the kitchen timer over. It was already counting down the seconds. "Mind if I crash here?" He gestured towards the bed.

"No. Go ahead." Gina tried to smother the next yawn, but she couldn't stop it. "Night." She glanced at the light edging in around the window. "Morning or whatever."

Seth laughed softly as he lay down on the bed. "Night'll do." He closed his eyes.

Gina stared down at him. It was hard to believe a couple of days ago she'd never met him. It felt like she'd known him forever. She forced her legs to move and headed for the kitchen. She grabbed a glass and opened the fridge. About to pick up the bottle of cold water, she noticed a cake box. She grinned when she saw the words that had been written on it with a marker pen. 'Gina- don't peek!'

Filling her glass, she put the bottle back in the fridge, a smile still on her face. She wondered if that was her present. A cake. And she wondered what other little surprises Seth had organised for them.

Feeling a bit hungry, she rummaged in the cupboards until she found some plain biscuits. She ate a couple, twisted the top of the packet closed and left them on the kitchen bench. The next half an hour passed quickly. She wandered around the house, picking up framed photos and glancing at the books lined up in the bookcase in a corner of the lounge room. She jumped a little when the kitchen timer went off.

After she'd woken everyone, she returned to the lounge room and flicked through the television channels. There was nothing worth watching. She paced the room restlessly. A glance out the window showed the occasional car pass. Nothing of interest. Wandering to the kitchen, she had another biscuit. Her stomach churned and it was an effort to keep it down.

Gina pulled a kitchen chair out from the table and slumped in it. Her stomach cramped with hunger, but revolted at the thought of food. The phone rang and she staggered out of the chair, her hand above the kitchen extension before she remembered she wasn't meant to be here. It continued to ring. Should she answer it? What could she say? No, best not to. It stopped. Silence filled the house again.

Gina sighed as she dropped back into the kitchen chair. It was possibly one of the last days of her life and she was bored and trying to make the time pass quicker. Resting her elbows on the table, she dropped her head into her hands. Most people who knew they were going to die chose to spend their last days with their family. She didn't have that option.

In her mind she could clearly see them. Her mum,

always offering comfort and ready to listen to anything no matter how unimportant. Her dad, his thick Italian accent, his ready smile and sense of humour. Her two older sisters who looked so much like her that everyone said the three of them looked like triplets. And Nonna. Outspoken Nonna who had an opinion on everything no matter how little you wanted to hear it. There were also aunts, uncles and cousins. Too many to count. A noisy crowd to fill family gatherings.

Chapter Eight

The kitchen timer went off, startling her. She blinked as she looked around the room. She had a bad feeling she'd fallen asleep. With a yawn and a stretch, she first went to wake Seth. The shadows under his eyes seemed darker. She lightly touched his shoulder and his eyes popped open.

Confusion filled his eyes for a second and then he smiled. "Hey."

"It's seven."

Seth sat up. "Wake the other two and tell them to meet me in the lounge room. Time for needles."

Gina groaned. She hated needles. "Okay." It took her a couple of minutes to wake Connor and Ashley. Connor was the hardest, rolling over and ignoring her no matter how hard she shook his shoulder. In the end, she pulled the pillow out from under his head and he turned to glare at her.

"I'm awake. Give me the pillow back."

"Then get up. Time for another needle."

Connor swore, but stumbled out of bed.

Gina headed for the lounge room and pulled a tissue from her pocket to gingerly blow her nose. She threw it in one of the paper bins and stopped as she saw the glasses of olive leaf extract and tablets lined up on the coffee table. She gulped when she glanced up and saw Ashley being given a needle. The world started to fade and Gina went cold and clammy, breaking out in a sweat.

Seth discarded the needle and looked over to Gina. "You okay?"

Gina opened her mouth to speak, but nothing came out. She swayed as the world grew dimmer. She felt Seth's hands on her as he led her to the couch and pressed her head between her knees.

"It's okay. Just sit there for a moment." Seth rubbed his hand across her back. "Ashley, grab a wet washer, please."

The clammy feeling started to fade and the world no longer seemed to be at the wrong end of a telescope. A wet washer was draped across the back of her neck. "Thanks."

"What's wrong with her?" Connor asked.

Seth moved off the couch. "You're next."

"What'd you do to her?" Connor demanded.

"Nothing. She's just a little light headed. Hurry up, Connor. We need to stick with the schedule."

Connor muttered under his breath, but Gina easily heard him swearing about Seth. She grinned as she heard his indrawn breath and some more muttered swearing. Her hearing started to buzz again and she couldn't make out what he was saying.

"You ready, Gina?"

She looked up to see Seth beside her, a hand held behind him. "I guess." She closed her eyes and leaned back in the couch. "Tell me when it's safe to look again."

"Okay." He took the opposite arm to the one he'd given her the needle in last time. "Cold for a second. Now for the little sting."

Gina tensed.

"Relax. It makes it less painful."

She relaxed for all of a couple of seconds and then tensed when she felt the needle. She hissed when Seth chuckled and tried to think of something else. Anything other than the fire invading her arm. "I've come to the conclusion that your dad is a sadist. Whatever he gave you to inject burns like hell."

"Just about done." Seth removed the needle. "I've

disposed of it in the sharps container. You can look now."

Gina opened her eyes to find Seth staring at her. "What?"

"How are you feeling?" Turning away, he picked up the tablets and glass. He held them out to her.

Gina swallowed the liquid and took the tablets from him. She stared down at the little orange disks. "Not too bad. Hungry. Queasy. Exhausted. Nose won't stop running and my head feels like it exploded hours ago. Just like I've got the flu." She popped the tablets in her mouth and chewed them.

Seth smiled. "Sounds like you're doing fine."

Gina shook her head slowly and winced when the movement made her head spin. "I'd hate to think what you'd call not fine."

"Douglas?"

"Great. I'm getting close to not fine."

Seth held out his hand and when she placed hers in his, pulled her to her feet. "Come on then. Let's get you back to bed. You look exhausted."

"And you don't?" She looked at the time on the DVD player. "It's nearly seven-thirty. You've hardly slept at all."

Seth shrugged. "I don't sleep much anyway. Six hours a day is usually enough."

"Well you certainly haven't had six hours. You sleep. I'll stay up a little longer."

Seth stared at her for a moment. "Okay. Even though it's probably only been ten or fifteen minutes since they left, I'll wake the other two so we're all on the same waking schedule."

Gina glanced around. "I didn't even notice them leave."

"I think you were a little preoccupied." Seth grinned.

She ignored his comment. It wasn't like she was the only person in the world bothered by needles. "I'll set the kitchen timer again." She wandered back to the kitchen where the timer was on the table. This time she didn't dare sit down. She walked through the house to stay awake. Everyone was counting on her to wake them in half an hour. She wasn't about to let them slip into a coma. She carried the timer with her and glanced at it every few minutes.

Time seemed to bend and twist. Sometimes it was only a minute that had passed, at others it was several. And then it was time to wake everyone up. Ashley woke easily. Connor was once again a problem and finding the energy to shake him was an even bigger one. She dug her fingers into his ribs.

"Hey!" He twisted to face her.

"You're impossible to wake."

"And you look like the walking dead."

"I feel like it." Gina forced her feet to move.

Connor staggered out of bed and took the timer from her loose grasp. "I'll take the next watch. Have you woken everyone?"

"I've just got Seth to wake. I'll go do that if you're sure you can take over."

"Yeah."

"Make sure you wake us. And keep moving. It helps you stay awake."

Connor turned her by the shoulders and gave her a gentle shove from the room. "I can manage. Get some sleep."

Gina staggered to the sewing room and sat on the bed beside Seth. He didn't stir. She lightly shook his shoulder. He stayed asleep. Fear skittered through her. Had she left it too long? She shook him harder. Adrenaline coursed through her.

"Seth." Her fingers wrapped around his shoulders and she pulled him towards her before letting him fall backwards onto the pillow. She put her lips against his ear. "Seth. Wake up." Drawing away from him, she saw his eyes slowly open and he stared up at her, disorientated. "I thought–" the words wouldn't come. She dropped her head onto his chest, the sound of his heartbeat loud in her ear. A shudder went through her.

Seth pushed her from him so he could sit up. "What's wrong?" He stared at her, concern clouding his gaze.

"I couldn't wake you." Her eyes watered and she sniffed. "I thought you were in a coma. Maybe we shouldn't sleep. You said lunchtime. That's only four hours away. We can stay awake that long."

Seth wrapped his arms around her and pulled her against him. "You need sleep. I'll stay up for a while."

"Connor is. But I couldn't sleep. What if I didn't wake up?"

Seth's arms tightened before he released her so he could meet her gaze. "I won't let that happen." He smiled. "Besides, there's cake in the fridge for tomorrow. You don't want to miss out on that, do you?"

Gina smiled reluctantly. "No, but is it really our choice?"

"Yes. We will survive this. Trust me."

"I want to."

Seth shifted over in the bed. "Lie down here next to me and I'll stay with you while you go to sleep."

Gina stared at the narrow space. "There isn't much room."

Seth grinned. "I know. Should be nice and cosy." He leered theatrically.

Gina laughed. "Is this the part where I flutter my eyelashes and ask what your intentions are?"

"Oh, the very worst," Seth assured her dramatically.

Gina became serious and reached for Seth's hand. "Whatever happens, I'm glad I met you."

"Nothing terrible will happen. Now get some sleep."

Gina lay down beside him and turned onto her side so she'd fit. "I probably won't be able to sleep."

"Try." Seth removed the hair band from her hair and brushed her hair back from her face. "I'm glad I met you too."

Gina lay quietly, her eyes closed. Her temperature was so high she barely felt the warmth of Seth's body. She listened to his even breathing and wondered if he'd fallen asleep. She heard the television turn on. It sounded loud enough she might as well be in the same room with it. She frowned and tried to dull the sound. It quietened. Startled by the suddenness of it, the volume increased again. She smiled. It was like zooming in and out with a camera. She tried a different direction and before she could exhale, she was listening in on the neighbours.

"What's so funny?" Seth asked.

Gina winced and opened her eyes. "Ow. I'm going to have to figure that out."

"What?"

"How to listen to conversations far away without increasing the volume around me. It felt like you shouted in my ear."

"Sorry. I didn't realise what you were doing."

"Not your fault. Maybe I should have hung out a 'do not disturb' sign."

Seth laughed softly. "So your hearing is improving?"

"Sometimes. What about your vision?"

"It comes and goes. It can be a bit disorientating. But eventually I won't need a microscope. Might even be able to manage without a telescope."

"That sounds handy. They aren't cheap equipment."

"Neither are listening devices."

Gina grinned. "I suppose not. I wonder what the other two can do."

"I don't know about Connor, but I'd say Ashley can control her body temperature. I don't know how useful that'd be though."

"Save on air-con and heating bills."

Seth laughed. "There is that." He was silent for a moment. "Weren't you going to sleep?"

"Yeah. I was distracted by the TV Connor turned on. Then I wanted to test out my hearing and eavesdropped on the neighbours."

"Remind me not to bother voicing any secrets. You could probably hear a pin drop in the next house."

"Possibly."

Connor burst into the bedroom. "They found the body. Guys in hazz suits carted him away and impounded my vehicle. They said he was from a lab where an experiment went wrong and he ended up with a highly contagious virus and our pictures were splashed all over the TV. People have been warned to avoid us and immediately call the police."

Gina sat up with a groan. "This keeps getting better all the time."

Connor looked from one to the other and grinned. "I didn't interrupt anything, did I?"

"Oh go away, Connor." She wished she had something to throw at him.

Connor continued to grin. "Just thought you'd want to know. We're on every channel."

Seth swore. "We won't be able to step outside the house without someone calling the cops."

"I'm going to tell Ashley." Connor turned away.

"Connor." Gina waited until he faced her again. "I

can hear whispers, Seth's eyes are like binoculars and we think Ashley can change her body temperature. Can you do anything?"

"My smell has gone stupid. Typical that I get the crappy ability. Now x-ray vision would have been good. How about it, Seth? Can you see through things?" Connor waited for Seth to answer.

He shook his head. "No. Only magnify things and see in the dark."

"That isn't very interesting." Connor turned to leave.

"Connor," Gina called out.

He turned back with a heavy sigh. "What now?"

"Are you feeling any better?"

"Nope. Still feel like crap."

"Oh." She guessed Seth had said lunchtime. That was still a few hours away.

Connor crossed his arms over his chest. "Can I go now?"

"Yeah." Gina watched him leave, sighing. She turned to Seth. "Now what? They're going to want to treat us like pincushions and they'll find out we're different. We won't be able to go home even if Douglas' friends let us."

"Let's worry about that later. Get some sleep, Gina.

No one can think clearly when they're hours past tired."

Gina stared at him. She wanted to argue, but exhaustion was seeping in again. She yawned. "But you have been thinking about it, haven't you."

Seth lay down and pulled her with him. "Yeah. Let's get through the next few days first."

"You don't know what to do either, do you?"

"Not yet. But I will."

Gina yawned again. "I hope so. My family are everything. They're part of who I am. They annoy me, help me, torment me and protect me. I have to be able to see them."

"I'll make sure of it. Now go to sleep."

"What about on my birthday? I want to be able to see them for my birthday."

"I don't know. We'll see if you're still contagious."

"How will we know?" she asked sleepily.

"You won't like the answer to that question."

"It involves a needle, doesn't it?" Gina mumbled.

"Sleep, Gina."

"Mmm… knew it."

Chapter Nine

"Gina."

She tried to push away the hands that shook her. "Leave… be."

"Medication time."

She opened her eyes enough to glare up at Seth. "Don't wanna move."

He held the tablets and glass out with a smile. She took them and handed back the empty glass before she rolled over to try and return to sleep. When he tapped her on the shoulder she rolled over enough to glare at him.

"What?"

"Keep your eyes closed."

Gina groaned. She guessed at least lying down meant she wouldn't fall if she passed out.

"Cold first. Okay. Now the sting."

Gina gritted her teeth, ready to snarl at him if he

told her to relax again. She felt the heat shooting through her arm, hotter than the last couple of times. She swore. "Is this something different?"

"No. Okay. All finished now. You can open your eyes."

Gina rubbed at her arm. "It still burns." She looked at the spot of blood that was on her arm.

Seth grabbed her hand when she went to wipe it off. "Leave it. I'll be back in a second."

Gina stared after him and wished she'd had time to ask what he was going to do. As long as it didn't involve another needle she guessed it didn't matter. He came back into the room with a microscope slide. She watched as he pressed it against the blood then held it up to peer at it.

"What can you see?"

"Shush."

Gina glared at him. It was her blood. Why shouldn't she know what was going on. Finally he lowered the slide. "Well?"

"I should have been doing this right from the start. I'm too tired to think straight. I can't tell anything conclusive from one test. The mutation has taken hold and the virus is taking over. I'll take another slide after the next needle."

Gina sighed. "None of that sounds good."

"Well, actually it does. It looks like your body isn't fighting as hard against the invasion. It's starting to think the virus is normal."

"How is that good? Wouldn't it be better to get rid of it?"

Seth shook his head. "You'd be destroying part of your body too. We want our bodies to accept the virus. I'll do another white blood cell count when I give you the next needle."

"They fight disease, don't they?"

"Yeah. But for some reason not only the cells that fight viruses, but also the ones that fight bacteria are in high numbers. That wasn't mentioned in the reports."

"You're always so full of good news, aren't you? Sure there weren't any other types of white blood cells in there?"

Seth grinned. "The parasite one wasn't high. Does that count as good news?"

Gina groaned and pulled the pillow over her head. "I wish I could sleep through all this and wake up when it's over." She felt the bed sink and the pillow was pried away.

Seth looked down at her, his expression serious. "Only three hours and we should have a better idea of what's going on."

"Would it help if..." Gina hesitated. She forced herself to continue. "Would blood samples taken more often help?"

Seth brushed her hair back from her face. "Thank you. I know how difficult you find needles. I'll take samples of my blood every half hour and everyone else's when I give them a needle. Not ideal, but I'm sure you lot don't want to be turned into my test subjects."

"I do. If it'll help us figure out what we can do and what's going on."

Seth looked thoughtful, then nodded. "I'll keep it in mind. I'll see what my results look like first. If I need any other information to help draw a conclusion I'll take you up on your offer."

"Okay."

Seth rested his hand across her forehead. "Get some more sleep. It'll be time to wake up again before you know it."

"Will you stay here with me? I don't want to die alone like Douglas did."

"You aren't going to die."

"Will you stay?"

Seth nodded. "Let me put the slides away first."

"Where do they need to go?"

Seth grinned. "Are you sure you want to know?"

Gina opened her mouth to say 'of course', then closed it. She had a bad feeling there was only one place they could be kept so they wouldn't dry up or go stale or do whatever it was that blood samples did when they were left out. She shook her head.

Seth laughed. "I thought not. I won't be long."

Gina watched him leave the room. Silence pressed in on her. She forced it away, seeking out noise. She followed the sound of Seth's footsteps to the kitchen.

"Are you sleeping with her?" Connor demanded.

There was a moment of silence before Seth answered. "That's none of your business."

"She's not bad looking. A bit too much weight for me," Connor said.

"I guess you prefer the girls who have as much shape as a boy."

There was the sound of a chair scraping quickly across the floor. "I'm not gay."

"I didn't say you were."

"Yes you did."

"No. I just commented on the body shape you prefer."

"Ashley's perfect. There's nothing boy-like about her."

Seth laughed. "There is a saying about protesting too much, Connie."

"Don't start with me, Lilly. You won't like how I finish things."

"Then watch what you say. I like every one of Gina's curves and it's idiots like you who make girls think they should diet until they're anorexic."

"That's crap."

"No. It's the truth. Now get out of my way, Connie."

"Why? You going to crawl back into bed with her? She's one of the girls at school that wouldn't have sex unless the end of the world was coming." Connor laughed bitterly. "But I guess it's on the way for us."

"No it's not. There's actually signs in the blood samples I took, to indicate mine and Gina's bodies are accepting the mutation."

"What about Ashley and me? Aren't we important enough for your precious little tests, Lilly?"

"I didn't think you were very fond of needles, Connie."

"Test me."

There was another silence. "Okay. Wait here while I get another slide and a needle."

Gina listened as Seth's footsteps took him to the lounge room. When he was halfway back to the kitchen her hearing was filled with a buzzing noise. She swore. Now she wouldn't know what happened.

She started to sit up then remembered Seth had mentioned the word needle. She hesitated. Torn. Maybe by the time she reached the kitchen they'd be finished with the needle. She stumbled out of bed and stopped by the door, her hand nearly on the doorknob. And maybe not.

She bit her lip. Being scared of needles was childish. There was nothing to be afraid of. It didn't help. She couldn't make herself take that one last step to open the door. It opened without warning and she jumped back. Seth stood in the doorway and looked at her.

After a drawn out moment, he grinned. "So how much of the conversation did you hear?"

Gina felt her cheeks grow hotter. "Until you went to the lounge room." She stared at her toes. The carpet beneath them was a serviceable mottled brown.

"Gina."

When he said no more, she looked up at him.

"Don't pay any attention to what Connor says. He's an insecure jerk."

"Yeah, I know."

Seth smiled. "I always knew you were smart." He took another couple of steps into the room so he could close the door. "How about you get some sleep. You really look like you could use it."

"Is that a polite way of saying I look like crap?"

Seth tucked a strand of her hair behind her ear. "Not at all. You just look tired. Nothing wrong with that. Hearing me compliment you when you weren't in the room wasn't good enough for you?" His smile became a grin.

Gina's lips automatically curved into a smile. "I guess not."

"Sleep. Compliments can wait until later." He guided her to the bed.

Gina turned to face him when they reached the bed. "What if there isn't a later?"

"There will be."

"I don't understand how you can be so confident about it."

"The scientific evidence indicates we have a higher than average chance of surviving."

"And what about the ones who died? I bet they thought that too."

Seth shook his head. "No, they didn't. They gave them a twenty-three percent chance of surviving."

Gina's mouth dropped open and she stared at him. "And they still went ahead with the experiments?"

"Yeah. Nice guys, aren't they?"

Gina shuddered. "These are the people who want

to track us down?" She groaned when Seth nodded. "We're as good as dead."

"No. If we're worth tracking down, it'll be because the virus did its job. We'll have the advantage. Faster, stronger, heal quicker. With your hearing and my sight we should know before they get close to us."

"I hope so." She didn't have much faith in his beliefs though. The four of them against terrorists? Yeah, right, like they could come out best in that fight. She yawned, her eyes closing as she did.

"Sleep, Gina. Before you collapse where you stand."

She dropped onto the bed. "You will stay, won't you?"

"Yeah. But you're not going to die."

Gina didn't answer. She didn't completely believe him, but she wanted to. She lay down and closed her eyes. The slight buzzing in her ears stopped and she smiled as she heard Connor and Ashley argue over whose turn it was to stay awake. Ashley thought it was hers. Her smile became a grin when Ashley won.

"What's so funny?"

Gina didn't answer. Instead, she called out to the approaching footsteps. "We're still awake Ashley."

"Okay. I'll be back in half an hour."

Gina had no trouble hearing the words. She might

as well have been standing beside Ashley. "Okay. Thanks." She listened as Ashley headed for the lounge room.

"So, you going to tell me what you were smiling about?"

Gina turned her head so she could look at Seth. "Ashley and Connor arguing over whose turn it was to stay awake."

"Ahh." Seth grinned. "Connor lost the argument. Guess that didn't sit well."

"No. He's still grumbling."

"I'm glad I don't have the habit of muttering under my breath. Who knows what secrets I might spill."

"Pity." Gina got comfortable again and closed her eyes. It seemed like only minutes before Seth was waking her. She looked around. "Ashley?"

"She woke me. You slept through that."

"Oh."

"Go to sleep. I'll be back in a minute."

Gina willingly closed her eyes. "Mmmm."

Chapter Ten

The next time Seth woke her, Gina couldn't stop shivering. She looked up at him when he pressed his hand against her forehead. "If you're checking my temperature, that's not very scientific of you." A bout of coughing made her curl up on the bed.

"Think I could take a blood sample?"

"I don't care," Gina groaned. When Seth returned and pricked her finger, she wished she hadn't agreed. Her stomach churned and she held her breath until the feeling passed.

"You can open your eyes now."

Gina looked up at him to see he peered at a slide with a smear of blood on it. Her blood. "What's the verdict, doc?" She tried to make light of the situation, but fear crept into her voice.

Seth peered at the slide for another minute before

he spoke. "Looking a little better. Not as much as I'd hoped though."

"I don't feel any better. I can't get warm."

"I'll see if Ashley has more blankets."

Seth left the room, taking the slide with him. Gina continued to shiver and cough. Better! She felt worse than ever. Was this how Douglas had felt when he'd tried to get warm by using a picnic blanket? Before she could dwell on it, Seth returned to the room with two blankets.

"It's odd adding blankets to the bed in summer." He smiled easily.

"It's not helping. I feel like I'm surrounded by ice."

Seth climbed into the bed and pressed his body to hers, draping his arm over her. "You're burning."

"It doesn't feel like it." Gina groaned. All she could think of was Connor's earlier talk with Seth. "I'm going to die a virgin."

Seth laughed softly. "No you're not."

"Why? Are you going to have sex with me?"

"No. You're going to live. But if you're still offering tomorrow…"

"Don't count on it." Gina tried to pull away from him.

"Gina. You're exhausted and sick. I couldn't take advantage of that."

She stopped trying to pull away from him. "You didn't mean a single word you said to Connor."

Seth leaned over her. "I don't say things I don't mean."

"Yeah, right."

Seth stared at her a moment longer before his lips lightly brushed hers. "I meant every word." He pressed his lips against hers again.

She forgot how cold she was and the sound of their heartbeats seemed to drown out all other sounds. A fast steady beat. Death was a million miles from her thoughts, but soon intruded again when she was forced to pull away to cough.

Seth drew her close to him once she fell silent again. "Sleep, Gina. Not much longer now and you should start to feel a lot better."

Her ear was pressed against his chest and she listened to his heartbeat. "I wish. I hate being sick."

"Everyone does." He ran his fingers through her hair. "Close your eyes and sleep."

"Don't let me sleep forever."

"I promise."

Gina drifted off, slowly growing warmer. When she was woken for her eleven o'clock needle, she found the blankets pushed to the floor and the room felt like a sauna. She didn't even have the energy to protest the injection or ask about the blood Seth smeared on the slide.

"How come you can still move? My body feels like it doesn't belong to me," Gina muttered.

"You'd move if you had to." He stared down at her for a moment. "I'll be back in a minute."

Gina didn't know if he was only a minute. It took her less than that to fall back to sleep. When Seth woke her at eleven-thirty, she was drenched in sweat and her temperature didn't feel as high.

"How are you feeling?"

Gina frowned as she thought about it. "I don't know. Hungry. Desperate for a shower."

He grinned. "I'm starved too. You have a shower while I make us something light to eat."

Gina nodded and struggled out of bed. She staggered as she stood up. She was glad to see Seth didn't do any better when he rose from the bed. She watched him stumble from the room before she attempted to take clothes out of the plastic bags. She grabbed another pair of knickers and a red cotton dress with a small flower printed randomly all over it.

Once she'd showered and changed, she felt a little better and walked steadily to the kitchen. She took the mug Seth held out to her and looked into it.

"Chicken noodle soup. There were packets of it in

the cupboard and I thought they'd be light enough." He took a sip from his mug.

Connor stepped into the kitchen. "I can smell that in the lounge room. Is there any left?"

Seth gestured towards the cupboard. "A few more packets in there. The kettle's still hot."

Gina was relieved her stomach didn't twist and turn and threaten to eject the soup. She had another mouthful, savouring the warmth as she swallowed it. Usually she didn't like soup in summer, but after days of so little food it tasted heavenly. She looked over to the doorway as Ashley entered the kitchen.

"You lot having a party without me?" Ashley grinned.

"Nah, that's tomorrow." Seth glanced at Gina.

"I noticed the cake in the fridge." Ashley grabbed a mug out and placed it in front of Connor who was making his cup of soup. "Please?" When Connor nodded, she leaned against the kitchen bench and faced Gina. "When's your birthday?"

"Tomorrow."

"Wow. This was rotten timing for you." Ashley took the mug Connor handed her and stirred it with the spoon sitting in it.

"I'd buy you a present, but it's a little hard to go

outside when your face is plastered all over the TV," Connor said.

"That's okay." Gina drank more of her soup, surprised to see she was halfway through it.

"I could go and get something. No one knows about me," Ashley suggested.

"Not until I'm sure we're not contagious," Seth said.

"How will you know that, Lilly?"

"That's what all the blood samples have been about, Connie."

Gina groaned. "I guess we'll have to put up with more of this posturing now we seem to be getting better."

"I'm just using his last name," Connor said.

"It's the tone of voice you use." Gina drank the last of her soup and wished there'd been more. She guessed she shouldn't overdo it though.

"Aw, that's crap. You're just sticking up for him. He's the one who uses a girl's name for me."

"Who cares?" Ashley put her mug in the sink. "We're alive. And I don't know about you lot, but it feels good to be alive."

Gina grinned. "I know. I'm actually starting to think we mightn't die."

"We can't stop being vigilant yet. We've still got

another couple of injections and we shouldn't sleep more than half an hour," Seth said.

"But I feel heaps better," Ashley protested.

"Let's keep it that way." Seth put his mug in the sink. "Time for blood samples."

Connor muttered under his breath and Gina glanced away as she tried not to smile. It hadn't been complimentary to Seth, but she guessed if it made Connor feel better, who was she to argue? She wasn't keen on needles either.

Once Seth had taken the blood samples, he stood near the kitchen table and peered at the slides, scribbling notes on a piece of paper. The other three sat at the table and watched. Impatiently.

"Hurry up, Lilly. If this waiting is payback, it's not funny."

"Shush." Seth scribbled more notes.

Ashley rose from the table. "I can't bear to sit any longer. This is driving me insane." She wandered aimlessly towards the sink, glanced at the mugs in there and turned away.

Seth placed the slide on the table. "Ashley, you seem to be healing the quickest."

Ashley grinned. "Really?"

Seth nodded. "But we're all improving. I'm

thinking at this rate it'll be late afternoon before we're definitely not contagious."

"Yes! I hope it's before the shops shut. I need some major retail therapy." Ashley linked her arm through Seth's and danced him around the kitchen, her head thrown back as she laughed.

"Then what?" Connor pushed away from the table. "We still don't have our lives back. We might as well be dead." He glared at Ashley. "You might be able to go outside, but we can't."

Ashley stopped her dance to glare at Connor, hands on her hips. "Oh don't be an idiot. You can wear disguises. I'll buy some this afternoon."

"What kind of disguise will let me see my parents tomorrow?" Gina asked quietly. "It's not like we can walk up and knock on the door without making whoever is watching the place suspicious."

"I don't-" Ashley broke off to grin. "Oh. I do know." She laughed. "Religious dudes. You know, the ones who knock on your door on the weekend."

Gina grinned. "You're brilliant, Ashley."

Ashley tilted her head back slightly so she could look down her nose at everyone. "Of course I am." She ruined her haughty look by bursting into laughter again. "Wigs. I'll have to buy wigs for everyone." She brushed her fingers across Connor's lip. "And one of those nasty little moustaches for you." She spun to face Seth. "And maybe we'll put glasses on you, Genius." She raised her hands and spun on the spot. "I feel amazing. Like I could run to the coast and back without a problem. I've never felt like this in my entire life." She danced around the room.

"Might be the virus mutation. Can you do anything out of the ordinary?" Seth looked Ashley up and down.

Ashley pursed her lips. "I don't know. But I feel like I could do cartwheels down the hallway."

"Go for it." Connor grinned at her and his gaze dropped to the hem of her dress she'd put on earlier.

"I've never been able to do cartwheels." Ashley laughed. "But you know, I think I'm going to give them a go." She dashed into the hallway, a holler of excitement floating behind her.

Gina reached the doorway first. She watched as Ashley finished a cartwheel off with a forward flip. "Thought you said you couldn't do them."

Ashley grinned broadly. "What a buzz. Wow. I could do them along the entire street. Out of the way, I'm coming back."

Gina pressed against Connor and Seth who also crowded the doorway. She watched Ashley almost fly down the hallway, moving so quickly the hem of her dress stayed in place. It reminded Gina of the way a glass of water could be turned upside down without losing a drop if you spun it quickly enough.

Ashley landed in front of them. "Yes." She was grinning, her eyes lit with excitement.

"I think you better take it easy. You don't want to burn up all your energy," Seth said.

"Sure thing, Genius."

Gina yawned. "I'm exhausted from watching Ashley."

"You lot can sleep. I've got too much energy to be able to sit still let alone sleep," Ashley said.

"Make sure you wake us in half an hour." Seth returned to the table to put away his slides and notes.

Gina grabbed a glass of water and took it with her to the sewing room. She felt extremely thirsty, but guessed that was to be expected after drinking so little today. She had several mouthfuls before sitting the glass near the wall at the head of the bed. The sheets felt slightly damp and she wrinkled her nose at them. It would take too much effort to change them. She dropped onto the bed.

Seth stepped into the room. "You want me to stay with you?"

Gina stared at him. She wanted to say yes, but

could she? It wasn't like they were dying now. Well, not from the virus anyway. She had so many other worries she didn't want to think about and she knew she would if she were on her own.

"I can crash on the couch."

Gina shook her head. "No."

Seth stepped further into the room and closed the door. "I can bring in cushions from the couch and sleep on the floor if you prefer."

She shook her head again. "No. It's okay. I'll share the bed. I just don't want to be alone. I start thinking about things when I am. Like the men who were after Douglas."

"We'll figure it out." Seth lay down beside her. "Didn't I tell you we wouldn't die?"

"You were talking about the virus."

"They're not going to get us, Gina. We will figure this out. Now get some sleep. There'll be a lot to do once we're no longer contagious."

Gina sighed. "All I want to do is see my family."

"You will. But we've got to make sure we don't lead the terrorists to them."

His words sent a chill through her. "No. Definitely not." They fell silent and Gina closed her eyes. It didn't take long for her to fall asleep.

Chapter Eleven

Seth declared them all well at three twenty-two. He also explained the virus didn't survive long out of the host so none of their gear was contagious either. With a shopping list and some of the money from Douglas' wallet, Ashley took the car and headed out. Unable to sit still, Gina first stripped the bed in the sewing room and put the sheets on to wash, then headed for the kitchen. By the time Ashley returned home, Gina had baked a loaf of bread, put a casserole on for dinner, made a chocolate slice and an apple teacake.

Seeing the food on cooling racks on the kitchen benches, Ashley grinned. "Oh good. I'm starved." She helped herself to the slice. "I've never been so hungry in my entire life."

Connor came into the kitchen. He hovered in the doorway as if worried Gina would chase him out again. "Now can I have some? The smells have been driving me crazy."

Gina nodded as she took a bite of cake. She'd chased Connor out of the kitchen three times. She didn't find cooking as much of a stress reliever as her mum did, but she couldn't think of anything else to do to pass the time. Filling the house with the scents of cooking food had also made her feel a little less homesick.

"Not much of a dinner." Seth came into the kitchen and glanced at the food everyone held.

Gina swallowed her mouthful. "Dinner's still cooking. But I'm starved and bored and have so much energy I don't know what to do with it."

"Yeah, I'm hungry too." Seth frowned. "Unusually hungry."

"I don't know about that." Gina grinned. "I still remember what you ordered at Macca's and how much of it you ate."

Seth shrugged. "I eat heaps. Fast metabolism. But I could probably eat everything on the bench and still be hungry."

Ashley picked up another piece of slice. "How about we don't find out if you can. I'm hungry too."

"Do you think it has anything to do with the mutation?" Gina asked.

"I don't know. It's possible." Seth took a piece of cake and some slice. "I guess if we're still eating non-stop tomorrow I'll probably have to say yes."

"Great. What'll we do for food when we run out of Douglas' money? We can't eat all of Gran's food. She also won't be in the hospital forever, so where will we go when she comes home?"

"You don't have a problem. No one's after you," Connor said.

"Doesn't matter. We're sticking together," Ashley said.

"You don't have to leave your life behind. Surely you've got plans for the year." Seth reached for another piece of cake.

"Nothing important. I was just starting a boring job at the beginning of next month. A brain dead, go nowhere job. I wanted to go to uni," Ashley said. "Anyway, sticking with you lot will be more interesting."

Seth stared at her for a moment. "And more dangerous."

"I'm not stupid, Genius. But sometimes, a little danger in life is what makes it worth living."

"You're mad," Connor said.

Ashley turned to him, hands on her hips. "Would you cut and run if you had the chance?"

"That's different-" Connor began.

"Why? Because you're a boy?"

"Well… ahh…" Connor looked towards Seth who shook his head and took a step back, hands held up as if to ward him off.

Ashley jabbed Connor in the chest with her finger. "You're an idiot. Sometimes brains are better than muscles to get a job done."

Connor grabbed Ashley's hand and glared at her. "Don't poke me."

Gina worried the argument would get worse. "What about the disguises you bought? Can I have a look at them, Ashley?"

With a last glare for Connor, Ashley turned to Gina. "Sure, but we might have to cut your hair a little shorter to get it to fit under the wig."

Seth reached out to tuck Gina's hair behind her ear. "We'll pin it back. She doesn't need to cut it."

Gina grabbed his hand when she saw her hair band on his wrist. "I wondered where that had got to. My hair was in the way while I was cooking." She slipped it off his wrist and pulled her hair back into a ponytail.

Ashley looked at Gina's hair carefully. "I guess we can try and pin it. I bought a couple of packets of hairpins. Should we give it a go?"

It took some time, but they finally managed to pin

Gina's hair flat enough for her to wear the wig of mousy brown, shoulder length hair. She stared at the mirror. "I look different."

"Wait until you're wearing those boring black and white clothes with the little badge and I've done your makeup. Hopefully even your mum won't recognise you."

Gina grinned at Ashley. "That would be an achievement." Her grin faded. "How are we going to let her know what's going on if they're watching the house and listening?"

"I've got a few magazines from a church. You can write inside one. They sell them you know."

Gina nodded. "Yeah. That's a great idea."

"You want me to help you get the wig off?"

Gina shook her head. "I'll leave it on for a while. Get used to it. I think I'll work out what to write to my family."

"Okay. I'll see if Connor or Seth want to check out their disguises."

Gina was still working on her letter when dinner was ready to be served. She returned to writing it once they'd all eaten. Finally she was happy with what to write in the magazine and asked Ashley for a copy.

'Mama, don't say anything to let the people watching know I'm here. Buy this magazine, please.'

Gina turned to the next page and again started to write between the lines. This time she didn't need to write so large.

'We don't know who to trust or who to avoid, so we're playing it safe and staying out of sight. The man who kidnapped us was part of a group of scientists experimenting on humans. We don't know if the group wants us for guinea pigs or to destroy us like the rest of the test subjects of the experiment that mostly went wrong. I'll try and keep in touch with you, but it will be difficult. There are people watching you and listening to what's going on. Mourn for me and let people think we haven't survived. It'd be safer for us right now if they believe we died from the experiment. Hide this letter and don't speak aloud of what I've written. If you need to get in touch with me, see Seth's father. But don't speak of it. There are people listening to everything you say, even in our home. I love all of you, Gina.'

She sat back and stared at the magazine, wiping at her cheeks with the back of her hand.

"You okay?"

She turned, startled to find Connor in the lounge room with her. "I guess. I can't help wishing things turned out different. I don't know how, but just different."

Connor sat down beside her. "I'm kind of glad to be here."

"Why?"

"It beats being at home."

"I miss home."

"I don't."

Gina stared at Connor. "But, your parents are probably frantic. Don't you want to let them know you're alive?"

Connor shook his head. "They wouldn't understand. Somehow this'd all be my fault. I should have done something. Even though Douglas had a gun, they still would have expected me to have done something. Anything."

"But, that would have put your life in danger. You don't argue with a man holding a gun. You treat him like his word is law."

"Yeah, but now I'm not normal so I've lost value for them. You can't imagine how hard it is to have to reach milestones on time. Catch a ball at the correct age, be interested in girls, hit puberty, everything all at the correct age. And if I didn't, there were specialists poking and prodding at me, checking to see if I was normal. You should have seen the amount of specialists they brought in the year I was kept back a grade."

Gina reached out and placed a hand on Connor's shoulder. "I'm sorry. That must have been tough. All my parents expect is that we keep on breathing every day and enjoy life."

"I wish. Nope, I've got a family tradition to uphold. There have always been doctors in my family. For generations on both sides. My whole future is mapped out for me. Even if I'm not interested in the path they've chosen."

"Not anymore. Instead of being the doctor, you're more likely to be the patient. Or maybe the test subject." Gina grinned fleetingly. "But hey, if you want family, I'll share mine with you. There's certainly plenty of them to go around."

Connor's laugh was forced. "I can't say I ever wanted a sister. A brother, yeah, but under the circumstances, I could probably make do."

"My dad always said he wanted a son. Someone to take his side in an all girl household. He'll welcome you with open arms and immediately ask you to back him up in his latest argument. I suggest agreeing with my mum, because she's always right." Gina winked.

Connor laughed more easily. "I'll keep that in

mind." His smile faded. "It must be nice knowing they are there for you."

Gina nodded. "Yeah. Always. No matter what and no strings attached."

"Strings! Don't get me started on them. There are so many strings attached to everything my parents give me I spend my days tangled in them."

"There must be something you like about your family. Something small, maybe?"

Connor fell silent. "The endless supply of cash. Is it any wonder I'm shallow?"

Gina protested, "You're not shallow."

"Really? Think back to last year. You were talking to that really tall skinny girl with the dreads. Something about so shallow you could see there was no gold in the creek."

Gina blushed. "Oh. You weren't meant to hear that. I was annoyed with you. You and your mates were picking on Mary."

"Who?"

"Tall skinny girl with dreads."

"I didn't know her name."

"Why were you picking on her?"

"Because I'm shallow."

"No, really."

Connor smiled wryly. "Really. If I'd stuck up for

her, my shallow mates would have turned on me and I would have been alone in a pack of wolves."

"Why hang with them?"

"Because they're the crowd my parents expect me to be seen with."

"Oh."

Ashley waltzed into the room. "I can't sit still for a minute. Does anyone else have that problem?" She glanced from Gina to Connor. "Sorry. Was I interrupting anything? Want me to leave again?"

Gina took her hand off Connor's shoulder. "No. We were talking about families. I guess I was a little sad after writing a letter to mine."

"I'm glad to have a break from mine. I have two annoying younger brothers who won't stay out of my things," Ashley said.

Seth stepped into the lounge room. "What are we all gathering in here for?"

"Complaining about families," Ashley said.

"I wasn't complaining," Gina protested.

Ashley grinned. "I was." She yawned. "I'm tired all of a sudden."

"You can sleep straight through now. No need to be woken every thirty minutes," Seth said.

"Yes!" Ashley waltzed towards the doorway. "I'm

going to bed to enjoy ten hours of uninterrupted sleep."

Connor rose to his feet. "Me too. Well, maybe not ten, but eight sounds good."

"Night, Connor." Gina reached out and rested her hand on his forearm for a second.

"Night." He brushed past Seth who still stood near the doorway.

When it was only the two of them in the lounge room, Seth came closer. "What was all that about?"

Gina smiled slightly. "Not much. So, what do you think our chances are of pulling this disguise off tomorrow?"

"High. You'll see your parents, we'll have a few doors slammed in our faces and be back here by lunch."

"I hope so. Not so much the doors slammed in my face, but the high chance of things going well." She yawned. "Ashley's not the only one who's suddenly exhausted."

"Get some sleep."

"Will you stay with me? You're better than a night light."

Seth laughed softly. "I certainly haven't been compared with a night light before."

"Will you? You keep the nightmares away."

Seth dropped an arm across her shoulders. "Yeah. Come on then."

"I need to get this wig off first."

"I'll give you a hand."

Chapter Twelve

Morning arrived before Gina was ready to face it. With Ashley's help, she transformed herself into another person and the four of them headed for her neighbourhood. Gina looked at each of them in the car. A slight smile formed when her gaze fell on Connor with his 'nasty little moustache'. All of them looked different. The boys had black hair in a tacky bowl cut and Ashley had the same mousy brown hair she wore, only a little longer.

When they pulled up at the end of her street, Gina's stomach churned and she breathed through her mouth, hoping she'd manage to keep down the large breakfast she'd consumed earlier. After having front doors slammed in their faces a couple of times as they worked their way down the street, Gina's nervousness fled. One elderly woman bought a magazine, a man abused them and a couple of houses ignored their knocks, their whispers of pretending to be out clear to Gina.

Nervousness returned as they walked down the path to her house. Her mouth dried and her palms became sweaty. She stumbled on the uneven paver. She hadn't done that since she was a little girl. Her gaze was drawn to the mass of flowers brightening the front of the timber house, lacy curtains shifting in the slight summer breeze. She could hear Nonna in the kitchen, arguing over how to prepare lunch, which was still a couple of hours away. Her mum, as usual made non-committal noises and continued to do things her way.

Seth knocked on the front door and Gina listened as her mum warned Nonna not to touch the food before her footsteps travelled through the house. The moment Gina met her mum's gaze she knew she recognised her.

Gina quickly held up the magazine and opened it to the first page. "Would you be interested in buying our religion's magazine, ma'am?" Her voice broke on the last word and tears filled her eyes. All she wanted to do was throw herself into her mum's arms.

There was silence while Ariana read the warning on the first page. "Come in while I get my purse.

Maybe a cool drink after being out in this hot sun would be nice."

Gina opened her mouth to speak, but Seth shook his head and spoke first. "No thank you, ma'am. We have other people we need to see today."

"Oh." Ariana stood in the doorway and continued to stare at Gina.

"Did you wish to buy a copy of our magazine? It's only two dollars," Ashley said.

Ariana nodded jerkily. "Yes. Yes. I'll get my purse. Give me a minute." She moved away from the door, frequent glances behind her as if worried Gina would disappear.

Gina clenched her jaw, tensing as she tried not to run after her mum. She closed her eyes so she didn't have to watch her mum vanish from sight. When she heard the footsteps return, she opened her eyes.

Ariana pressed a coin into Gina's hand and something angular. "Thank you." She took the magazine and continued to stare at Gina.

"Thank you, ma'am." Seth tugged on Gina's arm.

Gina walked automatically down the path, her gaze falling on the uneven paver as she reached it. She stepped carefully this time. Before she was ready to, they had left her yard and were walking up the path to the next house. She couldn't speak. Her hand was still closed over whatever her mum had pressed into it.

Connor spoke to the next person, who shook their head and politely closed the door. The next people were out and the ones after that slammed the door in their faces. They visited house after house as they worked their way to the end of the street and to the houses in the street behind. Each door brought them closer to the car. And no matter how hard she tried to hear what was happening in her house, no one spoke. There were tears and footsteps, but no words.

Gina sagged in the back seat the moment they reached the car. She opened her hand and stared at the contents. A two dollar coin and the necklace her mum had received for her confirmation from her parents. A gold cross with a diamond chip in the centre. It had once belonged to Gina's great-grandmother. Her eyes blurred so she couldn't see the cross. She couldn't recall her mum ever taking the necklace off before.

"Gina? You okay?" Seth asked from beside her.

"It's my Mum's. She never takes it off. It was my great-grandmother's. I never knew her."

Seth gently took the necklace from her and undid the catch. He slid it around her neck and did it up. "She worries for you and wants to keep you safe."

"I know. I wish there was some way I could make it easy for her."

Seth took her hand. "Until the ones who started this experiment are out of the picture, it won't be easy for her."

"What are we meant to do? Kill them?" Gina demanded.

"Might be the easiest solution," Connor said from the driver's seat.

"No way!" Ashley exclaimed. "I could never kill anyone."

"What if they had a gun to your head and were about to pull the trigger? If you had a gun on them, would you pull your trigger first?" Connor asked.

"That's a stupid question," Ashley said.

"No, it's not," Seth said quietly. "It'll probably be one we have to face before this is over."

"But I couldn't... it'd be..." Ashley's voice trailed off.

Seth looked at Gina. "What about you?"

"I don't know."

"How about we change the scenario then." Seth continued to look at Gina. "They've got a gun to your mum's head and are about to pull the trigger. Could you shoot first?"

There was no hesitation in Gina's answer. "Yes. They're not bringing my family into this."

"If they kill you, do you think your family will let it drop? Mourn you? Get on with their lives and let them get away with killing you?" Seth demanded.

Gina shook her head. "No. They'd want vengeance. Particularly Nonno. There's always been rumours he was in the mafia before he came to Australia. He believes in an eye for an eye."

"We've got to find out who ordered this experiment and where they are," Seth said.

Connor pulled up at a red light. "And how are we meant to do that?"

Seth grinned. "Follow the mouse back to its hole."

"How are we supposed to do that?" The red light became green and Connor drove forward.

"Tonight we put a tracking device on whoever is watching my house. But for now, we've got cake waiting for us." Seth turned to Gina again. "Happy birthday."

"It doesn't feel like a birthday."

Seth linked his fingers in hers. "The day hasn't finished yet."

* * *

Once the last of the chocolate cake and the pizza they'd picked up on the way home was eaten, they all drifted away from the table. Gina wandered to the sewing room, not sure what to do. Night was hours away. She ran her fingers through her hair that hung loosely down her back. She was glad to have the hairpins out and the wig off.

"Have you got a minute, Gina?"

She turned to face Seth, who stood in the doorway. "Yeah."

He stepped into the room and closed the door behind him. His lips slowly curved into a smile. "Does it feel a little more like a birthday yet?"

"I guess it did for a bit. Thanks for the cake."

"Would a present help?"

"I thought the cake was my present."

Seth drew a small thin packet from his pocket. "Happy birthday."

Gina took the packet and slid her fingers under the tape. She unfolded the end and tipped the contents into her hand. A slither of gold links slipped out to lie in a heap, a tiny gold apple sitting amongst them.

Seth took the bracelet from her hand and undid the

catch so he could put it on her wrist. He tapped the apple that hung from one of the links. "There was a goddess in Norse mythology called Idunn whose name means 'forever young'. She had golden apples that when eaten gave eternal youthfulness." Seth grinned. "Maybe she was an ancient scientist who injected her apples with some mutating gene. But whatever she was and however she managed it, what she gave was considered a gift. A very precious gift."

"Thank you."

"Douglas might not have meant it to be, but this can be a gift if we choose to see it that way."

"I doubt I'll be able to see it that way until I'm back with my family."

"Tonight we take the first step in bringing that about." He let go of her hand.

"Seth."

"Yeah."

"I haven't thanked you for everything you did to make sure we survived the virus."

"I wanted to survive too."

Gina smiled. "I know. But you helped the rest of us. Thank you."

"I was glad to."

Gina sighed as she heard footsteps outside her door. "What's wrong, Connor?"

Connor swung the door open. "Why don't we put on some disguises and go see a movie or something? We can't sit around here all day just waiting for night."

Gina turned towards Seth who shrugged. "Well…"

"Ashley said she'd be interested in getting out for a while. Anything. She's sick of seeing these walls," Connor said.

"Will you come, Seth?" Gina waited for his answer and smiled when he nodded. She turned back to Connor. "A movie it is. I guess I better put my wig back on."

Connor laughed. "Ashley has a different disguise. It involves red hair, torn jeans and a tonne of jewellery."

"Ahh… great?" She looked towards Seth for help.

"Don't look at me. I didn't pick it out. I dread to think what she's got lined up for me."

Connor laughed again. "All she'd say to me when I asked what I'm wearing, was did I know much about heavy metal."

Seth draped an arm around Gina's shoulders. "Let's find out what she's got in mind."

By the time they had on their new disguises, it was late afternoon. They wore shirts with heavy metal bands printed on them, torn jeans, long hair and clip on and stick on earrings. Ashley had even given them fake tattoos. Gina stared at herself in the mirror, her eyes heavy with eyeliner. Her lipstick was blood red and a stick on stud earring glittered on her nose, looking very realistic. She barely recognised herself. She doubted anyone else would.

Seth drove this time and Connor sat in the back with Gina. Ashley was again in the front, turning constantly so she could talk to them, her fake lip ring catching the last of the sunlight as she moved.

After talking for a while about the latest disguises she'd created and what she liked best about them, Ashley said, "I should work in the movies. Maybe in special effects."

"Are you going to use us on your resume?" Gina asked.

Ashley grinned. "Sure, why not?"

Seth chuckled. "Experience- disguises for three people on the run from the law."

Ashley nodded. "See, perfect addition on any resume."

"Oh, totally." Gina barely managed to keep her expression serious.

Seth parked the car and glanced from Ashley to Gina. "I hope you don't expect to watch a chick flick."

"Oh no, that wouldn't suit this afternoon's image

at all." Ashley glanced down at herself. "Nope. This look screams horror or action if there's no decent horror."

"I can live with that." Connor opened the car door.

"I hope there's an action you can't live without seeing," Gina said.

Ashley linked arms with Gina. "You don't like horror?" When Gina shook her head she sighed heavily and dramatically. "I'm so disappointed in you, Gina. You don't know what you're missing. There's nothing like being scared out of your mind when you know you're not in any danger."

"I think there's enough horror in our lives right now," Gina said.

Seth fell in beside her. "A bit hard to argue that comment."

Connor walked a little ahead of them and glanced back to speak. "So the vote's for action?"

A boy stepping out of the cinema ran into Connor. "Watch it, will you?"

Recognising him as one of Connor's crowd, Gina quickly stepped between them. "You are the one who should watch it." She grabbed Connor's hand. "Come on. Let's see what's on."

"Hey!"

Gina dragged Connor with her, ignoring Connor's mate.

Chapter Thirteen

Ashley strode along beside Gina. "Something I miss?" She glanced behind them.

"Yeah. A friend of Connor's," Gina muttered.

"Not good." Ashley glanced behind again. "And he's talking to another three boys and pointing in our direction."

"Let's get some tickets for whatever's playing next and get out of sight," Connor said.

"Maybe movies weren't such a good idea," Ashley said. "I thought it'd be fun."

Seth rested his hand momentarily on Ashley's shoulder. "It will be fun. Once we're out of sight."

"I'll grab tickets." Ashley strode towards the short line and within minutes was back with tickets. She wasn't back soon enough.

Four of Connor's mates strode over to them. Gina recognised each of them and hoped they didn't recognise her or Connor. She leaned close to Connor. "Don't say anything. We can't afford for them to recognise your voice."

"I'm not an idiot," Connor whispered.

Gina tried to remember everything she could about the boys headed their way. None of it was good. Will, David, Marcus and Neil had been amongst the boys who'd teased Mary. Pack of wolves was too nice a term for them.

"Neil here reckons you need to learn some manners." Will stood in front of Gina, invading her personal space.

"And he thinks he can teach me? Yeah, right." Gina refused to step back.

Seth moved closer, wrapping his fingers around her upper arm. "If you knife another kid while you're on parole it won't go down well."

Gina turned her head slightly towards Seth, getting into the scenario he'd provided for her. "You think they're going to say a girl got the better of them? I doubt they'd talk."

"Blood usually does the talking for them," Seth said dryly.

Ashley gave Seth two tickets. "I don't care about you two, we're going to see the movie." She linked her arm around Connor's and looked over the four boys. "There's nothing here you can't handle." She pulled Connor with her.

"Looks like your mates have run out on you." Neil grinned.

"Only because they know I can handle you four while my friend watches the entertainment." Gina saw the manager head across the foyer towards them. Relief coursed through her. It had taken him long enough to figure out what was happening.

"You're full of shit," Will snarled.

The manager reached them. "Is everything okay here?"

Gina smiled. "Yeah. Just letting our friends know we'd see them after the movie." She glanced back to Will. "Later." She turned away, Seth at her side, and headed into the movie, handing over the tickets as they did. The lights had been dimmed and the movie was just starting.

"Near the front." Seth pointed towards Ashley and Connor.

"Glad you've got such good eyesight," Gina whispered.

"Anything happen?" Ashley asked as they sat down next to her.

"I doubt it. I can't smell any freshly spilt blood," Connor said.

"You were waiting to smell blood?" Gina stared at him.

Connor shrugged. "Not like I can hear what's happening from that far away."

Gina smiled. "Nah. The manager came along like I thought he would." Hoped was probably the more accurate description.

"Are you going to talk all through the movie," an irate voice asked from behind them.

Ashley giggled and turned around. "Probably. I'd suggest moving if you don't like it."

Gina watched as the man stood up and moved away, a woman following him. She was surprised he hadn't argued. Unlike Connor's friends. Thinking of them, she listened, searching the area for them. It wasn't hard to find the four boys. They were bragging about what they would have done if the manager hadn't shown up. She sighed.

Seth leaned in close so he could whisper. "What's up?"

"They're talking about waiting around to deal with us after the movie. They know which direction we arrived from."

Seth laughed softly. "I guess the element of surprise will be on our side."

Connor leaned forward. "What's happening?"

"Your mates are idiots," Gina muttered.

"I could have told you that," Connor said.

Seth grinned. "They're talking about waiting around to deal with us after the movie."

"I'll smell them coming. Marcus always drowns himself in aftershave. It won't be a problem, Gina."

"Guess it'll give me a chance to see if I can do more than cartwheels. Now sit back so I can see the movie." Ashley pressed against Connor's chest until he sat back in his seat.

Even though she'd missed the first few minutes of the movie, it didn't take Gina long to figure out what was going on. Partway through the movie, Seth linked his fingers through hers and she glanced over at him. He smiled and turned his attention back to the movie. Gina's fingers brushed the cross that hung under her shirt. She might not be surrounded by family this birthday, but she was with people who were friends. People who'd faced death with her. It was right they should also celebrate life together.

When the movie ended, Seth and Gina followed behind Connor and Ashley as she explained her favourite action scene and why. Connor argued that another scene was better. They stepped out into the early evening, senses alert. Ashley continued to argue for her scene and Connor slowly turned his head. He glanced back towards Gina and whispered the word left.

Gina nodded. She could hear them plotting. She wondered if they should suggest Connor stay back in case he was recognised. She watched as he eagerly changed direction. His stride lengthened and there was a bounce in his step. Nope, she doubted he'd be happy with that suggestion. He looked keen for a fight.

"Males," Gina muttered under her breath.

Seth laughed. "He does look rather happy, doesn't he? But have you noticed Ashley?"

Gina's gaze fell on the girl who almost danced beside Connor. "Think we should leave them to it? They look like we'd only ruin their fun if we helped."

Seth shook his head. "No. I want to give something a try. I'll come at them from the other direction. Meet you there."

Gina's mouth dropped open at how quickly Seth moved. Ashley turned to walk backwards so she could talk to her. "Was that Seth?"

Gina nodded.

"Wow, he can move. I wonder if I can run that fast." Ashley faced forward again.

Gina picked up her pace until she was beside

Connor. "He's going to come up behind them. Take them by surprise."

"As long as he doesn't start without us," Connor said.

Gina stared at him. "These are your mates we're talking about."

"The guys I hang out with." Connor hesitated. "I guess you could say I've really only got three mates."

"Let's go kick some butt." Ashley wrapped her arm around Connor's waist. "I haven't had a good fight in weeks."

Gina shook her head. Ashley didn't seem the sort to wade in fists first, but she guessed looks could be deceiving.

Will stepped out of the shadows, the other three boys behind him. "You did say something about meeting up later, didn't you." His comment was met with laughter from his companions.

Gina nodded. "Yep. What took you so long?"

"You won't be so confident when we finish with you," Neil said.

Ashley laughed. "I'm gonna make you regret those words." Before Gina could blink, Ashley was in front of Neil, her fist connecting with his jaw. He hit the footpath with a crack. She swore. "Guess I should pull my punches. I wouldn't want to kill someone."

Seth appeared behind them. "Thanks for the warning. The last thing we need are even more cops after us."

Marcus bent over Neil. "I think we better call an ambulance. He's bleeding."

Ashley swore again. "Well that takes all the fun out of fighting."

"Let's get out of here. We need to avoid cops like they're the plague," Seth said.

Gina grinned at him as she recalled his earlier tale. "Yeah, wouldn't want to get caught while I'm still on parole."

Marcus took his phone out and dialled for an ambulance. Connor looked at his mates who now all knelt around Neil. Ashley grabbed him by the arm and pulled him away, Gina and Seth followed.

Reaching the car, Ashley hopped in the front seat. "Guess this disguise is compromised."

Connor sat in the back with Gina. "Do you think Neil will be okay? He's a complete jerk, but well…"

"I'll listen out for when the ambulance arrives and let you know what they say." Gina rested her hand on his forearm for a moment.

"Thanks." Connor glanced away and cleared his throat. "You know, I think I might be able to track people."

Ashley turned in her seat to look at him. "What do you mean?"

"I could smell where they'd walked. The closer we got to them, the stronger it was."

Ashley laughed. "Neat. Our own personal bloodhound." She frowned. "Wish I had a useful ability. Knocking someone out with one punch doesn't count. I bet all of you can do that. Big deal that I'll never need to bother with an air-con or heater ever again."

"I didn't think being able to smell better would be any use either," Connor said.

"Well I hope we find something changing your body temperature is good for."

Connor grinned. "Can you make your body ice cold?"

Ashley stared at him suspiciously. "Yeah." She drew the word out.

"Great. No need to keep the beer in an esky when we go camping. Just give them to you to hold for a few minutes." Connor moved closer to the door when Ashley tried to hit him.

"Can we pull over? I can barely hear Connor's friends. If we go much further I won't be able to hear what happens," Gina said.

When Seth pulled over, she continued to listen

to Connor's friends, relieved when the ambulance finally arrived. Neil was conscious when they arrived and she listened as he answered questions and the ambulance staff checked him over. She eventually turned to Connor with a smile.

"Neil's on the way to the hospital. He's cranky and not talking. Guess he doesn't want to say he was knocked out by a girl."

Ashley laughed. "They never do."

Seth pulled out onto the road again.

"So he'll be okay?" Connor asked.

Gina nodded. "Yeah. Minor concussion. He'll need a couple of stitches and have a killer headache. They'll keep him in overnight for observation, but he should be home in the morning."

"Always knew he had a hard head." Connor grinned.

Gina could hear the relief in his voice and didn't blame him. She didn't like his friends, but was glad Neil hadn't been badly hurt.

"Shush. We're getting close to my house," Seth said.

Chapter Fourteen

They fell silent as Seth parked the car. He pointed to a house in darkness halfway down the street. Across the road from it was a dark coloured sedan. Gina focused her hearing on the car.

"Two men, bored senseless and thinking they're wasting their time sitting outside when the occupant does nothing interesting and goes to bed early every night." Gina smiled. "And they're dying for a hit of caffeine."

Connor wrinkled his nose. "Smells like they've already had far too much."

Seth opened the car door and stood up to peer at the sedan. He swore as he sat back in the front seat and quietly closed the door. "They're using thermal imaging so nothing can get near their car without them knowing."

"What's that exactly?" Ashley asked.

Seth stared at her for a moment then smiled. "It picks up heat given off by things, including humans and animals. Looks like we've found something your ability is good for after all."

Ashley grinned. "Finally. What do you want me to do?"

Seth took a small round object out of the centre console. "Put this behind the number plate on the car. It's magnetic so it won't have a problem staying on. Make sure your body isn't giving off any heat and stay low to the ground. They seem to be mainly relying on the screens inside the vehicle rather than doing an external visual check."

"You expect me to scurry along the ground in these tight jeans?"

Seth shook his head at Ashley. "Just stay low. I don't care how you manage it."

Ashley took the tracking device and hopped out of the car. They watched as she bent low and dashed down the street, little more than a blur. Gina listened in to the men in the sedan, nothing of interest to hear. She breathed a sigh of relief when Ashley returned.

Ashley slid into her seat, a grin on her face. "Simple. Nothing to it."

"Easy for you to say. Being a bloodhound wouldn't have got me that close to the car."

"I think the different abilities are going to help in the long run. I don't know how they randomly occur or what triggers each one, but something must," Seth said.

"You can work on the problem later, Genius. How about we figure out what our next step is?"

"Getting out of here before anyone notices us hanging about." Seth started the car.

"So what do we do next, Lilly?"

"We wait. Until the mice move we won't be able to follow them to their mouse hole."

Ashley sighed. "I hate waiting. Give me action any day."

Connor nodded in agreement. "Yeah, I know what you mean."

A beeping in the front caught Gina's attention. "What was that?"

Seth took a mobile phone from his pocket. "The phone my dad gave me. I thought it was best not to use Connor's. We don't want to risk being tracked down by it."

"Was that a message?" Ashley leaned close to him.

Seth nodded. "Yeah. An address. I guess we check it out." He handed the phone over to Ashley. "Put it in the navigator for me, will you?"

The address took them to a high rise building in

the city. Seth keyed in the pin number, that had been sent with the address, to access the underground parking. They were quiet as they made their way to the elevator. Seth pressed the button for their floor and Gina glanced around, listening.

Everything seemed normal. But what did she know? How would she recognise a threatening conversation? It wasn't like someone would be sitting around going into detail about what they'd do when they caught them. Nor did she expect some mad scientist muttering under his breath about his psychotic plans. Gina smiled ruefully.

Seth glanced at her, a raised eyebrow. She shook her head, her smile widening. The elevator pinged and the doors opened. Connor stepped out and glanced around the corridor. They followed him, alert and ready. It was deserted. They encountered no one as they made their way to the last door on the floor.

Seth knocked on the door and grinned when it opened to reveal an older version of himself, the man a little taller and just as slim, his hair starting to thin. The man stared at each of them, returning Seth's grin after a moment. "The eyes give you away."

Ashley swore. "We need coloured contacts."

The door opened wider and they were ushered

in. The man locked the door behind them. "You lot made good time."

"Dad, this is Gina, Ashley and Connor. This is my father, Anthony."

Anthony held out his hand and shook each of theirs. "Glad to see you're all looking so well. If a little bit different from the photos I have of you." His gaze rested on Ashley. "Although this could be the way you normally look since I don't have a photo of you."

"Why would you have photos of us?" Connor asked.

"I think every police station in Australia has photos of the three of you."

"Oh, yeah," Connor mumbled.

Gina frowned. "How did you get here before us? And how did you give your followers the slip?"

Anthony laughed. "I haven't been home since just after dark. I've been here every evening while they think I'm safely tucked up in bed."

"What is this place?" Connor glanced around the sparsely furnished living area.

Anthony crossed the room to open one of the three closed doors. "Step into my lab."

Gina groaned. "Not needles."

"Sorry." Anthony looked apologetic.

She sighed. "Do we really need more tests? Seth said we're not contagious."

Anthony nodded. "I know, but there are other things I need to look at. I particularly need to know how your blood tests would look if someone tested you for contagious viruses. We want you to be able to return to your lives, but you're currently suspected of being infected with a highly contagious disease."

"Okay. Let's get it over and done with before I have too long to think about it." Gina stepped into the room and was surprised to see it was set up like a laboratory. "Where'd you get all the gear from?"

"Due to the sensitive nature of my work the lab is regularly relocated. During the day other scientists work in here, but we all have access at any hour. I've rigged an alarm to warn me when the pin for this room is used to access the underground parking." Anthony made his way to a workbench as he spoke.

Seth guided Gina to a chair. "You better close your eyes. I'll tell you when it's safe to open them again."

Gina sat down with a weak smile for Seth. "Thanks." She fiddled with the apple on her bracelet as she waited. "I'm beginning to feel like a pin cushion."

"It'll be over before you know it," Anthony said from close by.

"He's putting a strap around your arm. Keep your eyes closed. Okay, cold now," Seth warned.

Gina sighed. She knew what warning came after that one. She couldn't help tensing when Seth gave it.

"A little sting."

"I'm glad you were never bothered by needles, Seth." Anthony released the strap and was quiet for a moment. "All done now."

"Keep your eyes closed," Seth warned. "And was it any wonder, Dad? Didn't Mum always call me your favourite experiment? You were forever taking blood samples so I'm probably completely desensitised to them."

"Can I open my eyes yet?" Gina asked.

"No. Dad's taking a sample from me."

Anthony chuckled. "How could I resist? It was the perfect opportunity to study the changes in a baby. Besides, I never heard her complain unless we were having an argument. She'd demand to know the results, mainly wanting to know if you were coming down with something. I've never known a woman so obsessed with germs. Or should I say obsessed with eradicating them."

Seth took one of Gina's hands. "It's safe to open your eyes now."

She opened them to see him looking down at her, his lips curved in a smile. "Are you laughing at me?"

Seth shook his head. His smile disappeared, but the corners of his mouth looked like they were trying to curve upwards again. "Never. Come on then. Or do you want to stay in here while the other two have their blood tests?"

Gina tugged her hand from Seth's and rose to her feet. She hurried from the room, careful to only look at the doorway. She didn't want to risk seeing a needle. She glanced around the living area, uncertain what to do next. Ashley and Connor sat on the couch having a quiet yet intense conversation. Gina made sure she didn't eavesdrop.

Seth paused in the doorway. "Connor, Ashley, you're both needed in the lab." When they nodded in acknowledgement, he made his way to a laptop set up on the kitchen bench.

Not knowing what else to do, Gina followed him. She watched as he brought up a program that seemed to be a street directory with a stationary black dot on it. "What are you doing?"

"Checking on our mouse."

"It's a black dot." She watched as Seth typed on the keyboard and the dot became the shape of a mouse.

He turned to her with a grin. "Happy?"

Before Gina could reply, Anthony strode into the room followed by Ashley and a pale Connor. "One of the fellows I work with has turned up. You need to leave immediately."

Seth exited the program and met his father in the middle of the room. They briefly hugged. Anthony took a key, a piece of paper and a credit card from his wallet.

Seth looked at the objects his father gave him. "What are these for?"

"The card is in the same name as the car, you'll need to sign the back of it. I used your date of birth for the pin. The key is to a house I've set up for you and the address is on the paper." Anthony stared at Seth, quiet for a moment. "Be careful. These people don't play nice."

Seth nodded as Anthony led them to the door. "Make sure you be careful too. Just remember the car we're tracking is the one watching you. If they discover the tracker they might blame you."

Anthony unlocked the door and rested his hand on the doorknob. "Use the stairs for a couple of floors before you get on the elevator." He swung the door open.

They stepped into the corridor and headed for the stairs. Gina glanced back to see Anthony watched them. He smiled briefly before he closed the door. Connor, who was in the lead, opened the door to the stairwell and they hurried down the stairs, their footsteps echoing around them. They passed three doors before Seth went ahead of Connor to open the next one.

Chapter Fifteen

The wait for the elevator seemed overly long and Gina examined the area. When she was about to check it out again, Seth wrapped his arm around her waist and pulled her close. He smiled down at her before his lips grazed her ear.

"Look like you haven't a care in the world. There are cameras here. And don't bother looking for them. They're really small."

Gina glanced around the elevator when they entered, relieved it was empty. She couldn't resist looking for hidden cameras. She glanced at Seth who laughed softly. "What?"

He shook his head and turned towards Ashley. "You know, that movie we saw earlier was good. That guy who thought that everywhere he went he was being watched or listened to really could act."

"But–" Connor started to say.

Ashley rounded on him. "Don't you dare say he couldn't act. I mean, he could act so well that I've spent most of the night feeling like someone's watching me."

Connor's puzzled expression cleared. "I wasn't. I just wanted to say that next time I pick the movie. I hate crap like that."

The elevator pinged and the doors opened. They stepped out into the underground parking. No one was around. Everything was quiet except for their footsteps on the concrete. Gina listened carefully. They were definitely alone. But she guessed most people had better things to do, after midnight on a Saturday night, than hang about an underground car park. Within minutes they were back in the car and on the road.

"I'm so glad to be out of there," Ashley said.

"Why didn't someone warn me the place would be full of hidden cameras?" Connor demanded. He was once again in the back with Gina.

"Sound and pictures. I didn't think of it. It wasn't until I saw them that I could warn you." Seth handed the piece of paper Anthony had given him to Ashley. "Put this address in the navigator, would you? We probably should check out what he's put together for us."

"I hope there's food there. I'm starving," Connor said.

Gina smiled. "Actually, I am too."

"I'd say our food bill is going to be ridiculous." Seth glanced at the navigator. "Good thing Dad gave me a credit card. That money from Douglas isn't going to last forever."

"Who pays back the money on the credit card?" Gina asked.

Seth shrugged. "It'll be some research institution. Probably a top secret one that doesn't even know all its own secrets."

Gina frowned. "Isn't that kind of like stealing?"

"We're running for our lives." Seth met her gaze briefly in the rear vision mirror.

"I suppose."

"There's a twenty-four hour Macca's over there." Connor leaned forward to point it out. "I'm starving."

Seth indicated and changed lanes. "This'll be the only stop. I need to see if there's a computer at the house so I can check on our mouse."

They ordered enough food to fill six paper bags and were glad to have the credit card when they heard the bill. Gina bit into a burger as they pulled back onto the road.

She swallowed her mouthful. "What do we do if there's no computer at the house?"

"Find an internet café that's still open at this time of night," Seth said.

"Wouldn't it be morning since it's after midnight?" Ashley rummaged in one of the paper bags at her feet, already finished a burger.

Seth shrugged. "Semantics. We've got to find out who's behind this. Until we do, no one's safe. Not even our families. And we've got to make sure none of them link Ashley to us."

"And then what? After we've found the bad guys, what do we do?" Gina waited as the silence dragged out.

"Well, Lilly? You think you have all the answers."

Seth pulled up in the driveway of a house surrounded by a tall fence. The gates swung open as the car stopped in front of them and he drove along the curved driveway towards the double garage that also opened. As soon as the engine was off, he turned to look at Gina and Connor. "I don't know. But I'm guessing none of us are going to like the choices we'll have to make."

"Why did everything open up like that?" Ashley gestured towards the garage door as it closed behind them. "Is someone here?"

"Security system. It reads the number plate." Seth pocketed the car keys.

Connor pushed the car door open and paused. "How do you know, Lilly? This could be a trap. Someone might be in here already and opened it for us."

Seth shook his head. "No. Dad would have let me know if the security was compromised. We have the same system on our house."

Gina continued to sit in the car as the other three climbed out. Each door closed loudly. She looked up when Seth opened her door and stared in at her. When he said nothing, she glanced away from his study of her. "Guess I managed to survive my birthday."

"I promised you would."

"Do you always keep your promises, Seth?" She met his gaze.

Seth stared at her silently for nearly a minute. "I try not to make promises I can't keep."

"Would you be willing to promise we all get through this alive?"

"How about I promise to do everything I can to make sure we survive?"

Gina looked away. She stared straight ahead and

a soft sigh escaped. "How can you see this as a gift? Look at all the problems that come with it."

"We'll deal with them."

Ashley reappeared in the doorway that led from the garage into the house that she and Connor had disappeared through. "Found a computer and a laptop. You two coming?"

Another sigh escaped and Gina forced herself to move. "I don't know if surviving my birthday is a good or bad thing."

Seth stepped back from the car. "It's good."

Gina could only look at him. She didn't have his optimism. If being alive put her entire family in danger, wouldn't she have been better off dead? How could saving one life compete with risking an extremely large family?

"Well?" Ashley demanded impatiently from the doorway. "I thought you were keen to see what those dudes watching your house are up to."

Gina turned away from Seth. There was nothing she could say to him. She guessed only time would tell if being alive was good. She walked quietly beside him and glanced down when his fingers linked with hers. Her gaze travelled up his arm, stopping at his face.

Seth smiled slightly. His lips barely moved and

his words were little more than a sigh on the air. But Gina heard them clearly. "Survival is good. Do you think these people are going to quit their experiments? Even if we'd died, they would have gone back to the research stage. Who knows what disasters they might create? No one is safe while they're still playing god."

"Come on you two. You can gaze into each other's eyes later when I'm not standing around watching." Ashley turned away and entered the house again.

Seth grinned. "Well? Are we going to check on the 'dudes' or stand here gazing into each other's eyes?"

Gina couldn't help smiling. "Let's make sure there's not a single bit of information left they can use. I don't want to risk them accidentally making a virus that'll wipe out the entire country."

Seth continued to hold her hand as they entered the house. They walked through a laundry, along a hallway and stepped into an open plan area that contained both a dining table and a lounge suite. Gina's jaw dropped as her head slowly turned to take in the entire space.

"You sure we're in the right house?" She turned to Seth.

He chuckled. "Yeah."

"It's massive. It didn't look this big when we drove

in. But I guess I only caught glimpses of columns and arched windows through all the trees and shrubs growing around it. What are we meant to do with all this space?"

Connor stepped out of a doorway towards the far end of the room on their left. "Kitchen's fully stocked." He leaned against the doorframe. "You know this place would be perfect for holding parties. There's enough space to fit all the seniors at our school. Even though most of them aren't worth inviting."

"Study is this way." Ashley stood at the start of another hallway behind Gina on her right. "Can I take first pick of the bedrooms?"

"No way." Connor pushed away from the doorframe and crossed the room. "You'll want the master bedroom."

"The bathroom has a spa bath. I've never been in one before." Ashley smiled up at Connor, peering at him through her lashes. "You don't really want it, do you? Each of the bedrooms have their own bathroom so it's not like you'd be missing out on having one."

"Flirting won't change my mind." Connor stopped in front of Ashley.

Ashley placed her hand on his chest. Her smile

never faltered. "Me? Flirting? Now would I do that to get my own way?"

The sound of Seth moving towards the study distracted Gina from the conversation. With a last glance at Ashley and Connor, she followed Seth. She stopped in the doorway and watched as he flipped open the laptop sitting on the large polished desk and sat in the high backed, swivel chair. Her gaze took in the bookcases that dominated one wall and the heavy drapes at the five windows in the angled room. There was a second desk with a desktop computer and printer as well as a handful of pens in a container and a notepad. A cordless phone sat in a cradle beside the pens.

Seth shook his head as he gazed at the internet page he'd opened. "Surely they'll have to swap sometime. They can't expect the same men to watch the house constantly."

Gina moved across the soft carpet and stood at his shoulder. The mouse was still at the same spot on the map. "You don't think they've discovered we're trying to track them, do you?"

Seth stared at the screen. "I don't know." He opened another window and typed in the address bar. Moments later he was looking at the car parked across from his house.

"How did you do that?"

Seth grinned up at her. "Accessed the security cameras at my home."

Gina was speechless for a moment. "Doesn't it bother you?"

Seth looked puzzled. "What?"

Gina waved towards the screen. "The security. Surveillance cameras, codes in emails, people watching you."

Seth shrugged. "My life's always been that way. Sometimes it's annoying, but mostly it's interesting."

"Interesting." She could only stare at him.

Seth nodded.

"And what has the last few days been for you? A mild diversion?"

Seth pushed back the chair and stood up. "No." He reached out and took her hand.

Gina pulled away from him. "Then what?"

"Gina, it's part of who my dad is. I've had to learn to put up with it. It's either that or live with my mum and her second husband. And trust me when I say putting up with all the security stuff is preferable to him. Rod's only a couple of years older than me."

"Twenty?"

"Okay, maybe a bit older than that. Twenty-two."

"How old is your mum?"

"Thirty-five." Seth laughed. "That got your attention, didn't it? You should have seen your expression."

Gina made a face at him. "Well, I'm not used to all this cloak and dagger stuff." She dropped onto the seat Seth had vacated and sighed heavily. She shook her head slowly. "I don't know what to do. I thought all I had to do was survive the virus. But I should know life's never that simple."

"It'd be boring if it was."

"Huh. Give me boring. I love boring."

Seth smiled. "No you don't. There's been moments you've enjoyed having these abilities." He pressed a finger to her lips when she started to speak. "Don't argue. Admit it."

Gina leaned away from Seth. "Maybe. But that doesn't change anything. I'm worried about my family. I have cousins that are still babies. If anything happened to them because of me…" she shook her head, unable to continue.

"Gina." Seth reached out and clasped her hands in his. "We'll–" he swore as his gaze fell on the screen of the laptop. He let go of Gina to push the chair to the side so he could access the keyboard.

"What's happening?"

"Shush." A sharp shake of his head was her only answer.

Gina leaned forward and watched as two men stepped out of a car that had pulled up behind the one they were tracking. The men in that car were already on the footpath. She watched as they greeted each other, exchanged words and the new men got into the car that their tracking device was attached to.

Gina pointed at the screen. "They're swapping people, not cars."

"Shush."

"What are we going to do? How are we meant to find them?" She watched as Seth opened up another page and frantically typed in the address bar. She rose from the chair and pushed it behind Seth so he could sit down.

"Thanks." He didn't even turn his gaze from the screen as he sat. He swore again.

"What's going on?" Ashley asked from the doorway.

Gina had turned towards the door the moment she'd heard the footsteps in the hallway. "They're swapping people instead of cars."

"Guess we'll have to tail them." Ashley stifled a yawn. "But not until after we have a sleep. You don't mind if I have the master bedroom, do you? Connor said if everyone wants it we'll have to flip for it."

Gina shrugged. "I don't know. I suppose not. It's just somewhere to sleep."

"Seth? What about you?" Ashley turned towards him.

"Yeah. Whatever. Shush."

Ashley grinned. "I get the master bedroom."

Connor joined her in the doorway. "I'm not sharing a room with him." He pointed towards Seth.

Gina frowned. "What do you mean?"

"There's only three bedrooms. You'd think with a house this size there'd be more," Connor said.

Gina looked at Ashley who smiled innocently and shrugged. She shook her head. "Convenient you didn't mention that before."

Seth turned to glare at them. "I'll use the lounge. Now can you all shut up and get out of here so I can concentrate?"

Gina ushered them from the room, closing the door. "Which room is mine?"

Chapter Sixteen

Gina's eyes popped open when she heard a sound in the bedroom she'd chosen. It was probably more accurate to say chosen for her since Connor had complained about using a single bed and wanted the room with the double bed rather than the two singles. When she rolled onto her side, Gina saw Seth grab a pillow and blanket off the other bed in her room.

He looked towards her. "Sorry. I didn't mean to wake you."

"You don't have to sleep on the couch."

"Are you sure?"

Gina smiled. "We've already shared a bed, is there a problem with sharing a room?"

Seth laughed softly. "I guess not."

"Did you manage to do whatever you were trying to do on the computer?"

He put the pillow and blanket back on the bed

before he faced her again. After a moment he shook his head. "No."

"What were you trying to do?"

"Track them using traffic cameras and other security cameras."

"Is it possible to do that? I mean, security cameras. Aren't they meant to be... well... secure?"

Seth sat on the edge of the bed and his lips curved slightly. "Something like that."

"Well?"

Seth shrugged. "It didn't help. I managed to follow them for a bit. But they were too quick. Not enough traffic on the road to slow them down. But then again, if there was a lot of traffic on the road, I might have lost them in it."

"What now?"

Seth drew the mobile phone from his pocket and set the alarm. "We get up in about an hour and watch the watchers."

"Seth, you need more than an hour's sleep."

He shook his head. "No. We have to move while they're still uncertain of our survival. We don't want to risk them finding us first."

"But-"

"Think we can have this conversation later? Otherwise I'm going to get less than an hour's sleep."

Gina fell silent and watched as Seth lay down and pulled a sheet over himself. She listened to his breathing as he closed his eyes and was surprised at how quickly he fell asleep. She quietly rose from the bed and checked the time. Nearly seven. There was no way she could go back to sleep. Not now. The worries and fears were crowding back in. Her earlier sleep had been dreamless since she'd been exhausted. Now she was partly rested, she didn't think she'd be so lucky.

* * *

Gina was in the kitchen putting the plate of pikelets, she'd just finished cooking, on the table when the alarm on the mobile phone went off. Before she went to wake Connor and Ashley, she put jam, butter and syrup on the table. Connor arrived in the kitchen as she was about to leave it.

"Something smells good."

She grinned. "Don't eat all of them. The rest of us are hungry too."

"I woke Ashley. She'll be here in a minute." Connor sat at the table and grabbed a handful of pikelets from the stack in the middle of the table.

"Thanks. I'll let Seth know breakfast is ready."

His mouth full of food, Connor only nodded.

Gina strode to the bedroom, pausing in the doorway. The room was empty, but she could hear water running in the bathroom. She knocked on the door. "Breakfast is ready."

"I'll be there in five," Seth called back.

"Okay." Gina returned to the kitchen and slid into one of the empty seats. Ashley was already seated beside Connor.

Ashley nodded towards the half eaten pikelet she held. "These are good. I reckon you should be permanently on kitchen duty. I've never been so hungry in my entire life. Lucky you made a tonne."

"Tell me about it. I'm easily eating twice as much as normal. My parents have always bitched over how much I eat, bet they'd really complain now." Connor grabbed another pikelet and smeared it with butter and jam.

Seth entered the kitchen and headed for the kettle. "Anyone else for coffee?" He grabbed four cups and brought them to the table as soon as they were made. "Dad sent over another phone and vehicle this morning."

"What for?" Ashley took the cup off Seth.

"You and Connor can go back to your

grandmother's house and collect all our gear while Gina and I watch the men at my house."

"Why do you get to watch them?" Connor demanded.

"Because Gina's and my abilities are good for surveillance."

"I can track them." Connor glared at Seth.

Seth nodded in agreement. "I know. Which is why we need you to ditch the gear here and join us as soon as possible. If we lose them, you'll have to find them. But I'm not sending Ashley to get the gear on her own and she has to go in case someone checks on who's at the house."

"Who made you boss, Lilly?"

"You have a better plan, Connie?"

"No fighting." Gina looked from one boy to the other. "We're tired, scared and have every cop in the country looking for us. Not to mention the people who made the virus. Don't you think we have enough people against us without fighting amongst ourselves?"

Ashley pushed away from the table. "I need to water Gran's plants anyway. And I should call my family while I'm there. They'll worry if they don't hear from me. I'm going to sort out our new look. I'll be in my bathroom when you're ready." She rose to her feet and grinned. "You know, the one with the spa."

Gina smiled at Ashley's retreating back, relieved the tension at the table was broken. She turned to Seth. "What vehicle did your dad drop off?"

Seth glanced towards Connor before returning his gaze to Gina. "A four-wheel-drive."

"He didn't." Connor shoved away from the table and started to stride from the room. He turned back, grabbed a handful of pikelets then hurried away.

"Seth." Gina drew his name out and shook her head. "And don't try that innocent look on me."

"I don't know what you're going on about." Seth dipped a knife into the jam.

Gina listened as Connor's hand lightly hit the other vehicle and he swore. When he started swearing about Seth, she stopped listening and focused her attention on Seth again. "You told your dad to get the same vehicle that Connor had."

"Now why would I do that?"

"Come on, Seth. We have enough problems without you needling Connor."

"It's a different colour."

"That's not-"

"You think you're smart, don't you, Lilly?" Connor stood in the doorway, his hands grasping the frame.

Gina pointed at Seth when he started to speak. "Not a word." She rose from the table and moved to stand in front of Connor. "I'm sure he didn't mean anything by it."

"It's a bribe." Seth leaned back in his seat.

Gina frowned as she stared at Seth. "What?"

Seth rose to stand by them. "Think about it. What are we going to do once we sort out the people behind this experiment? Do you think the government is going to feel comfortable having an unbeatable army that's not on their side?"

"We're not an army," Gina protested.

"Really?" Seth raised an eyebrow.

"That still doesn't explain why they sent that vehicle. Someone must have said something. And I bet it was you, Lilly."

Seth grinned. "Of course it was me. I don't expect you to thank me, but it would be nice if you didn't take it as an insult."

Connor's eyes narrowed. "Are you saying you didn't mean it as one?"

"Not as an insult."

"How did you mean it, Lilly?"

Seth laughed. "Well, I guess it was too good an opportunity to pass up. I knew it'd piss you off initially, but I also know you didn't deserve to lose your own vehicle because of all this."

Gina hit Seth on the shoulder with the back of her hand. "If you'd explained everything first, Connor wouldn't have taken it the wrong way."

"I know."

"I'm gonna get you back for this, Lilly."

Gina pushed against Connor's chest to move him from the doorway. "The pair of you need to grow up." She glared at each of them in turn. "You're worse than a pair of toddlers." She stalked away from them. Partway to her room, she remembered Ashley waited for them and crossed the lounge room to enter the tiled foyer that the master bedroom, two walk-in closets and bathroom opened onto.

Chapter Seventeen

"About time," Ashley said as Gina stepped into the bathroom. "Hurry up. It takes ages to pin your hair up. Are you sure I can't cut it?"

Gina shook her head then stayed still when Ashley complained at her movement. She watched in the large mirror that took up all the area behind the vanity as Ashley transformed her into a redhead with a bob. By the time Ashley was finished, her skin was lightened with a scattering of freckles and she wore a green crop top with black jeans and low-heeled boots.

"Wow. You seriously should think about doing this for a living. How did you learn to do this?" Gina turned to face Ashley who had shiny black hair in a similar bob and matching makeup. Ashley's smaller nose, heart shaped face and wig colour was all that stopped them from looking identical.

"I was in Little Theatre for years. We all had to help out with behind the scenes stuff, including makeup. I'm also pretty good at costumes and scenery." Ashley's hands went to her hips. "Now let's round up the guys so I can work my magic on them."

"If they haven't beaten each other to a pulp," Gina muttered. She searched the house by listening for them and heard them in the study. "I'll send them in. Any preference to which one you want first?"

"Nah, doesn't matter."

Gina nodded and headed towards the study. Both boys were seated at the desk with the laptop, arguing. Connor turned as she stepped into the room.

"Wow." Connor's gaze travelled over her before meeting hers again. He rose from the chair. "Not bad at all. Ashley is a magician. I bet no one at school would recognise you. Nice top by the way." His gaze dropped to look at it again.

"Oh get stuffed." She walked over to the chair and pushed Connor out of the way so she could sit on it. "Your turn, Connor." She smiled sweetly. "And I hope she turns you into a toad. It'll match your personality perfectly." She elbowed Seth who laughed.

"Hey. How come you can pick on him and I can't?" Seth pushed her elbow away.

"If he gives you a sleazy look like that, you can pick on him too," Gina said.

"As if," Connor muttered before he stalked from the room.

Gina glanced at the screen. It showed the car still in front of Seth's home. "Anything happen?"

Seth shook his head. "No. And I went over the recording I made so we didn't miss anything while we had breakfast. I don't know how often they change, but hopefully it won't be until after we get there."

Gina turned away from the screen to look at Seth. "You want to explain your earlier comment about a bribe?"

"Dad thinks he's found an organisation that will protect us."

"Why would they?"

"Because we'd help them."

"And why would we do that?"

"Because alone we're targets."

"But…" Gina frowned. "Aren't we planning to deal with the people who are after us?"

"And what about the police? There's no way we can prove we haven't been exposed to some kind of virus. This organisation would swear we aren't infected. They have well known medical staff in their pay."

"What would they expect us to do for them?"

Seth looked back at the screen. "What we've been created to do."

"No." Gina pushed the chair back and rose to her feet, shaking her head. "No. I'm not a killer."

"How about a defender?"

"Now you're just playing with words."

Seth rose to face her. "No. There's a difference. Think about it. We don't have to decide now."

"And what if they want to make more like us?"

"We'll make sure they can't. The virus is too dangerous. We can't risk it getting loose. Think about it, Gina."

"I don't know."

Seth reached out and took one of her hands. "Aren't you the one who said you had no experience with cloak and dagger stuff?"

Gina nodded.

"Dad and I have. And we have to do something to keep ourselves safe. And our families."

Gina pulled away from him. "That was low. You know how I feel about my family."

"And it won't take long for others to realise. You can't protect them without help. We have to find some way to make the world think we're ordinary. We need to be able to slip back into our lives without causing any speculation. This organisation can help us do that."

"Where are they based?"

Seth shrugged. "I don't know. But they've got offices in every country and people worldwide. They've got their hands in everything. Military, scientific research, medical facilities, transport, agriculture, politics." He shrugged again. "The list is endless."

"They sound like they're trying to take over the world."

Seth laughed. "Not quite. They like to keep their dealings quiet, but everything they've done has been positive, or at least had positive results." He held up his hand. "Think about it. Until we deal with the creators of this virus there's no point in making other plans. Besides, I'm sure they'll offer more incentives to encourage us to join them. We wouldn't want to give in too soon."

"I don't know." She frowned. "Ashley's ready for you now. I don't know why she couldn't come and tell you herself instead of shouting for me to tell you."

Gina dropped into the chair when Seth left the study. She stared blankly at the screen. In two days school would start. Her last year of high school. Instead of worrying about how her final year would be and which teachers she'd get, she was faced with an organisation that had half the world in its palm and some madmen, or mad people, who'd love to kill her after they found out how she'd survived the virus.

A breeze. She should have that all sorted before Tuesday. Not! She dropped her head into her hands and groaned. What was she going to do? Incentives. Her hands dropped away and she smiled. If they really wanted to prove how badly they wanted the four of them to join their organisation, they could show it by making sure it was splashed all across the news that they weren't infected with any virus. Once the virus creators realised they'd survived. Until then, there was no point in letting them know they still existed.

Chapter Eighteen

Gina yawned and stretched. She wished she'd brought a book with her. Sitting in the car beside Seth was beyond boring. Even the men watching the house weren't speaking. Most of the houses nearby were empty. The few that were occupied contained people having the most boring of conversations. She looked over at Seth who watched the car that was too far from her to be easily visible. It was all right for Seth, he was at least doing something useful.

She glared out the window and wished there was a breeze. Sitting in a car on the side of the road in summer was the worst thing in the world. Gina dreaded to think how hot it would be by midmorning if it was this hot already. The jeans she'd thought looked good now felt hot and sticky against her skin. She wished they could leave the car running to use the air conditioner, but they didn't know how long they'd be stuck sitting around.

When the mobile phone rang, she jumped. She glared at Seth who grinned as he answered the phone, putting it on speaker mode.

"Yeah?"

"Crap collected and dumped off. Where are you?" Connor demanded.

"Sitting at the start of the street," Seth said.

"You sure they didn't swap while you were on the way there?"

"No. I recorded it and checked when we arrived. You two going to join us?"

"Yeah." Connor hung up.

Seth put the phone back in his shirt pocket. "Well, he sounded cheerful."

Gina tried to ignore his black and gold hair and colourful shirt. It was difficult. The look didn't completely suit him, but it certainly made him unrecognisable. "I don't blame him. This is so boring. Why didn't you warn me? I could have picked up a book on the way."

"You could always play solitaire on the laptop." Seth gestured towards the back seat where it sat.

"Yeah, right. Real exciting. Try again."

"What would you normally do on a Sunday?" Seth continued to watch the car.

Gina shrugged. "I don't know. Hang with mates. Go to the beach. See a movie. Anything other than sit around doing nothing."

"The beach is good."

"Of course it's good. It's summer. It's the best place to go in summer. And I'm meant to go for my license tomorrow. After that I won't have to rely on friends to give me a lift. At least I won't once I find a car I can afford."

"How much have you got saved?"

"Not as much as I'd like. Only-"

Seth held up his hand. "Shush. Listen."

Gina focused her hearing on the car ahead of them and heard another car pull up.

"About bloody time," voice one said.

"We're wasting our time. The kids are probably dead," voice two said.

Four car doors opened and closed. Feet sounded on bitumen and grass.

"Anything?" voice three asked.

"Not a sound. Maybe he's as dead as his kid," voice two said.

"Who knows? I just hope they call this off soon. Those kids are dead or smart enough not to go home.

I mean, would you? They'd make perfect thieves. They could be rich in no time at all," voice one said.

"I'll see you later at the lab," voice three said. Two car doors opened and closed, followed moments later by another two doors. The car engine started.

"They're going," Gina said.

Seth started the car and slowly pulled out onto the street. Gina held her breath while they passed the parked car, but she didn't hear a sound from them. She sighed in relief as they turned the corner.

Seth handed the mobile phone to Gina. "Call the other pair and let them know we're on the move."

Gina nodded. As they turned onto different streets, she relayed the information to Ashley. Within ten minutes, she saw the four-wheel-drive come towards them on the other side of the road. She glanced behind as Connor found somewhere to do a U-turn and follow them.

"Tell them to get up ahead of us and we'll pick them up. We don't want two vehicles following the mouse," Seth said.

Gina nodded and passed along the message, wondering if she should have put the phone on speaker. She watched as Connor sped up and passed them. He pulled up several blocks away. Seth parked in front of them and Connor and Ashley got into the back seat of the car. Ashley shifted the laptop to give them more space.

Seth pulled out onto the road and continued to follow the other car. He stayed far enough back that the car couldn't see them, but close enough in case they made a couple of quick turns.

Connor pressed the power window button until it was halfway down. "Get closer to them for a second. I want to make sure I have their scent if they lose us."

Seth nodded and sped up. He stayed close to the other car until Connor put the window up, then he slowly dropped back again.

"Do you think they realise they're being followed? It seems like we're going in circles," Ashley said.

"We are. It's probably standard procedure. Never take the same route, never go straight back," Seth said.

"Oh and I suppose you think you're an expert," Connor said.

Seth shook his head. "No, but I've been passenger often enough when those procedures were followed."

"Can everyone shut up?" Gina glared at both of the boys. "How am I meant to concentrate on listening? Do you want me to miss something they might say? Just because they haven't spoken since they left the house doesn't mean they won't."

Silence fell in the car as they continued to follow. When they reached an industrial estate the car turned into the driveway of a large facility surrounded by a chain wire fence. They drove past and parked nearly a block away. Gina listened as the other car parked and the men opened and closed their doors. They didn't speak and she nearly growled in frustration as they walked across the bitumen and opened the door of a building. She strained to hear their footsteps, but heard nothing. The closing door had immediately cut off the sound.

Gina sighed. "The building has some kind of soundproofing."

"Must be major soundproofing for you not to be able to hear through it," Ashley said.

Gina shrugged. How would she know? It wasn't like she knew everything about her new abilities. She turned to Seth. "So what do we do now?"

"Why do you always have to ask Lilly? It's not like he's in charge or anything."

"Go ahead, Connie. What's our next plan of action?"

"To get in there of course," Connor said.

"Really? I would have thought getting a closer look would have been our first step," Seth said.

"You pair are giving me a headache," Gina muttered.

Ashley waved towards the facility. "How do you expect to get a closer look at that place? I bet they've got security cameras all over it. You can't just pull up in front."

"That's exactly what I plan to do." Seth took a pocketknife out of the glove box and handed it to Ashley. "Puncture the back tyre. Make it quick and unobtrusive."

Ashley took the knife and unfolded it. "How's that going to help?"

"Connie's going to change the tyre while I have a look around."

"Why do I have to change it?"

"You think the girls should be the ones changing it?"

Connor shook his head. "No, but I don't see why you can't change it."

"Because I'm the one with the good vision. When we need a bloodhound, I'll whistle."

"Seth!" Gina glared at him.

"Yeah, well, his sulks and complaints are starting to piss me off," Seth said.

"And your 'better than everyone else' attitude has already pissed me off," Connor said.

"Do you want me to puncture this tyre or are we going to sit in the car all day? It's starting to get hot in here and this wig is making my scalp sweat. I've had to lower my temperature twice already."

"Puncture it," Seth said. "And everyone remember they could have listening devices around the building."

Ashley was out of the car in a blink and back in before the tyre had a chance to go down. Seth started the car when the door closed and did a U-turn as Ashley folded the knife shut and slipped it into a pocket of her jeans. He drove back down the street and pulled up in front of the facility.

Seth turned in his seat to look at Gina. "You want to pop your head out the window and check the back tyre for me?"

She suppressed a grin and checked out the window. "It's flat."

Ashley swung the car door open and hopped out. She stood, hands on her hips and stared at the tyre. "Just great. I hope you're not expecting me to help. It's too hot to change a tyre." She glanced around. "There isn't a single bit of shade."

The other three climbed out of the car and joined her on the footpath to stare at the tyre. Connor crossed his arms and glared at it while Gina stood there awkwardly. She didn't know what to do. How was one meant to act when they got a flat tyre? Swear? Shrug philosophically? She didn't know.

"Your turn to change the tyre, Connie. I did the last one," Seth said.

Connor glared at him. "Yeah, but it wasn't on a boiling hot day."

"Guess it's your bad luck." Seth grinned and turned away, his back to the car. He whispered under his breath, "Come stand in front of me, Gina."

She did as he asked, a question in her eyes as she stood in front of him. His hands rested on her hips and his lips curved into a smile. She opened her mouth to ask him what the plan was then stopped. What if they were listening?

Seth's lips brushed hers, his words nearly inaudible. "Put your hands on my shoulders. Give me a reason to stand here and look like I'm gazing into your eyes."

Gina grinned and slid her hands up to link behind his neck. "Why is it I think you're actually happy Connor is stuck with changing the tyre?"

Seth grinned. "Now what would give you that impression?"

Her grin became a laugh. "Gee, I don't know? Your excess of sympathy maybe?"

Seth's gaze continued to roam the area behind

Gina. "How harsh. I'm devastated you could think that about me."

"Yeah, right. I bet you're devastated exactly the same amount as you feel sympathetic."

Seth's gaze met hers. "Innocent until proven guilty in this country." His lips brushed across hers and he murmured, "Thank you." He turned back to Connor, one arm still around Gina. "Will you be much longer? It's hot out here."

"If you hadn't thought you knew where we were going and let me direct, we wouldn't have got lost and probably have been somewhere with a tree you could stand under." Connor took the spare tyre out of the boot. "If you're in such a hurry, why don't you put the flat away?"

Seth put the flat tyre away while Connor fitted the spare. It only took them a few more minutes and they were back on the road. Gina turned the air conditioner up and lifted the hair off her neck to cool down quicker.

Seth glanced in the rear view mirror. "Good thinking back there, Connor. I should have realised it wasn't an area we were likely to be in."

"Guess you're not a genius all the time." Connor grinned.

Gina rested her hand on Seth's thigh and shook her

head slightly when he looked over at her. She smiled when he gave her a slight nod. When she was about to pull her hand away from him, his hand covered hers to keep it there. She was conscious of the warmth of his skin through the fabric of his clothes.

Ashley leaned forward. "Did you see anything, Genius?"

Seth nodded. "Motion detectors, visual and audio devices and thermal imaging."

"And we're meant to get in there?" Gina demanded.

Seth nodded. "Yeah."

"Impossible," Gina said.

"No. Not impossible. We've just got to figure out how to do it." Seth handed the phone to Gina, letting her hand go. "Text the address to my dad and add the words all info and quiet. He has people he can contact. You'll find his number in the address book."

Gina sent off the message and handed the phone back to Seth. "What do we do while we're waiting?"

"If we didn't have to stay in disguise, I'd suggest going swimming at Southbank," Ashley said.

"I wish," Gina said wistfully.

"How about morning tea? Breakfast feels like it was ages ago," Connor suggested.

"As long as it's something better than fast food," Gina said.

Connor shrugged. "I don't care what it is, as long as it's food."

Seth gestured ahead. "Fish and chip shop?"

Gina looked where he pointed but couldn't see the shop. "I guess. At least it's better than fast food."

"I hope they do grilled fish. And have lemons. I love grilled fish drenched with lemon juice," Ashley said.

Connor groaned. "Stop torturing me. I feel like I haven't eaten for a week."

Seth pulled up in front of the fish and chip shop and they all piled out and headed in to order food. Seth paid with the credit card and they sat at the table and chairs out the front of the shop.

"Why should you be the only one with a credit card?" Connor asked.

"Only had time to get one. I'll let Dad know the rest of you want one too."

Ashley brightened. "Really? Is there a limit to what I can buy with it?"

Seth laughed. "No. Although I wouldn't try buying a car or house with it. That might raise alarms. Which reminds me of this morning's conversation."

Gina glanced around. "Do you think this is the place to be having it?"

"I don't know. You tell me. Other than a camera inside, there's nothing else around here I can see," Seth said.

Gina listened carefully. She heard someone hum to the radio in the back of the shop and the person who'd taken their order was now on the phone. The traffic was light on the road and being Sunday, the businesses on either side of the shop were closed. No one walked along the footpaths lining each side of the road and Gina couldn't blame them. It looked like it was going to be a stinking hot day. She could even hear someone snoring in one of the houses across the road and wondered if they'd been out partying the night before.

She looked at Seth. "Seems clear."

He nodded briefly and explained what he'd told Gina earlier. Their order was called as he finished. Gina headed inside to grab the food while the other two stared at Seth, obviously lost for words.

Ashley took one of the parcels of food and unwrapped the butcher's paper from it. "What do you think, Gina?"

"I don't know." She sat at the table. "I'm worried about what they'd expect us to do in return."

"Like shoot people or something?" Connor squirted tomato sauce on his chips.

Gina shrugged. "Yeah, I guess so."

"But what if the people they wanted us to shoot were," Ashley waved her hand as she looked for the word, "I don't know… bad people or something. Murderers. Terrorists. Whatever."

"But wouldn't that make us just as bad as them?" Gina asked.

Connor shook his head. "You're not going to make this some stupid morality discussion where there's no right answer, are you?"

"What do you mean?" Gina asked.

"You know, kill the murderer before he kills others and you're a murderer. Let him live and he murders someone and you're responsible for their death because you could have stopped him," Connor said.

Gina frowned. Surely there was a way around the problem. She looked over to Seth. "Is that what they'd make us choose between?"

"The other option is to capture the murderer and imprison him," Seth said.

Gina glared at Connor. "You did that deliberately."

Connor shook his head. "Nope. You'd have to blame my father for that one. It's his favourite morality scenario. I've always failed at answering it.

Guess next time he asks I'll give him the prison option and see what he has to say."

Ashley squeezed lemon juice over her grilled fish. The alfoil it sat in was turned up at the edges to keep the liquid from overflowing. "Can't we just tell them we're not assassins?"

Seth looked at Ashley thoughtfully. "That'd probably work. No planned killings, only casualties of war. I'm a lot more comfortable with that."

Gina nodded slowly. "Yeah, that doesn't sound too bad."

"And we get the right to refuse any job we find morally questionable," Connor said.

Seth grinned. "That would mean we could veto any job just by coming up with a moral reason."

Relief rushed through Gina. "Yes. Definitely add that to our agreement."

Ashley picked up a plastic fork. "And we're not guinea pigs. I've had more than enough needles to last me a lifetime."

"Me too." Gina shuddered.

Seth's phone rang and he wiped his fingers on a serviette before he answered it. "Yeah... okay... bye."

The conversation was so quick Gina didn't even

have a chance to listen in on it. "What was that about?"

"Dad emailed me some info. Just the basics. He'll have the rest of the details to us by tomorrow morning. So no need to rush. We'll finish lunch first."

"Lunch. You've got to be kidding. This is only a snack." Connor picked up a chip that dripped tomato sauce and popped it in his mouth.

Gina started to disagree, then stopped. Once this would have been lunch, but Connor was probably right. With the amount they'd been eating lately it was only a snack.

Chapter Nineteen

Gina looked at the other shadowy figures in the four-wheel-drive. They could have been ninjas with their black clothes and balaclavas that completely hid them. All that was visible were their eyes. Seth's phone rang once and fear and excitement shivered through Gina. It was hard to believe they were going to break into the place. They'd only learned about it yesterday. That didn't seem like enough time to plan properly.

"Places everyone," Seth whispered.

They carefully opened car doors and quietly closed them. The interior light stayed dark, having been turned off earlier. Gina walked along the side of the road and listened to the night, waiting. She heard a slightly louder buzz followed by silence as the electricity was temporarily turned off. She raced towards the fence, her companions keeping pace. They were over it in seconds and pressed against the front of the building. The steady hum of electricity sounded in the overhead wires again. She kept her breathing slow, listening and waiting, trying to tell herself she could do this. Or at least remind herself that Seth thought she was capable of it.

She heard the electricity stop again. A quick wave of her hand and Connor turned the door handle and the sound as the mechanism broke made her cringe. They slipped inside, heading for the corner of the room Seth indicated. Above them was a security camera. They pressed against each other in the corner to stay out of its line of vision. She couldn't believe she was doing this. Never in her wildest dreams could she have imagined breaking into a secret facility.

The sound proofing no longer stopped her from hearing what went on inside the building. She searched every area. There were sounds of people working, the steady beat of feet on floors as guards patrolled, the mutters of security personal watching as the electricity flickered out momentarily and the clatter of fingers on a keyboard.

They had four more minor power outages to get to the security control room. Hopefully they could manage. She pointed in the direction of the security personal and heard something that almost made her cheer.

"I brought you a coffee," a voice said.

"About damned time." It was the man who'd complained about the security system flickering out. "What about a lamington, or did you only think about yourself?"

"It was the last one. I could go and get you some fruit cake."

"You know I hate fruit cake."

Gina reached out to Connor and pulled him close so she could whisper in his ear. "One of them is eating a lamington and they've both got coffee."

Connor squirmed as she whispered, but nodded when she pulled away from him. He breathed in deep and turned his head slightly. He nodded again, a grin and a thumbs up telling them he had the scent.

Gina waited and listened for the next power outage, trying to remain calm. They could only stop the power momentarily or the backup generator would cut in. And they couldn't do it too often or that would also trigger the generator. She just hoped they didn't get caught standing around in a corner. She heard it go out again and raised her hand.

They raced down a corridor and slipped into another room, hiding below a security camera. Gina tried to slow her heartbeat. She was worried she wouldn't hear the power outage over the sound. The minutes dragged and she began to wonder if Anthony had been caught playing with the power. Finally it went off again and they raced through the building. The third outage brought them to the security control room and Connor and Ashley rendered the two men unconscious, using the pressure points Seth had shown them earlier. When he spied the untouched lamington, Connor drew down the bottom part of his balaclava. Grinning, he reached for the lamington. Gina shook her head at him.

"What? I was hungry." Connor dusted the coconut off his fingers before pulling the balaclava back up to cover his mouth.

Seth sat down at the panel. "Shush. And someone tie and gag those guards." He brought up a floor plan of the building and slowly checked each room using the floor plan number with the corresponding camera number.

There were eight more guards, two men sleeping and a man and woman working in a lab. The woman entered information on a computer.

Seth leaned back. "Right. Guards need to be brought back here when they've been dealt with. We'll leave the scientists till last." He pointed to one of the screens. "Connor, that's your first guard."

Another screen. "Gina." He pointed to yet another screen. "Ashley." He turned to face them. "Be careful."

They nodded and slipped out of the room. Once outside, they headed in different directions. Gina raced along the corridors, surprised at how quickly she could move. She heard the guard long before she saw him. Then she was behind him and had her fingers against the pressure points that would render him unconscious. She was glad Seth had warned them about the dangers of knocking people over the head. The last thing she wanted was to kill someone or cause them permanent damage. The guard slumped at her feet and she stared down at him, shocked at how easy it had been.

"Gina, snap out of it."

She glanced up at the camera Seth would be watching her through and gestured with her middle finger. She heard his laughter, but ignored him. It wasn't like she did this every day. Bending, she picked up the guard and effortlessly threw him over her shoulder. She hurried back to the control room and dumped him with the other guards.

"What did you think you were doing? Waiting for another guard to come and find you?" Seth bent to help her tie up the guard. "The other two have already gone to get their second guard."

"Well, sorry." Gina drew the words out. "It's not like I do this all the time."

"I was worried. But you're doing okay." Seth turned towards the screens. "He's your next guard."

Gina nodded and ran towards the location of the guard. This one faced her and pulled his gun as she ran at him. She grabbed his wrist and twisted his arm so he dropped the gun and punched him in the jaw. She winced as his head snapped back and he sagged to the ground. She'd only wanted to stun him, not knock him out. Hoping he'd be okay she tossed him over her shoulder. Bending her knees, she awkwardly picked up his gun and headed back to the control room. Maybe they could manage this. It was turning out far easier than she'd expected.

Seth took the gun from her. "Connor and Ashley are getting the last two patrolling guards. You can come with me to get the two that are asleep."

Gina nodded. The thought of attacking a sleeping man made her feel uncomfortable. But she had little choice in the matter. She hoped neither of the men woke and fought back. She could still hear the sound that the guard's head had made when it had snapped back. It wouldn't surprise her if it was a long time before she forgot that sound.

As soon as the two sleeping men were taken care of, they met up with Connor and Ashley in the control room. They watched the two scientists obliviously working.

"Now what?" Connor asked.

"We find out what the scientists know," Seth said.

"And you reckon they're going to spill their guts just because you ask?" Connor shook his head. "Stop speaking crap, Lilly."

"Shut up, Connie and get moving." Seth flung the door open and hurried along the corridor.

Gina ran after him, Ashley and Connor behind her. They burst into the lab. The two scientists turned to face them and the woman clapped her hand to her mouth. Gina frowned as she heard a sudden sharp sound. Like an alarm going off. But it was gone as quickly as it came and she couldn't tell what had made it.

"What's going on here?" the man demanded.

Seth stepped further into the room. "That's what we'd like to know. Who's in charge of this operation?"

The woman glanced towards the man, but closed her mouth when he shook his head. She pressed a button on the keyboard and the information that had filled the screen disappeared.

Connor swore and crossed the room in a second. He dragged the woman out of her chair and held her arms tight behind her back. "What did you just do?"

The woman shook her head vehemently, refusing to speak.

The man took a step towards Connor, a smile of satisfaction curving his lips. "It worked. What did you do? How did you survive? You were able to move faster than I expected."

"This is your research? You're the one who created the virus?"

Something in Seth's voice must have worried the man because he sobered and took a step back. "I was approached to do this. He has my family. You don't think I would have willingly done this, do you? But I'm glad it worked. I was running out of time to show them results. I have a little boy. He's two-years-old. I can't let them kill him."

"Douglas said everything was being destroyed because it didn't work," Gina said.

The man nodded. "Yes. Of experiment X-One-Six. We've started on X-One-Seven now."

Gina frowned and wished she could pull her balaclava off. It was starting to annoy her. Just like the man's manner annoyed her. Something didn't seem right, but she couldn't put her finger on it. "Who came to you?"

The man shrugged. "He never gave his name. He had his men move into my home and took me to the first lab they set up. What could I do?" He spread his hands. "He has my family."

"Where's your home?" Seth entered the information into his mobile phone as the man gave him a local address, then slipped it back into his pocket.

Gina finally realised what bothered her. The man's heart rate was normal. The woman's pounded away like it would burst from her chest, but the man was calm. Like he hadn't a care in the world. He waited for something. Before she had a chance to voice her theory, she heard the front door of the building burst open and an army of feet came pounding inside. "You set off an alarm."

Once again the man spread his hands. "What could I do? They had my family."

"What's your name?" Seth asked.

The man hesitated. "How can that help you? Please. I'll tell you everything if you can rescue my family. You can't stay here. The alarm I set off will bring an army to this room any time now."

Gina could hear the army closing in. "Let's get out of here. Now."

Seth grabbed the laptop off the bench and snapped it shut. "Which way?" He looked at Gina, ignoring the man's protests that he couldn't take the laptop.

Gina flung the door open and with a glance to see they followed, ran into the corridor. She paused to listen. The army had broken into smaller groups. They were going to have to pass several of them to get out of here. "Reinforcements have arrived. I'd say at least a hundred."

Seth swore.

Ashley punched the air. "Bring it on. Let's show them what we can do."

"Which way?" Seth asked.

Connor breathed in deep then pointed to the corridor on the left. "That way has the most if you're looking for a fight."

Seth headed right.

"Spoilsport," Ashley muttered.

They raced along corridors. The first handful of armed men barely had time to raise their weapons before they were through them. The second group was ready and the sound of gunfire filled the air. Gina dodged one bullet and nearly ran into another. They rounded a corner to face a dozen men already firing. She ducked, crashing into one of the men and knocking him into another. Beside her the other three helped disable the men.

She heard Seth swear and stumble slightly. She glanced at him, but he shook his head and gestured her onwards. She ran towards the exit, her heart pounding with fear when she heard men reach the security room and give their location. They burst out the front door and into another group of reinforcements. She swung at one man who tried to grab her and couldn't help smiling as Ashley shouted triumphantly. She didn't have time to see what had made Ashley happy. The fence was in front of her. The electric fence that still had power to it.

Chapter Twenty

Gina turned to face the army that surrounded them. She couldn't look at her friends who stood to her left. Her gaze wouldn't move from the guns pointed at them. At least they weren't firing.

One of the men stepped forward. "Hands up. Now!"

Gina started to raise her hands, listening to the power. She hoped Anthony could see them in the camera they'd planted across the road earlier and he turned the power off soon. No, better make that immediately.

"Drop that laptop."

More men poured out of the open front door and Gina felt her knees go weak. She wanted to yell at Anthony to hurry up. What was taking him so long?

"Now. Drop the laptop."

She heard the electricity turn off. Relief rushed

through her. "Go!" She was over the fence before the army noticed, her friends beside her. There was a burst of gunfire and she dodged more bullets.

"Hold fire! You'll draw attention."

Gina smiled when the order brought an end to the bullets. She pulled open the front door of the four-wheel-drive and climbed in, sinking back in the seat. She closed her eyes and listened as her friends climbed in the vehicle and orders were shouted to find them. She could hear the pound of feet, engines turn over and vehicles move off.

"Why can I smell blood?" Connor asked from the back seat.

Gina's eyes flew open. She knew she wasn't hurt. She looked from Seth to Ashley.

"I'm fine," Ashley said. "And I haven't got any of their blood on me. I'm learning to control my punches better."

Gina looked at Seth again. "Seth?"

"A scratch." He handed his phone to Gina. "Put that address in the navigator."

"It's more than a scratch. I can smell a lot of blood," Connor said.

"We don't have time to stop. We've got to check out the address he gave us, before anyone else gets there." Seth slowed to turn a corner then sped up again.

"Yet we've got time to let you bleed to death?" Connor demanded.

"Pull over and let Connor drive. There's a first aid kit in the back," Gina said.

"He can't see in the dark if we have to turn off the headlights and try to lose a tail," Seth said.

Gina put the address in the navigator. "Pull over and let him drive. Don't be stupid, Seth. You can drive again after we stop the bleeding." He remained silent, the speed of the car consistent. "Please, Seth." She heard him sigh.

He slowed the car and pulled over. "Swap places quickly."

Gina hopped in the back with Seth and reached over the back seat for the first aid kit as Ashley and Connor climbed in the front. Connor pulled out onto the road as Gina sat back in the seat, the first aid kit in her hands. She removed her mask, noticing the others had removed theirs.

Opening the first aid kit, she placed it at her feet. "Now show me where you're bleeding."

Seth lifted his shirt and pulled it over his head. The black gloves he wore came off with it. He held his left arm out of the way. "Once it's cleaned up, it won't look as bad."

"Yeah, right," Gina muttered. She wiped at the blood smeared across his side with a handful of tissues. Grabbing swabs from the first aid kit, she tipped an antiseptic liquid on them.

Ashley turned in her seat to look. "Wow. Looks like you lost half your blood."

Seth closed his eyes and gritted his teeth. "Then you don't know what three litres of blood looks like."

"How do you know how much blood you have?" Connor asked.

"Approximately eight percent of body weight." Seth hissed and pushed Gina's hand away from him. "It's clean enough."

Gina pushed his arm out of the way. "It looks like it needs stitches."

"Too bad. Bind it. That'll have to do," Seth said.

"Do you think there's a bullet in there?" She peered at the wound, wishing she had more than the flicker of streetlights to see it with.

"Worry about it later. Can you hear any pursuit?"

Gina shook her head as she grabbed a bandage, gauze and tape. The gauze darkened the moment she taped it on and she frowned as she wrapped the bandage around Seth. "Are you sure you're going to be all right? It won't stop bleeding."

Seth pressed his hand against the wound once she was finished. "It's slowed. Now are you sure there's no one following us?"

Gina listened. She located them in the distance. Only a handful headed in the correct direction. None of them close enough to find them. She wondered if they knew their possible destination or if they were now randomly searching the area. She continued to listen and then grinned. "They don't know where we went."

"Good. But regularly check for them." Seth turned towards Connor. "You want to pull over so I can drive?"

"You've got to be kidding. You stink of blood. I don't want to risk you passing out behind the wheel and killing the lot of us," Connor said.

Ashley gestured towards the navigator. "We're nearly there. No point stopping."

Five minutes later, they pulled up in front of a lowset brick house. A well maintained garden cast shadows across the darkened windows. They sat in the car while Gina listened. She could hear nothing. Not even the soft breathing of someone asleep.

"No one's home." She turned to Seth. "What do we do now?"

"It smells odd," Connor said.

"What do you mean by odd?" Seth pulled on his shirt and gloves.

Connor shrugged. "I don't know. Stale? Not sure. But I haven't smelt this before."

Seth stared at him a moment longer before slowly nodding. "Okay. Masks back on. No speaking unless absolutely necessary."

They piled out of the vehicle as soon as their faces were hidden. Seth looked around. At a gesture, they ran to the back of the house with him and waited while he scanned the area. He turned to Gina who nodded to let him know she couldn't hear anything. Next he turned to Connor and waved him towards the door, making a shoving motion with his hands. Gina cringed as the door flew inwards when Connor shouldered it open. The wood of the trim splintered around the three locks on the door.

"It's empty," Ashley said.

"Shush." Seth stepped inside the laundry and looked around.

Connor moved into the hallway with Gina close on his heels. He peered into rooms and came to a stop in what was probably a lounge room. Only the carpet and curtains were left. He sniffed the air. "Empty. That's the smell. Emptiness." He turned suddenly and ran into the kitchen, all of them close behind him.

"What's wrong?" Ashley asked the question first.

Gina listened carefully. Nothing had changed. All was quiet.

Connor pulled the stove away from the wall, reached behind it and held up a small sneaker. One that would probably fit a two-year-old. "This is the only scent of people left in the place."

"Let's get out of here," Seth said.

They returned to the car in silence, Connor putting his arm in front of Seth when he would have hopped in the front seat. They stared at each other for a moment. Seth shrugged and climbed in the back. Gina hesitantly reached out to touch his hand the moment she was buckled in beside him.

Seth turned to her. "I'm fine."

"Are you sure?" She wished she could see as well as him in the dark.

"Yeah."

"Should we take you somewhere to see if the bullet is still in there or get it stitched?"

Connor laughed derisively. "Yeah, sure. He gives himself needles. Want to bet he'd be willing to sew himself up too? Did you want to be Rambo when you grew up, Lilly?"

"How long do you think the house was empty, Connie?"

"I don't know. How long does it take for the smell of humans to go from a place?"

"I'm not sure. Bloodhounds can track a scent a week old. Maybe it can last longer in a closed environment. Unless they cleaned it with something to remove all trace of the occupants."

"Why would they do that?" Ashley asked.

"So people can't track them." Seth turned to Gina. "Speaking of, is there anyone following?"

Gina shook her head. "I don't know. I can't hear any familiar voices or conversations. Can you see anything?"

"No." Seth turned towards Connor. "Head back to our house."

Ashley picked up the shoe Connor had left on the dash. "What are we going to do now?"

Connor took it from her and returned it to the dash. "Don't play with it. You'll ruin the scent."

Ashley laughed. "You make it sound like a new perfume. Eau de toddler."

"You'd want a good marketing campaign if you hoped to sell it," Gina said.

"You're all so bloody funny, aren't you?" Connor muttered.

"Yep." Ashley leaned forward and keyed their address into the navigator. "Twelve minutes. I can't wait to get back in my spa bath."

"It's too late at night for that. You might fall asleep in it again," Connor said.

"I didn't fall asleep. I was resting my eyes."

Gina turned to Seth who had his mobile phone out, ignoring Ashley and Connor's argument. "What are you doing?"

"Letting Dad know we're fine."

"Did you tell him about getting shot?"

"I'm fine."

"I want to have a look when we get home."

"Home?"

"You know what I mean, Seth."

"Yeah. But I'm fine."

"We'll see."

Seth refused to let her have a look the moment they arrived. He checked to see if the car still watched his father's house before he headed to their bathroom for a shower. Gina sat on her bed and waited for him to finish. She tried not to listen to the water as Seth washed. With her improved hearing, it was like she was right next to him. Instead, she checked on

Ashley and Connor to see if they were still arguing. It took her a moment to realise the argument had become making up and she shut down all sound in that direction.

Unable to sit, Gina paced the room, freezing as the sound of water stopped. She really tried to ignore the sounds in the bathroom. The soft sound of a towel against skin was followed by jeans being shaken out before they were pulled on. At the sound of the zip, Gina turned away from the door and stared at the closed curtains. The door opened behind her and she looked towards Seth, his hair still damp. Her gaze dropped to his bare chest then to where he'd been wounded.

Gina opened her mouth to speak, but no sound came. She took the couple of steps that separated them. Her hand brushed across the red puckered scar on his side. At Seth's indrawn breath, her gaze met his. There was no pain in them like she'd feared.

"I told you I was fine." His words were a whisper.

Gina could only nod, her hand still against his scar, her lips parted. She listened to the sound of his heart, surprised it was as fast as hers.

"Gina?"

She forced herself to drop her hand and turn away, uncertain what to say. She heard him step close, the sound of his heartbeat loud in her ears. Her gaze was drawn to the golden apple at her wrist. A confusion of thoughts filled her head. Was Seth like Connor? Proximity the only requirement. Should she have warned Ashley? Although she seemed to know her own mind and wasn't some naive kid.

Seth's hand rested on her shoulder. "Gina?"

She turned to face him, his hand trailing across her back to rest on her other shoulder, his skin warm against hers. "What happens if we ever figure all this out?"

"What are you trying to ask me?"

She couldn't meet his gaze. "Isn't there some kind of mental thing? You know, hostages and danger and stuff like that. Like with hostages and captors, but just between hostages." She watched his lips curve into a grin and had to meet his gaze. She glared at the amusement she saw in them. "Oh forget it." So what if she hadn't made much sense. He didn't have to laugh at her. She started to turn away, but his grip tightened on her shoulder.

"Stockholm syndrome."

"What?"

"When a hostage becomes sympathetic to their captor. It's called Stockholm syndrome."

"Oh."

His hand skimmed across her shoulder and rested against her neck. "Tell me to back off and I will."

"I don't know."

Seth grinned fleetingly. "I can't help you with that answer. You'll have to figure it out for yourself."

"I don't know what to think. Everything is too confusing. I just want to go home."

"I know. I do too."

"How can we? We're no closer to figuring this out than we were before."

"It mightn't feel like it, but we're making progress." Seth smiled. "Don't look so sceptical."

"I am. Our only lead gave us nothing."

Seth shook his head. "You're wrong. It gave us a face, a laptop, an address and the scent of a child. We will track down whoever is responsible for this."

"But what happens if we hand them over? What if they talk the so called 'good guys' into the benefits of their experiment?"

"I don't know, Gina. I really don't know."

"Why do I feel like we're screwed no matter what happens?"

His hand moved to cup her cheek, his other hand doing the same. "We'll figure something out. I promise."

"You really don't break your promises?" She held

her breath waiting for his reply. When it came it was a whisper.

"Never." He bent his head to press his lips against hers. Burying his fingers in her hair, he deepened the kiss. He slowly pulled away enough that he could meet her gaze. "It isn't the situation. My life has been filled with odd situations, death defying experiences and secrets."

"Mine hasn't."

"Tell me to back off if that's what you want."

"I don't want to be left alone."

His hand returned to cup her cheek. "I won't leave you alone. You can still tell me to back off."

Gina turned her head so her lips grazed his palm. She heard his indrawn breath and she faced him again. "How about I tell you to keep it slow instead?" Her lips curved slightly. "I like the kisses."

Seth laughed softly. "Me too." He lowered his head again.

Chapter Twenty-One

Gina was woken abruptly by a sound in her doorway. She blinked as she slowly focused on Connor standing there. As soon as he saw she was awake, he beckoned to her before he hurried away. Gina tried to slip out of Seth's arms without waking him, but the moment she started to move, they tightened around her. His lips nuzzled at her neck and warmth filled her.

"Seth." His name came out as a whisper.

"Mmmm."

"I have to get up. Connor wants something."

"Can't he wait?"

She felt the vibration of his words against her throat and she was tempted to say yes. "I thought you didn't need much sleep."

Seth sat up enough that he could meet her gaze, a grin forming. "I didn't plan on going back to sleep."

She laughed softly as she pushed him away. "That is not slow."

He sighed and lightly kissed her. He pulled back to stare at her, his gaze a caress. "Okay. Slow it is." He slid over her so he could get out of the bed then glanced over his shoulder at her. "You want to remind me how Connor ended up with the double bed while we got the single?"

Gina yawned and stretched, her hands brushing the bed head. "I thought you found single beds cosy."

"A double bed will have to go on the to do list."

"If you're so worried about space, why not get a king?"

He held out his hand to draw her to her feet. "I don't want to give you that much space to get away." He wrapped his arms around her. "But we can get a queen-size if you want."

Before Gina could reply, she heard Connor say her name, impatience and irritation in his tone. She glanced towards the doorway and realised he was much further away. Probably the kitchen.

"What's wrong?"

Gina pulled away. "Connor's getting impatient and I need to use the bathroom before I see what he wants."

"I'll put the kettle on. Do you want coffee?"

Gina shook her head as she retreated to the bathroom. She listened as Seth walked away, greeted Connor and Ashley and put the kettle on. She smiled as Seth whispered, "Are you listening in on us, Gina?" Finished in the bathroom, she headed for the kitchen and her smile became a grin as she met Seth's gaze.

Seth laughed. "I guess that was a yes."

Connor looked between the two of them. "What is a yes?"

Gina shook her head. "What did you wake me for?"

Connor took the cup of coffee Seth handed him. "I think we should talk to the organisation that wants us to join them. We need to be able to move about during the day without worrying half the country want to call the police about us."

Ashley took a mouthful of coffee. "God this is good." She eyed her empty plate. "I can't believe I'm still hungry." She slid her plate across the table. "Put more toast on for me before you sit down, Seth." When he took the plate, she smiled. "Thanks." She took another sip of coffee. "Surely the dudes your dad knows can do something about telling everyone we're clean. I mean, if they want us to work for them, they're going to need us to go about in public, aren't they?"

Seth put bread in the toaster and pushed the lever down. "I doubt they'll want to advertise the fact we're working for them. But they should be able to do something about making the world believe we're not infected."

"Does that mean we'll all go home?" Connor crossed the kitchen and opened the fridge. He pulled out an apple and leaned against the closed door of the fridge. "How are we meant to do anything with our parents breathing down our necks?" He took a bite.

"I'm sure they can come up with some reason why we can't return home. It'd probably be best if we don't anyway. No need to advertise to the mad scientist where we are." Seth placed the two pieces of toast on Ashley's plate and laid a knife across them. The butter and jam she'd used earlier were still on the kitchen bench. He put it all on the table in front of her.

Connor pushed away from the fridge. "Tell them they need to bring in a million specialists and my parents will be thrilled."

"There's no way I could tell my parents we're going after the bad guys. They'd freak." Gina took a bowl from the cupboard, eyed it, returned it to the cupboard and took out a small mixing bowl instead.

"Will they have a problem about you not returning home?" Seth put more bread in the toaster.

Gina shook her head. "Not if they're told it's for my safety." She poured cereal and milk into the bowl, grabbed a spoon and sat at the table.

Connor threw the apple core in the bin and gestured towards Gina's bowl. "Is there another one of them?"

Gina shook her head as she swallowed her mouthful. "There's a slightly larger one."

Connor pulled the larger mixing bowl out of the cupboard. "Perfect." He emptied the last of the cereal into the bowl. "Who's going to do our grocery shopping?"

"Don't even think about looking at me," Ashley warned. "I hate grocery shopping."

"I'll arrange it." Seth put in more bread then spread the two pieces of toast he'd dropped onto the bench.

"If they want us to work for them, I'm going to need somewhere permanent to live," Ashley said. "My parents live too far from here to make it practical to keep living with them."

"Maybe we should make a list of wants before we see them," Seth said.

Ashley nodded slowly. "Sounds like a good idea."

She paused and stared at Seth for a moment. "Do you think they'd pay for uni?"

Seth grinned. "Ashley, we're unique. We could start a bidding war if we went open market. Keeping us a secret is to their advantage. If we don't like what they offer, we can easily suggest going elsewhere. I reckon we can get a little pushy on what we want."

"A car too?" Ashley looked hopeful.

Seth nodded. "Better put down living expenses since our food bill is going to be astronomical."

"And someone to clean this place." Ashley eyed the spilt milk Connor had left on the bench. "I am not cleaning up anyone's mess."

"I don't mind staying here for now, but I want to go home eventually," Gina said.

"I don't," Connor said.

Gina stared at him. "Won't you miss your parents?"

Connor laughed. There was no humour in the sound, only bitterness. "Not likely."

"I'm sorry," Gina said softly.

Connor grinned. "Don't be. This is a much better option than doctor."

Ashley pointed a warning finger at him. "If we're going to share this place you're not going to hold parties here. I'm not having the place trashed. I wasn't impressed by your friends."

"Acquaintances." Connor lifted the nearly empty bowl and drank the last of the milk from it.

"Pig," Ashley muttered, a barely suppressed smile.

Connor turned from Ashley. "Where are you going, Lilly?" For once, Connor didn't use his usual derisive tone to say Lilly.

"To start my list and get in touch with my dad. Should we aim for this afternoon?"

"That soon?" Gina stared at Seth who nodded. "But I haven't even thought about what to ask for."

"Think big," Seth said.

"But what if they say our big is far too much?" Gina asked.

Seth pulled his t-shirt over his head.

"Do you have to, Lilly?"

Ashley eyed Seth's chest and grinned. "Isn't it a bit early in the morning for a strip show? Although I'm not complaining. Should I put some music on for you?"

Seth laughed and held his left arm away from his side. "You're meant to be checking out my gunshot wound, not my body, Ashley."

Ashley swore as she rose from the table. "What happened to it, Genius?" She did a slow walk around him.

Gina stared at the feint white line that had been

an open wound last night. "It's gone. Last night it needed stitches. Today it's," she swallowed, her gaze meeting Seth's her voice becoming a whisper. "Gone."

"That's going to be handy." Connor grinned. "Do we tell them? Hadn't we better keep some stuff secret?"

"We keep it all secret. Even when they find out things, we don't confirm it. The less they know the better it is for us," Seth said.

"Are you saying we shouldn't trust them?" Gina asked.

Seth nodded. "Trust no one. Look how countries fight over nuclear technology. We're the human version of a nuclear weapon."

"Wow, Genius. You're certainly full of good news this morning." Ashley pushed away from the table. "If the strip show is over, I'm going to work on my Christmas list. And Santa better be very nice this year."

"But have you been a good girl?" Connor asked.

Ashley paused to glance over her shoulder before she left the kitchen. "I don't know, Connor. Have I?" She grinned before she turned and strode towards her bedroom.

Seth pulled on his t-shirt. "I'll let you know when the meeting is arranged."

Chapter Twenty-Two

Gina watched Seth leave the kitchen before she turned to Connor. She stared at him trying to find the words she wanted to say. He looked so familiar, and yet he didn't seem the same boy she went to school with.

He grinned. "A pic would last longer."

Gina laughed. "I wasn't admiring, I was trying to ask you something."

"So ask."

Gina glanced away. "There's a rumour at school that your longest relationship is two weeks." She forced herself to meet his gaze. "Does Ashley know that?"

"I'm glad to know you don't hear all our conversations."

"I try not to. Why?"

"Because if you did you might be having this talk

with Ashley and telling her not to break my heart." His flippant tone became serious. "We know what we're doing, Gina."

"I hope so. I think we're going to be stuck with each other a long time."

"Is that so bad?"

Gina stared at Connor, weighing the question. She slowly shook her head. "Not as bad as I first thought it'd be." She grinned. "You're not as unbearable as you pretend."

"What? Did you think you glimpsed a hint of gold in this shallow creek?"

Gina laughed. "You're never going to let me forget that comment, are you?"

"Probably not. Now how about we write up our lists?" He draped an arm around her shoulders. "Do you think a Ferrari would be too much to ask for?" They headed for the study. "Actually forget about the Ferrari. I want a Bugatti Veyron."

"You do remember you're only on your P's. That means no powerful vehicles."

"Maybe they can get me an open license." Connor pushed the study door open.

Gina shook her head. "The four-wheel-drive is more practical."

Seth spun his chair to face them. "Good. Just got an

email from Dad. Can someone get Ashley?" He spun back to the laptop, his fingers flying over the keys, his right hand occasionally moving the mouse.

Gina slid out from under Connor's arm. "I'll get her. You can start on your fantasy list."

Connor grinned. "I wonder if they can get me an invite to the playboy mansion."

Gina hit him on the shoulder. "Be serious."

"I am."

Gina shook her head as she headed for Ashley's suite, which took up most of one side of the house. She was sprawled on her bed, chewing on the top of a pen as she stared at the notepad in her other hand. "Seth got an email from his dad."

Ashley rolled over to stare up at Gina, one arm going behind her head, the notebook left to lie beside her. "Do you think we can turn that lounge room into a home gym? We can make the dining room at the front of the house our lounge. The eating area in the kitchen is more practical than carting food halfway across the house anyway."

"I don't mind." Gina shrugged. "And it's probably a more sensible request than Connor's."

"What does he want?"

"A Bugatti and an invite to the playboy mansion."

Ashley laughed and rolled her eyes. "Boys!" She

grabbed her notebook and hopped off the bed. "Why get a car you can't legally drive yet?"

"That's what I told him."

They reached the study. "An old RX7 would be nice. But for something newer a Series 1 Lotus Elise would be sweet."

Connor looked up from where he sat at the second desk, the keyboard pushed out of the way of the paper he wrote on. "I never thought of them." He turned back to his paper, ran a line several times through one of his points and wrote next to it.

Gina looked from Connor to Ashley. "You two can't be serious."

"What do you want?" Ashley perched on the desk Connor used.

Gina didn't even have to think about it. She wanted an end to her biggest fear since this had started. "I want my family safe."

"Ask for a lot of money so you can install security systems for them," Ashley said.

"Forget about lists for the moment and look at these." Seth held out some papers he took from the printer.

Ashley slid off the desk. "How did you get pics of the mad scientist?"

"Neighbours talk. Especially if they think they're

being interviewed by the Australian Federal Police. None of the family has been seen at the house we were at last night for about a month. A fortnight ago a removalist and cleaning crew came in and emptied the place." Seth took another page from the printer. It consisted of four photos. "This is the house his wife and son are in. That's them. And again here. And this one was taken this morning as she went shopping, the nanny pushing the kid in his pram."

Connor took the page of pictures. "This house doesn't look like a prison. Or the people like prisoners."

"That's what I was thinking." Seth took the page from the bottom of the pile Ashley held. "This is a list of his known aliases, but no one knows who he really is or where he came from. The current name he uses is Raymond King. He's used the name Raymond three times, Ray five times and Ralph twice out of the twenty-three aliases he's had. No similarities have been found between the other names."

Ashley touched several last names. "King, Prince, Rex. Someone thinks highly of themself."

Seth grinned fleetingly. "I've been thinking over what he said last night. Several times he said 'he has my family' but the last time he said had, rather than has. And he seemed too calm. Something about this doesn't add up."

"The woman's heartbeat was racing, but Raymond's was normal. His breathing was even and his tone conversational," Gina said.

Seth nodded. "I think he's one of the main players. Maybe he started out as a hostage, but he isn't anymore."

"Yeah, he was pretty hyped to hear we survived," Ashley said.

"And it won't take him long to figure out the one thing we all have in common," Seth said.

"Our age." Gina's words were soft, but they caused the room to fall silent.

"We've got to find him before he changes the direction of the experiments," Ashley said.

Seth gestured towards the laptop that sat closed on the floor beside him. "Dad will pick the laptop up later and see what he can find out."

"Why can't we do it?" Connor asked.

"I don't want to risk losing information if there are any traps on it. Dad has access to the right equipment," Seth said.

"Can we trust him?" Connor asked.

"Of course we can," Seth said. "He's my dad."

Connor shook his head. "That doesn't always mean

anything. I wouldn't trust my parents with any of this information."

"I wouldn't tell my parents either," Ashley said. "But not because they'd hurt me. My mum would be so excited she'd plaster it all over Facebook, probably tweet about it for days and run the phone bill up talking to all her friends." She grinned. "And I bet she'd even find some way to get on a stack of talk shows."

"Two families down." Connor turned to Gina. "What about you?"

"I'm not going to tell all my family, but that'd mean hundreds of people. I will tell my parents and grandparents. They need to know why I'm different. I don't want them to worry."

"Well those statistics suck," Ashley said.

Gina frowned. "What do you mean?"

"Let's hope the real statistics are better than what we've got in this room. Otherwise, fifty percent of kids can't rely on their families."

"You're such an optimist, Ash," Connor said.

"I know." Ashley grinned as she held up her notebook. "Now if you've got no more cheerful news to share with us, I have an organisation to bleed dry."

Seth shook his head. "We're still waiting to hear what time the meeting will be."

Connor took Ashley's notebook. "What are you asking for?"

Ashley snatched it back and headed for the door. "You can wait and see."

"Come on, Ash. Don't be like that. I need some ideas." Connor followed her down the hall. "My list is only half a page long."

Gina dropped onto the seat Connor had vacated and stared at Seth who had returned to the laptop. "When will I be able to talk to my family?"

He turned his chair to face her. "Dad's working on it. I know how important they are to you. He's keeping them informed and drops in regularly to supposedly commiserate with them. He gives them notes to let them know you're safe and they haven't found you."

"Thank you." Her attention was drawn to the laptop when it pinged to let Seth know an email had arrived. She watched as he opened it and her gaze was drawn to the date. "School starts today."

Seth rolled his chair across the floor and took her hand. "I'm sorry."

"It's not your fault." She tried to smile, but it failed. "Besides, isn't every teenager meant to be thrilled when they get days off school?"

"Not for this reason." He reached out and tucked her hair behind her ear.

This time her smile didn't fail. She slid the hair band off his wrist. "You keep stealing it on me." She pulled her hair back into a ponytail.

Seth grinned. "I like it down." He tugged lightly on her ponytail. "Will you be okay?" He gestured towards the laptop. "I've still got some information to go over."

Gina nodded. "Yeah. I should probably start my list."

Seth slid open a drawer and pulled out a notebook and pen similar to Ashley's. "Go overboard. That way we have negotiating room."

Gina took the items and rose to her feet. She started to move away but was halted when Seth pulled her to him. She stood between his legs, the soft cover of the seat pressed just below her knees, Seth's arms around her as his head rested on her chest. She ran her free hand through his hair.

He tilted his head to look up at her. "Remember my promise." He drew her head down to him and lightly kissed her. His lips curved slightly as he pulled away. "Now go and outdo Ashley's efforts to bleed them dry."

Gina couldn't resist returning Seth's smile. She ran

her fingers across his bottom lip. "The first thought I had when I met you was nice smile."

His smile became a grin. "What was your second thought?"

She thought of how she'd wanted his number. That had been more of a plan. Running her fingers across his face, she stopped beside his eyes. "I wanted to comment on how blue your eyes are."

"When you smiled back at me, I wanted to ask you for your phone number. I was trying to figure out how to do that when Connor walked in."

"Do you still want it?"

"Do you have a mobile phone?"

Gina shook her head.

"Put that on your list. And stop procrastinating." He turned her towards the door. "Get that list written."

"I wasn't procrastinating. Someone distracted me."

Seth laughed. "Are you complaining?"

Gina only grinned back at him before she stepped out the door. When she reached the end of the hall she headed for the dining area Ashley wanted to do away with. She sat in a hard backed dark timber chair and flipped opened the spiral notebook. Staring at the lined page, she tried to think about what she wanted.

Chapter Twenty-Three

Anthony arrived at around the time school would normally be finishing for the day. Gina couldn't help thinking about how different today had been compared with her usual first day back at school. Creating a list had been about as school like as the day had been. The rest of the day had been filled with consuming a ridiculous amount of food, flicking through numerous television stations only to find nothing worth watching and logging into her Facebook to stare at posts she couldn't answer. It helped to see how worried everyone was for her. She wanted to tell them she was fine. A little different, but fine. Okay, maybe more than a little different.

Connor came out of the study, pulling his shirt back on and smiled weakly at Gina who paced back and forth in the foyer. "Your turn."

"There was a needle, wasn't there?"

Seth took her hand. "It's okay. I'll go with you."

"Your dad does realise we're not going to like him very much if he keeps sticking needles in us, doesn't he?" Gina walked down the hallway, her hand tightening on Seth's the closer they came to the study.

Seth laughed. "Nope. Dad doesn't know that at all."

Anthony looked up from where he typed on his laptop, the one already on the desk pushed to the side to make room for his. "What don't I know?"

"That shoving needles in someone won't make them your friend," Seth said.

Anthony grinned, his smile very similar to his son's. "Unless you're a drug dealer trying to befriend a junkie."

Seth laughed. "Since that scenario doesn't apply, I think Gina is going to start dreading your visits."

Anthony waved to the chair. "Sit down and I'll make it as quick as possible."

Gina took a step back and looked up at Seth. "How about you go first?"

Seth shrugged. "I don't mind, but you're only postponing the inevitable."

"Shirt off. Sit down." Anthony rose to his feet, a stethoscope around his neck, a blood pressure cuff in his hands.

Seth pulled his t-shirt over his head and threw it to

Gina as he sat down. "Just make sure you warn Gina before you start playing with sharps."

Anthony nodded as he used first the blood pressure cuff and then the stethoscope. He made notes on his laptop before he turned back to Seth. "What's the scar from?" He pointed to his son's left side.

"I was shot last night."

Anthony motioned Seth to stand and hold his arm away from his body as he poked and prodded at the feint white line. "Any pain?"

Seth shook his head.

Anthony lifted Seth's arm above his head. "Pulling?"

"It feels normal. Not the slightest bit different," Seth said.

"How bad was it?"

"Normally it would have needed stitches. And I probably would have needed a blood transfusion."

"You said it was a scratch," Gina accused.

Seth smiled. "It's not even that now."

"Do you think you can be a little more careful next time?" Anthony's tone was mild, his gaze sharp.

"I thought I was considering we were running from a small army."

Anthony stared at his son a moment. "I better take

some samples. The meeting is only half an hour away."

Seth turned to Gina. "That's your signal not to watch."

She faced the door, her hands tightening on the shirt she held. "Tell me when it's done." She cut sound to that area, not wanting to hear the process. To distract herself, she tuned in to Ashley and Connor.

"I can't see why he had to take our cars off the list," Connor said. A piece of paper vibrated as it was shaken.

"We'll each get a car, just not a sports car," Ashley said.

"Practical is boring." Connor slapped the paper against the table.

"We're going to earn a fortune. You could save up for one."

"The contract is only for two years. What do we do after that?"

Ashley laughed. "Negotiate for a sports car next time."

Anthony interrupted Gina's eavesdropping. "Your turn now."

"Seth?"

"You can't see anything," Seth said.

She turned and threw his shirt to him. He pulled it over his head, but he wasn't quick enough to hide his smile. "I don't have to take my shirt off, do I?" She sat in the chair Seth vacated.

Anthony shook his head. "Lean forward and raise it at the back for me." He listened with the stethoscope. "Okay. Let it go. Now sit back and lower the front a bit." Once he'd finished with the stethoscope and blood pressure cuff, he smiled ruefully. "Now comes the forget about being friends part."

"Great," Gina muttered as she closed her eyes. She tilted her head back and wished the back of the chair was higher. She felt hands on her arm and was tempted to open her eyes to see if it was Seth.

"Strap going around the arm." Seth's words were a whisper near her ear.

She tilted her head in his direction and rested her cheek against him. She had been right. She was starting to recognise the sounds of everyone. Heartbeat, breath, movements. They were all different.

"Cold. And now for a little sting." His lips brushed her cheek as he spoke. "Relax. Almost over."

She was tempted to headbutt him for the relax comment, but guessed it would hurt her too. How was she meant to relax when someone kept jabbing needles into her? She felt the needle being drawn from her arm and waited for the all clear.

"You can't see anything now," Seth said.

Gina opened her eyes to glare at Seth. "Relax? Seriously? Do you have to keep telling me that? How can I relax when someone keeps jabbing me with needles? It isn't in the least bit relaxing."

Seth grinned. "Do you want me to kiss it better?"

Gina pushed Seth away as she stood up. She couldn't help checking what Anthony was doing. He tapped away on his laptop, reminding her of Seth. "What are all the tests for anyway? We're better, aren't we?"

Anthony glanced up at her. "I want to make sure there are no problems. Regular tests will ensure any possible problems are discovered in plenty of time to deal with them." He turned to Seth. "Can you check some slides for me?"

Seth grinned. "I was wondering when you'd start to find a walking microscope useful."

Anthony turned back to his laptop.

Gina gestured towards the door. "I think I'll join Ashley and Connor." Blood might not be as bad as needles, but she'd rather not see how much had been collected.

Seth's grin remained in place as he stepped close

to her. "Call me when it's time for the meeting." He kissed her lightly then turned to the small esky sitting on the floor.

Gina hurried from the room, but paused halfway down the hallway to listen in. She knew she shouldn't, but couldn't resist. She heard Anthony's chair turn, him still in it.

"Anything you want to tell me, Seth?"

"I haven't even looked at the samples yet, Dad. Microscopic vision, not x-ray. They're still in the esky." There was amusement in Seth's voice.

"You and Gina?"

Seth laughed. "You do realise she's probably listening in."

"Is she?"

"Yeah. But that's okay. I like her. A lot."

Gina smiled, barely suppressing the laugh that wanted to escape.

"Should I have put condoms in the stuff I got for you? You didn't have them on your list."

Gina's smile evaporated and her face heated.

Seth laughed again. "It's fine Dad." His voice lowered to a whisper his father couldn't hear. "Gina, you still listening?" There was a pause in the conversation. Seth spoke again, still in a whisper. "I'm about to talk blood test results now, just in case you'd rather not hear those details."

That was enough to make Gina shut out the conversation and walk to the end of the hallway. She paused to locate Ashley and Connor. They were in the lounge room, discussing how to set up their home gym. It was something they both wanted. Not wanting to be a part of that discussion either, Gina wandered to the kitchen. She was always hungry these days. She had no sooner opened a tub of chocolate ice cream when she heard her name spoken.

"Gina, how about sharing. I'm starved," Connor said.

"What's she got?" Ashley asked.

"Chocolate ice cream."

"Oooh. Yes. Me too, Gina."

Gina grinned as she pulled out three various sized mixing bowls and split the two litres between four, one serve left in the container since she guessed Seth would want some too. She heard him open the study door. When he reached the lounge, Ashley spoke to him.

"Did you want ice cream too?"

Gina grabbed spoons and two of the bowls. What she really needed was a tray. She grinned when Seth appeared in the doorway. "I was just thinking a tray would be handy."

Seth laughed. "Should I feel insulted?" He picked up the other bowl and the container.

"Should I?"

"About?"

"How did your dad jump to the conclusion of condoms when you said you liked me?"

"He's my best friend. We talk about everything."

Gina stared at Seth a moment. "What else have you said about me?"

Seth shook his head. "Barely anything. I haven't had much time to talk to him. Or even email him about anything other than X-One-Six. But he knows me Gina. I just finished telling him you were listening. And I still told him I like you."

"Gina. You pair better not be making out in there while my ice cream melts," Connor said from the lounge room.

"She better not be eating it all herself," Ashley said. "Maybe we better go get it off her."

"Connor and Ashley are going to be in here in a second if we don't take them their food," Gina said.

Seth smiled. "Saved by the bell." He headed for the lounge room.

"About time," Connor said.

Ashley took a bowl from Gina as she dropped onto the couch beside her. "We could probably live on junk food without getting fat." She had a mouthful of ice cream and closed her eyes a moment. "Maybe we should test that theory. You know, for scientific purposes."

Seth laughed. "Should we do cholesterol tests too? All in the name of science."

"Now don't go taking the fun out of my project," Ashley said.

"Why do I get the feeling Seth's ideas on science always involve needles?" Gina scooped up some of her ice cream, starting with the melted area first.

"Facts are important in any experiment. Facts, recording data and comparing results. You can't have an experiment without them," Seth said.

Gina froze. "Comparing results."

"What about it?" Connor asked.

"X-One-Six. Where are all the results for the other fifteen experiments? They'd want to compare their results with earlier data. Was there anything on Douglas' laptop?" Gina asked.

Seth shook his head. "References only. No actual data like he'd recorded for X-One-Six."

"We're going to have to find all that information

too, aren't we?" Gina asked. Her ice cream dripped off her spoon and back into the bowl.

Seth nodded.

Ashley gestured towards the list lying on the coffee table in front of them. "Maybe you should make a list of what we need to do since you're so keen on them."

"Item one, destroy mad scientist. Item two, find needle in a haystack in the form of notes for sixteen experiments," Connor said.

"Wouldn't item one be interrogate mad scientist?" Ashley asked.

"And how do we go about doing that? Carry a lie detector in our back pocket? I really think they're a little too large to carry around with us," Connor said.

Seth stared at Gina. "Maybe not."

"What's that supposed to mean?" Gina eyed him warily.

"You knew there was something wrong when we spoke to Raymond. I bet you could learn how to do a lie test. It's all to do with things like heart rate, blood pressure and respiration. You could also listen to how things are said. I can help. I can watch for tics, perspiration and other visual responses," Seth said. "We can check online for what to look for."

"Not right now. Our front gate just opened," Gina said.

"I can smell two different people," Connor said.

Ashley laughed. "We sound like freaks. Like something that belongs in an asylum."

Connor tossed a pillow at her. "Speak for yourself."

"Nope. I'd rather speak for all of us." Ashley continued to grin. "You have to admit life's been pretty interesting this past week."

Gina rose to her feet as she heard a car pull up and a car door open and close. "I could do with a little less interesting." She headed for the front door, the others joining her. "Only one is coming in." She opened the door before anyone could knock.

A man in a black suit stood in front of them. He had short, neat brown hair and hazel eyes. He held out his hand to Gina. "Nicholas Smith."

Connor started to laugh. "Smith? You've got to be kidding. Right? You can't be serious that's your last name."

"If you're going for the men in black look, you forgot the dark glasses," Ashley said.

Nicholas remained expressionless. "I believe you initiated this meeting." He glanced at the watch he wore. It had a dark face with a black leather band. The numbers and hands were gold.

Ashley tugged Gina out of the doorway. "Sure.

Come inside, Nick." She smiled up at him. "Is your friend coming inside, or staying in the car?"

"She's welcome to come inside," Seth said.

"She will wait in the car." Nicholas stepped inside and scanned the area.

"This way." Gina gestured towards the dining table. There was no need to take him on a tour of the house, the dining area was the closest.

Chapter Twenty-Four

As soon as they were all seated, Seth slid his list across the table to Nicholas. "Since you seem pressed for time, we'll get straight to the point. We feel we've been extremely reasonable in our demands considering the nature and uniqueness of our situation."

Nicholas perused the page in front of him. "You can forget the first demand. This isn't a classroom where you can say you don't feel like doing a job."

"It's not a question of liking the job. It's the right to refuse any job we find morally questionable," Seth said.

"We're not assassins," Ashley added.

Nicholas turned his gaze on her. "Yet."

Ashley rose to her feet. "Well, I can't say it's been nice meeting you, Nick. But that's one point we won't budge on."

"Sit down." Nicholas gestured towards the chair.

Ashley continued to stand. "Why?" There was only curiosity in her tone.

"I thought you might be more comfortable having this discussion while you were seated," Nicholas said.

"You've already turned us down," Seth said. "I believe the discussion is over."

"And this is why I dislike working with kids." Nicholas tapped the paper. "You can't expect us to agree to these terms with no idea of what you're capable of."

"I guess that's going to be a bit of an issue. Our second point happens to be that we're not test subjects, experiments or willing to be," Gina said.

Nicholas tapped the figure they'd named. "And yet you expect us to provide you with a substantial income, house you, pay for living expenses, education and transportation. This all sounds very one sided."

"It's not like we asked for a Bugatti Veyron," Seth said.

Gina barely managed to hold back a laugh. This was made more difficult when she caught Ashley's gaze.

"Quit playing games and give me your real demands." Nicholas slid the paper towards Seth.

Seth smiled and rose to his feet. "I guess Ashley was correct. The meeting is over."

Ashley still stood at the table, arms crossed, most of her weight on her right leg and her left foot angled and slightly forward. "I'm always right." She sounded smug.

Nicholas rose to his feet also. "Give me the list. I need some reason to give when I tell my superiors negotiations failed."

Seth held it out to him. "If the people you work for were serious, they would have sent one of your superiors, not an errand boy. And if you really want to know what we can do, why not offer us a job that your organisation is having trouble completing. Something we wouldn't find morally questionable."

"You want me to believe you'd do a job for free after the demands you've presented? Who are you working for?" Nicholas asked.

Seth strode towards the front door and held it open. "No one."

Nicholas stared at him a moment before he crossed the room and stepped outside. "This house, the cars, all of it, will be taken back. We expected you to be reasonable in your demands." He looked at each of them where they'd stopped at the front door.

"We were very reasonable. The problem is you

don't know what you're trying to buy. Offer us a job. We fail, we'll reduce most of our demands. If we get it done, the list is accepted as is," Seth said.

"Any job?"

"As long as it isn't morally questionable. And we expect proof that it isn't," Ashley said.

Nicholas stared at them a moment longer before he turned and strode to the dark coloured sedan. He slid into the passenger seat and the woman drove towards the front gate. They watched them leave then closed the door. Gina leaned against the door and listened as the car stopped two streets away. She was glad Seth had warned them what was likely to happen in the meeting. She would have given in and negotiated. She grinned.

"What's happening?" Ashley asked.

"He's making a call. Quiet," Gina said.

"They were stringing us along, sir," Nicholas said. He paused and Gina wished she could hear the other end of the conversation. It was little more than a hum though. "Yes, sir. I have a list of their demands here. I'll photograph them and send them through." Another pause. "Give me a minute." As the silence extended, Gina quickly filled them in on the conversation then waved them quiet when Nicholas spoke again. "Did you receive that, sir?" He laughed softly. "Yes, they are very ambitious. But they did offer to complete a job that fits their first demand and if they complete it, we concede to their every demand." He laughed again. "It'd be worth it just to take those arrogant little bastards down a couple of pegs." Silence again. "Have the paperwork ready for me to collect. We'll be there in thirty. Have someone contact the children and arrange for me to see them in an hour and a half." Silence. "Yes, sir."

"The office?" the woman asked.

"Yes."

"Which job?"

"Waltham."

The woman laughed as she started the car. "Do you kick puppies and kittens too?"

Nicholas laughed. "You wouldn't say that if you'd been the one stuck dealing with the little bastards. They have it coming to them."

Ashley laughed when Gina relayed the conversation. "Oh, we really have to make him eat his words. I hope it isn't a job we'd find morally offensive."

"Maybe it's an impossible job," Gina said.

"Perfect. We're impossible people," Ashley said.

"Yep, just ask Nick. He'd certainly agree to that," Connor said.

Seth's phone rang. "I guess this is them now." They all fell silent as he answered the phone. He grinned. "Sure. We look forward to seeing what job he thinks would make an appropriate test." Seth paused. "We'll see him then." He disconnected and grinned at them. "Shall we show him what the little bastards can do?"

Connor laughed. "Sounds like a plan to me."

Anthony stepped out into the foyer and glanced around at them, Raymond's laptop under his arm, his own in a case held by one hand, the esky in the other hand. "They've gone already?"

"Nicholas Smith. And he'll be back in an hour and a half. He just got permission to offer us the Waltham job," Seth said.

Anthony nodded. "I'll email you if I find out any details about it."

"Thanks, Dad."

"I better go. This laptop needs to be examined. Get the door, Seth?"

Seth opened the front door and stepped outside with his father. Gina watched them walk to Anthony's car and she wished she could see her family. There had to be some way. Seth opened the door to his father's car and helped him put his gear on the passenger seat. They hugged, patting each other's backs as they did. Seth pulled away with a grin and made a laughing comment. Gina gave them privacy. She waited in the doorway as Seth strode back towards her. She shook her head at the questioning look in his eyes.

Seth closed the front door behind him. "I bet that was a strain."

Gina laughed. "You have no idea." She heard Ashley and Connor walk towards Ashley's room.

"Do you want me to tell you what we said?"

"That's okay. I don't mean to always invade your privacy."

Seth took another step and wrapped his arms around her. "I'd tell you if it bothered me."

"Okay." Gina relaxed against him. "What are we going to do while we wait?"

Seth laughed softly. "I'm really tempted to make a completely different answer to that question. But I think we should see what we can come up with online about Waltham."

Gina grinned. "Need any help with that?"

"The research or my completely different answer."

"Research."

"Sure. I'll turn the desktop on too." Seth led the way to the study and they were soon researching the name. They came up with several local newspaper articles about a Hubert Waltham who skated very close to the edge of the law and complained he was an innocent man and the police had it in for him.

Gina pushed away from the desk when she heard the car come up their driveway. "Nick's back. I'll go and get Ashley and Connor."

Seth nodded. "I'll let him in."

Gina couldn't help noticing that Nicholas looked almost cheerful as he placed a thin pile of paperwork on their dining room table. "There doesn't seem to be a lot of information there." She took the first page from the pile. It was one of the newspaper articles she'd already read. She handed it to Seth with a smile.

He nodded and glanced down at his phone when it beeped for an incoming message. He handed the phone over to her and she read the confirmation from Anthony that the Waltham job was suitable. She handed the phone along to Ashley and Connor who eventually handed it back to Seth.

"If you are finished your show and tell, can we get on with this?" Nicholas asked.

"Go ahead, we're listening," Seth said.

"Articles and proof for your first demand." Nicholas took a handful of pages off the top of the pile. "Details about the area and security measures." Half the pile was set aside. "What we need confirmation of." A smaller pile. "Known habits and associates of Hubert Waltham." The last of the pile.

Seth picked up the security measures pile and flicked through it. "How long do we have to complete the job?"

"Four weeks."

"How many teams have failed?" Seth asked.

"Seven."

"How many years have you been trying to get this information?"

There was a long pause. "What makes you ask years? It could be weeks."

"If it was only weeks you wouldn't have bothered to offer it to a bunch of kids. How many years?"

"Nearly two."

Connor grinned as he looked up from the paper relating to what they needed confirmation of. "If we get the info within the week I reckon we should double our wage."

Ashley laughed. "Does that mean we should triple it if we get it done tonight?" She had the pages of habits and associates.

"I don't think you realise the seriousness of the situation. The roof is covered in pressure plates. Guard dogs and guards patrol the outer perimeter. A thirty second break between them. Motion detectors and heat sensor beams make a complicated pattern that has a twenty-two second break every eight minutes when the pattern randomly resets with one of the thirty patterns in the system. Doors and windows have alarms on them. If they are open longer than five seconds without the code being keyed in, they go off. Even the house has random security measures from motion detectors, security cameras and heat sensors. Realistically, you would have at the most thirty seconds to get from the outer wall to inside the house. It can't be done. And all the security has backup systems. They go down for more than five seconds and the backup kicks in. Do you honestly think you can complete this job?"

"Yes," Seth said.

"Why else do you think we're making what you call outrageous demands, Nicky," Ashley said.

Gina watched Nicholas as he stopped breathing for several seconds. He inhaled slow and deep, held his breath and let it out again. His expression remained neutral. It was only her exceptional hearing that allowed her to notice. She wondered what names he was mentally calling them. A smiled curved her lips. "That name doesn't bother you, does it? It's not as if it's something nasty like arsehole or… hmm, I don't know. Maybe bastard?" She listened as his breathing halted again and he went through his calming process.

"Are you trying to tell me something?" Nicholas asked.

Gina nodded, annoyed by Nicholas' attitude towards them. "Yeah, be a little nicer to us, Nicky. I've got a feeling your job will be to keep us happy. Your boss is going to want us to renew our contract in two years time."

"You haven't completed the job yet. You've got two weeks to show some results. Completion within four weeks."

Ashley smiled. "We'll get it done. We'll start the planning stage as soon as we see a story on the news that confirms we weren't infected by the virus."

"That wasn't in your list," Nicholas said.

"You do expect us to be able to work unhindered, don't you?" Seth asked.

Nicholas rose to his feet. "Watch the late night news."

"Which channel?" Connor asked.

"Any of them. Don't bother to show me out. I know the way." Nicholas strode to the front door, shutting it softly behind him.

Gina listened while he walked to the car, that door

closing a little more loudly. She smiled and waved her hand for quiet when Connor was about to speak.

Nicholas didn't speak until he was at the end of the street. "We have to find out more about them."

"If we agree to all their demands we won't be able to use surveillance equipment or techniques on them without their permission. If they can pull this off, the boss won't want them to be able to get out of their contract." It was the same woman who'd been with him earlier.

"A tip off that someone plans to break in tonight might ensure things go in our favour."

"Nicholas–"

"No. They want those kids. But they don't want to meet all the demands. There's too many strings. It's not the money. It's the other demands that bother them. They want to be the ones in control. You make the call. Just after the late night news tonight. I'll make sure there's an extraction team ready to get them out of there."

"What if they don't make their move tonight?"

"We keep watching until they do."

The woman sighed. "If you think it's best."

Nicholas was silent a moment. "I do."

When the silence stretched out, Gina relayed what she'd heard. Silence filled the house.

Seth broke it first. He looked up the sunset time on his phone. "Right. That gives us three hours to pull this off. Let's go over the details."

"We could do it tomorrow," Connor suggested.

Seth shook his head. "Tonight. Before they make the call." He spread out the pages relating to security. "Right. We have five seconds to get over the fence. Twenty-two to cross the front yard. Has anyone seen details on the distance?"

Ashley handed a page to Seth. "If we can cross it during the twenty-two second break between patterns it'd be easier than learning them."

Seth nodded as he pulled his phone out to use the calculator function. "Ashley, Connor, can you find out how far you can run in twenty seconds?" When they rose from the table, he turned to Gina. "Can you email my dad and ask him to cut the power tonight. Only for four seconds. We'll email him the time when we've figured it out. His email address is listed in my contacts." He turned back to the paper scattered across the table.

Gina smiled as she watched him for a moment. He was completely absorbed. When he looked up, a slight look of confusion on his face, she grinned and headed for the study. It didn't take her long to send the email and the reply was almost as quick. She read it over.

'Let me know the time to the second. Twenty minutes notice at least.'

Chapter Twenty-Five

Once again they were dressed all in black and wore balaclavas. Seth stared at his watch, waiting for the correct time. Gina didn't bother with time. She waited for the sound of electricity to stop. She heard it go out the same moment Seth gave the signal to move. They reached the house with seven seconds to spare before the next motion detector and heat sensor pattern started. Plenty of time for Seth to get the window unlocked and open and for them to enter and close it again before the five second alarm went off. Now to get what they came for and be out in eight minutes in time for the next twenty-two second break in the pattern. Gina grinned even though no one could see it. She couldn't wait to ruin Nicholas' night. They stood still and silent as Seth did a visual search of the room. He pointed out the security, which Gina could barely see in the shadowy room. They followed Seth as he sprinted through the room, paused in a hallway then took off again.

The journey through the house consisted of the same technique. Each room was visually searched by Seth. He took several photos along the way as something caught his attention. When they reached the study just over a minute later he pointed out the security measures to avoid then turned on the desktop computer. Gina moved around the room, tapping on the walls and furniture, listening to the sound and comparing it to the others. She pointed to the two areas that sounded different and Seth soon found a secret compartment and a wall safe. Using the information she had researched online, Gina soon had the safe open, amazed at what extremely sensitive hearing could accomplish. They were in the study less than five minutes. Data was collected from the computer and stored on an external hard drive, photos were taken of a copious amount of paperwork as well as all items in the safe and secret compartment.

Within a minute they were in the room they'd first entered. Seth checked his watch. He sent a text with his phone and waited. As soon as the power went off he opened the window and they hopped out after him. Gina wanted to throw her head back and laugh with excitement. They were nearly out. No one had seen them. She tried to rein in the adrenaline that coursed through her. They hadn't left the property yet.

They ran across the yard stopping at the perimeter fence. She automatically listened for the hum of electricity. As soon as it was quiet, they clambered over the fence. Once outside, she couldn't stop grinning. She wanted to tear the mask off and dance around shouting. Instead she continued to run, following Seth as the four of them headed down the street to where the four-wheel-drive was parked.

Connor hit the central locking button and got in the driver's seat. He pulled his mask off as he closed his door. "Man, I want to do that again. Are we good or what?"

Gina finally let her laugh escape as she sat beside Seth in the back seat. She pulled off her mask and wiped at the bead of sweat on her forehead. "I can't believe how easy that was." She was surprised at how exciting it had been.

Ashley stripped off her black outfit to reveal a wine coloured dress so short it barely covered her. It plunged low in front and she wore black fishnet stockings and pulled on black, knee high stiletto boots. "Are you sure you don't mind me having the fun of delivering the results to Nicky?" Her hair was already pinned and she pulled on a wig that matched her dress. The sleek bob curved towards her cheeks. Lipstick finished her disguise. Her eye makeup had been done earlier.

Seth handed her a necklace, what looked like a diamond in a gold setting. "There's a device in this that records both picture and sound. Press the jewel firmly and it'll start. It has a maximum of one hour, but even if it takes you longer we can continue to pick up the signal and watch what's happening on the laptop."

Ashley slipped the necklace over her head and it hung in the vee of her dress. "Sweet. Something for us to watch next time he's annoying us."

Connor drove around the block, his window down. "They must be pretty keen to get us out of there. I can smell about fifty people, including Nick."

Seth finished backing up their information onto his laptop before sliding the external hard drive and SD card from the camera into a beaded velvet drawstring bag. He handed it to Ashley. "Only give this to Nick. Make sure someone else sees you give it to him and let him know there's a backup copy in case he loses it."

Connor parked on the side of the road past the pool

of light given off by a streetlight. "Accidentally on purpose loses it."

"There was nothing in the information that made any of you think Waltham's innocent, was there?" Gina asked. She hadn't seen anything, but she wanted to make sure before they gave all the details to Nicholas.

"He's guilty." Seth angled his laptop. "Shush. Late night news is starting."

They all crowded in as close as possible, the light of the screen bathing their faces. Two news reporters sat behind a desk, covering the main highlights. Ten minutes into the program, straight after a round of ads, the male news reporter adopted a serious expression.

"There have been many concerns in the community this past week about the children who were recently kidnapped." The news reporter was momentarily replaced with photos of Gina, Connor and Seth, but he continued his spiel. "There were reports of a highly contagious virus. The man who kidnapped them was on the run from a laboratory, where the safety measures of an experiment were compromised. This has raised the community's concerns regarding the safety of experiments that involve dangerous materials. We now go live to speak to the doctor whose care the children are under."

The image changed to show the front of a local private hospital followed by a reporter who held a microphone in front of a white-garbed doctor. "Can you tell us how the children are?"

The doctor nodded. "They're doing extremely well. When they were found they were suffering exhaustion and dehydration. Luckily for them Finney had dropped them in a deserted area as soon as he had no more need of them as hostages. Extensive tests have been performed and each child has come up with a clean bill of health. They were kept under observation for several days. Rest and plenty of liquids were all they really needed."

The reporter held the microphone in front of himself. "Can you tell us about the seriousness of the virus they came in contact with? If it was so contagious, why didn't they contract it?"

"It could have been any number of reasons. Limited contact with their kidnapper helped. So too is the fact the virus is not airborne and once away from the host dies rapidly. The community should have no concerns there's an outbreak, but if they do, a course of antibiotics to ward off secondary infections, plenty of rest and fluids is the best plan of action," the doctor said.

"If the virus was easily treated, why did the kidnapper, Douglas Finney, die?" the reporter asked.

"He failed to follow those simple precautions. The man was on the run. He was afraid to see a doctor for antibiotics, he didn't get enough rest and as the autopsy showed, he didn't drink enough fluids and died of a secondary infection rather than the virus."

The scene returned to the television station where the news reporter now smiled, white teeth gleaming. "And there you have it. Antibiotics, rest and fluids. Nothing to be alarmed about. The children are on the mend and will probably be back at school within a few days with a harrowing story to share with their friends. Coming up after this break we talk to an expert on what you can do if you are ever at risk of being kidnapped."

"Gee, how thoughtful of them. Now they're going to tell us. A bit too late though," Ashley said.

Connor laughed as he sat back in his seat. "I hope I had a sexy nurse while I was in hospital."

"Yeah, he was tall dark and handsome and said he'd love you forever." Ashley grinned at him.

"Haven't you got somewhere to be?" Connor eyed her up and down. "Some street corner or something?"

Ashley continued to grin but changed the tone of her voice. "You couldn't afford me, honey." She kissed her fingers, pressed them against Connor's lips and opened the car door.

"Be careful," Gina said.

Ashley turned to look into the back of the vehicle. "I'm not worried. You lot can be with me in seconds. I know you'll be listening." She grinned. "Besides. Do you know how much damage these boots can do? They call them stilettos for a reason."

Seth's fingers tapped across the keyboard. "Don't worry, we'll have eyes on you as well. Now turn that camera on."

"Yes, captain." With a grin, Ashley saluted, closed the car door and sauntered down the road, the small beaded bag hanging from her wrist.

Gina watched the screen of the laptop, which remained black for several seconds before becoming a blur of lights and sounds. She guessed Ashley must be running. She looked up as Connor opened the front door of the car then opened hers.

"Move over. Why should I be the only one who can't see the screen properly?" Connor slid in beside her.

"Shush." Seth gestured towards the screen.

The sound quality wasn't the best so Gina reached

out to hear it for herself. She could hear the breath and heart beat of every person that was hidden, waiting to rescue them. It made it a little difficult to focus on a single person, but Ashley and Nicholas were fairly easy to pick out as she knew the sound of them. Nicholas leaned against a gum tree, his shoulder making the peeling strips of bark crackle softly as he breathed. He spun as he heard a sound behind him. The heartbeat of a man off to his right sped up.

"Hi, Nicky. I hope I haven't kept you waiting too long," Ashley said. "Did you miss me?"

Gina heard a strangled sound that she guessed was a smothered laugh. She heard Nicholas go through his calming routine.

"What are you doing here?" Nicholas' expression remained neutral, his tone even.

"Why meeting up with you, Nicky." Ashley's hand ran down the front of Nicholas' suit coat, undoing the buttons when she reached them.

He grabbed hold of her wrist when she opened one side. "What are you playing at?" He kept his voice low, leaning forward to keep their conversation private. His grip on her wrist tightened, but Ashley easily broke free.

"Behave." She tapped his nose and laughed. She

opened one side of his coat again to expose a gun. She let it close and checked the other side, sliding the beaded bag from her wrist into the inner pocket revealed. "Don't worry if you misplace anything. We've got a backup copy. I look forward to seeing you tomorrow morning. Ten. Don't be late." She started to turn away, then turned back again. "And Nicky, we aren't signing any agreement unless you get on your knees and tell us you're very sorry and beg us to sign." She slowly walked away.

Chapter Twenty-Six

Gina listened as Nicholas went through his calming routine four times. It obviously wasn't helping since he swore under his breath. "Get me a laptop. Now." He almost snarled the words. She listened as someone radioed for a vehicle followed by fingers tapping on a keyboard. Nicholas swore again. "Call them all in. We're done here."

"What's going on?" a male voice Gina didn't recognise asked.

"We're done. Wrap it up," Nicholas said.

"They delivered, didn't they?" the woman who'd been with him earlier asked.

"Little bastards," Nicholas muttered.

The woman swore. "Have you seen this? Nicholas, the boss is going to go crazy over this. I'd wear an old suit tomorrow."

"Why?" Nicholas asked.

"Because you won't want to wear the knees out of a good one."

Nicholas swore while Gina laughed and had to explain to everyone what was happening.

Ashley, who was already back, grinned and executed a half bow from where she sat in the front of the car, Connor again in the driver's seat beside her. "Thank you, thank you. You've been a wonderful audience."

Connor started the car and pulled out onto the street. "He's not going to want to kneel and beg. That was really low, Ash."

"So was calling us little bastards. The self righteous prick." Ashley removed her wig. "You're not sticking up for him, are you?"

Connor shook his head. "Nah, but he's going to absolutely hate us."

"We're not going to make him kneel," Seth said.

"Why not?" Ashley asked.

"You've had your fun. At least leave the poor guy some dignity," Seth said.

"Oh, all right. But he better not annoy me tomorrow or he is going to kneel and beg." Ashley pulled her boots off and started to roll down her fishnet stockings.

"You do realise I'm trying to drive here, Ash."

Ashley laughed. "Having trouble focusing, Connor?" She took a pair of jeans from the bag at her feet and started to slide them on.

Gina turned to Seth who still worked on his laptop. "What are you doing?"

"There'll be a contract lawyer at our place tomorrow morning at a quarter to ten. Dad has sent him our list so he'll know what to compare their contract against. Dad's also managed to retrieve all the information from Raymond's laptop."

"What did it say?" Gina was aware of the sudden silence in the front of the car.

"It's encrypted."

Ashley swore at Seth's answer. "Now what?"

"Now we wait until the data's been decoded," Seth said.

"Everything always happens so much quicker in spy movies. Do you ever see James Bond sitting around for days on end waiting for the next lot of action?" Ashley asked.

"Nope. He finds the nearest woman and the closest bed." Connor glanced towards Ashley. "What do you say, Ash?"

Ashley laughed.

"Was that a yes?" Connor asked hopefully.

"It was a, you don't deserve an answer after perving on me while I was getting dressed."

Connor stopped at their gate and waited for it to swing open. "I'm starved. Did you do something about groceries like you said, Lilly?"

"Yeah. Dad organised a housekeeper."

"Where are we going to put her?" Connor parked in the garage.

"Him. And he'll come in each day." Seth closed the lid of his laptop. "Leave messages for him on the door of the fridge."

Connor opened his door and froze. "Either I've died and gone to heaven, or our housekeeper has already been. I can smell lasagne." He was a blur of movement as he headed to the kitchen.

"Don't you dare eat it all." Ashley ran after him.

Seth turned to Gina. "You've been really quiet."

Gina nodded. "Are we doing the right thing? I mean, we're going to be stuck with some unknown organisation for an entire two years."

"And they're going to want us to stay with their team so they'll make sure they treat us like a priceless treasure," Seth said.

"Trying to make sure we fail isn't the way you handle a priceless treasure."

"That was before he knew we were priceless." Seth

grinned. "Now he's going to want to do everything he can to stay on our good side."

"I can really understand where Ashley is coming from. Are you sure we can't make him beg? Just a little bit?"

"No. Now let's get something to eat before Connor and Ashley eat it all."

When they reached the kitchen they found two large trays of lasagne that had been pulled out of the oven, steam curling from them. A message had been scrawled across the fridge with a whiteboard marker. 'Dinner in the oven. Turn it off when you're finished. In fridge- plate of salad to go with dinner, fruit salad for dessert, salad rolls for snacks. Let me know meal preferences. Shopping list inside pantry door. Todd.'

Ashley stood at the kitchen bench, eating from the half a tray Connor had left after he served himself. She pointed to the food with her fork. "This dude is amazing." She grabbed the whiteboard marker off the top of the fridge and scrawled 'thanks' under his message.

Gina opened the fridge once Ashley had returned to her food. "Do you want your salad?"

Ashley shook her head. "I'll have it later."

Gina served her food and moved over to the table to give Seth space. She sat across from Connor who looked like he was in heaven. She grinned at the questioning look he gave her for staring at him so long.

"Are you sure you don't want a pic?" Connor asked.

Gina shook her head with a smile. "Nah, I'm right."

"I am never going home again. The moment we get the all clear to go home, I'm telling my parents I'm moving out," Connor said.

Ashley sat on the bench and laid a tea towel across her lap so she could sit the hot tray there. "I emailed my mum earlier and told her I'd got an office job and I was moving in with friends. She had a million questions and was a little disappointed when I said I basically made coffee and did office filing."

Seth had just finished putting the kettle on. "Made coffee? I think I'm the one who mostly does that around here."

Ashley grinned. "But I did do the filing earlier. I filed it under 'pocket' for perfect job. Although I'm pretty sure Nicky wasn't impressed with my filing methods." She slid off the bench and dropped the empty tray in the sink. "Are you sure I can't make him do a little bit of begging?"

Seth took three large mugs from the cupboard. "Positive."

"You're no fun. I think I might go and soak in my spa." She twirled on the spot. "I love saying that. My spa." She grabbed one of the coffees Seth had made and waltzed out of the room. "My spa. I adore my spa."

Gina yawned. "I'm going to take a shower and head to bed."

Connor grabbed his serving of fruit salad from the fridge. "Have you had enough to eat? What about the rest of your lasagne?"

Gina waved towards the small serving still in the tray. "Go for it. I'll have my fruit salad and salad roll if I get hungry later."

Connor didn't need any urging. The rest of the lasagne was gone in moments and he took the coffee cup Seth handed him.

Seth had a sip of his coffee. "I'm going to go over some of Douglas' notes. See if there were any place references I missed."

Gina nodded before she headed for their bedroom. She stopped in the doorway when she saw the new bed in the middle of the room. She heard Seth stop behind her and take another sip of his coffee. "Who put that there?" She turned to face him.

"Todd. He waited until we left so he didn't get in our way."

"How did he know we'd left?"

"Dad told him."

"Are you sure it's going to be safe to have him around? Can we trust him?"

Seth nodded. "His father has worked for Dad for decades. Dad asked Todd if he wanted to work for us. He's not just a housekeeper. He's a bodyguard. But he's done all sorts of things because sometimes you need a cover when you're a bodyguard."

"What about Connor and Ashley? Weren't you going to tell them?"

"Yeah. Tomorrow. I've still got a lot I want to go over tonight and I know they'd have a million questions."

"Okay." Gina took a step into the room.

"Gina."

She turned to face him.

"Are you sure that's okay?" Seth gestured towards the bed.

Gina grinned. "Just don't tell my mum. She'd freak."

Seth laughed. He covered the couple of paces that were between them, one arm going around her, the other held away from them with his hot coffee. "That's a deal."

His lips met hers and Gina's eyes closed as she clung

to him. She stared up at him when he drew back a little. "Don't stay up all night. We have a meeting at ten."

"I won't." His lips brushed hers again before he slowly pulled away. He smiled fleetingly then turned and strode towards the study.

Gina listened to him go. She heard him sit in the office chair and scratch around in a drawer. His fingers tapped on the keyboard and after a few moments she heard a pencil scribble across paper. She smiled as she headed for the bathroom. It would be ages before Seth called it a night. It didn't take much for him to forget his surroundings and immerse himself in whatever he was studying.

* * *

Gina woke the moment the front door opened. She tensed as she heard footsteps travel through the house and into the kitchen. Crockery was moved around and water was run in the sink. She frowned. There was no way a burglar would break in at, she turned her head to look at the new alarm clock on the bedside table, six in the morning, to do their dishes. She eased away from Seth, who muttered in his sleep and reached for her. Gina pushed her pillow towards him and smiled as he snuggled up to it. Within seconds she stood in the kitchen doorway and watched as the man at the sink spun to face her.

He relaxed instantly and dried his hands on his worn jeans. His heartbeat dropped back to a normal pace as he stepped forward to greet her, his hand held out. From Ashley's room, she heard the sound of Connor stumble out of bed, sniffing the air. The man in front of her had dark brown hair that hung untidily around his face, tanned skin, blue eyes that seemed to have a permanent squint from being out in the sun and looked like he'd needed a shave a week ago. He appeared to be in his mid to late twenties and as if he belonged on the beach or a boat, not in a kitchen.

"I'm Todd." He shook Gina's hand.

"Gina. You're not what I'd have pictured a bodyguard to look like." She heard Connor's indrawn breath and moved out of the doorway so he could enter the kitchen too.

Todd shook Connor's hand. "I'm sorry I woke you. I'd hoped to get in and finish up before you were all out of bed."

"That's okay." Connor, wearing only boxers, turned to Gina and took her arm. "Excuse us for a minute." He strode to his room, closing the door the moment they were in there. "When were you going to tell me? Am I the last to know he's a bodyguard?"

Gina shook her head. "I only found out when I was heading to bed last night. And Ashley still doesn't know. Seth planned to tell the two of you this morning."

"You can't go keeping secrets from us. It's the four of us now."

"I know. And we weren't keeping it a secret. Seth planned to tell you this morning."

"And what if I'd said how great a housekeeper he is? Were you hoping to make me look like an idiot?"

"No. That's why I said what I did. I wanted you to know. I'm sorry. We didn't expect him to turn up so early."

Connor ran his hands through his hair and turned away. "I thought-" he broke off and turned back to her. "Just don't keep secrets. Okay?"

Gina reached out and rested her hand on his bare shoulder. "We're a team." She smiled up at him. "And I like being part of this team. It sucked at first. Being sick and all of that. But it certainly hasn't been boring."

"Even though you can't go home?"

"We're working on that. After last night, I believe we can do anything. We're going to track Raymond down, get the notes and deal with anyone else who's looking for us." Gina heard Seth whisper her name. She grinned. "Come on. Seth is awake. You can hassle him for all the details." She opened the bedroom door.

Connor put his arm across the doorway when she was about to leave. "Are you sure?"

Gina studied Connor's face, surprised at how uncertain he looked. Even when death had seemed a distinct possibility he'd never worn such an expression. "About what?"

"Are we a team?"

Gina gave Connor a quick hug. "Of course we are. Now come on. Seth keeps calling me and he sounds like he's starting to get worried."

Connor lifted his head and scented the air. "Breakfast. Smells good. I'll wake Ashley. We can have the full discussion after breakfast. I'm starved."

Gina grinned. "When are you not? I heard you get up twice last night for a snack. Maybe you need a fridge beside your bed."

"Sounds good." Connor dropped his arm so she could leave the bedroom.

Chapter Twenty-Seven

By the time Nicholas was coming up the driveway, Todd had long gone and the house was spotless again. Breakfast had been French toast, orange juice and fresh fruit. Morning tea had been an entire chocolate cake and half a litre of ice cream each. Todd warned them he'd be back in the afternoon to prepare dinner and apologised again for disturbing them. Gina and Connor didn't bother telling him it was only because he'd been a different sound and scent that either of them had woken. They left the contract lawyer at the dining room table with a coffee and a stack of paper he'd pulled from his briefcase and the four of them headed for the door.

Ashley opened the front door and grinned at Nicholas. "Is it too late to add something else to the contract? I really think I should choose your clothes.

Do you wear the same suit each day or do you buy them by the dozen?"

Nicholas ignored her question and stepped inside. He glanced around, his gaze pausing on the contract lawyer who returned the paperwork to his briefcase. He turned back to them. "Was he necessary?" He nodded in the direction of the lawyer.

Before anyone could answer, the lawyer strode across the room. "Nicholas." He held out his hand.

"Francis." The handshake was probably the shortest one in history. Nicholas handed the contract to Francis. "I guess this is the reason you're here." He turned to Seth. "Should we take our conversation elsewhere?"

Ashley glanced towards Francis who headed back to the dining table. "Surely you have nothing to say to us that can't be said in front of our lawyer." Her face held an innocent expression. The glint in her eyes was all that wrecked the image.

Gina heard the uneven breath Nicholas drew in and took pity on him. "We planned to sit in the kitchen." She gestured in the direction. "It's at the other end of the house." With a nod, Nicholas stepped forward, using his calming technique. Gina was tempted to tell him he'd probably need to permanently use that technique, especially around Ashley. She loved to stir.

Nicholas sat at the end of the table and Ashley perched on the table, crossing her legs. "So Nicky, what did you think of my little present? Did it make good bedtime reading? And you didn't forget our agreement, did you?" She looked down at the slate tiles in the kitchen. "Although these tiles look like they're going to be pretty uncomfortable." Nicholas started to rise out of his chair and Ashley reached out and put her hand on his shoulder to press him back into his chair. She grinned as she slid off the table. "Only kidding." She walked behind him and around to the other side of the table where she dropped into an empty seat beside Connor. Gina was across the table from her.

"Now that you've had your fun, what do you want?" Nicholas asked.

Seth put the kettle on. "Do you want a coffee, Nick?"

Nicholas turned to stare at him. There was a fleeting moment of confusion before it was masked with his usual neutral expression. "Coffee?"

Seth nodded. "How do you have it?"

"White with two sugars," Connor said.

Nicholas turned to Connor. "How do you know that?"

Gina also wanted to know the answer to that question, but guessed it had something to do with his sense of smell. "We know a lot of things, Nick. And yes, we do want something." She heard his breathing return to normal and his pulse slow. She almost felt sorry for him when her comment made him feel comfortable. "We want you to treat us decently. We're young adults, not little kids. Would it hurt you to treat us that way?" She heard his pulse pick up. She had made him uncomfortable again. "Or is that too naive of me?"

Nicholas took the coffee Seth gave him. "I don't understand any of you. One minute you're demanding a contract that'd make a lawyer rub his hands in delight, then you turn around and want to be best friends. What is really going on here?"

Seth sat beside Gina. "We had help with the list. You don't think we came up with all of that on our own, did you?" He grinned.

"What do you want?" Nicholas looked at each of them in turn.

Gina spoke first, just as they'd planned. "We want you to not try and sabotage any of our future efforts and in turn, we'll do the jobs you give us and let you get a pat on the back for the planning we do." She could have sworn his heartbeat stopped for a moment. She made a mental note to look online later to see if that was possible.

"Sabotage?" Nicholas appeared confused.

Gina smiled. If she hadn't known he'd tried to sabotage them last night she might have fallen for his act. "Don't try it."

"We really don't appreciate being lied to, Nicky," Ashley said. "You know it's not too late to do that grovelling."

"I believe it was begging, not grovelling," Nicholas corrected her.

Ashley shrugged. "A girl is entitled to change her mind." She grinned. "I like the sound of grovelling so much better."

"We understand why you tried to sabotage us, but from now on, you're on our side completely or," Connor's voice lowered. "I guess you're our enemy."

"If you sign that contract, you're one of the team. That means we can't be enemies." Nicholas gestured towards the dining room.

Ashley shook her head. "Not quite. Maybe it's been a while since you were in high school, but kids can be ruthless, devious and really good at stabbing people in the back. And our favourite technique is humiliation and leaving people open to major ridicule." Ashley paused before she used the information they'd learned that morning. "And I really don't think that will help you get from level two clearance to level one."

Seth continued the conversation. "We know you're a team leader. And the leader is only as good as the team under them. Those fifty people won't get you level one clearance as quickly as we can. Providing, we're all willing to play on the same team."

Gina frowned, finally realising what the odd sound was she'd been hearing since Nicholas had arrived. She pinpointed it and in the blink of an eye, she removed the slim digital recorder from his inner coat pocket and placed it on the table in front of him. She listened as his heartbeat went into overdrive and she shook her head. "I don't think he knows how to play nice. He's breaking the contract before it's even signed." She heard him swallow.

"Exactly. It isn't signed so it isn't in effect yet," Nicholas said.

"I don't know that we can work with him." Ashley turned to Nicholas. "You really disappoint me, Nicky. We could have had such a beautiful friendship." She sighed theatrically.

"So you'll what? Ask for someone else? I'm listed as your team leader in the contract."

Connor grinned. "Didn't you point out the contract isn't signed yet?"

Gina listened to him carefully. "If we can't trust you, we can't work with you."

Silence filled the room as Nicholas stared at Gina. His heart rate slowed. "How do you want to organise this? Do you want to interview other team members? See resumes?"

Gina shook her head when Connor was about to speak. Taking it as his answer, Nicholas started to speak, but Gina put a finger to her lips and continued to stare at him. His breathing was completely back to normal. She tried to figure out what it meant. It came to her. That weary sigh her dad sometimes made when he'd had a difficult day at work and finally got home only to find there was yet another problem to deal with.

"I think he's given up." Seth's words were a whisper for Gina only.

She nodded slowly. "You think we've been stringing you along, don't you?"

"Haven't you?" Nicholas asked.

"No." Seth glanced down at his phone when it beeped. "Contract is fine."

"What has this all been about?" Nicholas demanded.

Gina heard the feint hint of anger in his voice. "Some minor tormenting to satisfy Ashley. She likes to make sure she gets her revenge, even if it's only a fraction of what she thinks she's entitled to. But mostly we wanted to know how you planned to treat us if you were our team leader, Nicky."

"Then why do you keep calling me Nicky?"

Gina grinned. "Because you're too stuffy. It must be that rebellious teen thing coming out. I guess we could promise that we'd try and remember not to call you that in front of the rest of your team." She heard a hitch in his breathing.

"How long are you going to play with me?" Nicholas glanced around at them. "I've seen cats take less time to kill a mouse."

"Maybe you should have made up one of your lists for him, Lilly."

Seth grinned. "You could always have a go at spelling it out for him, Connie."

Connor reached for the digital recorder. "Point one." He glanced around the table. "What was point one again?"

"Respect," Ashley said.

Gina nodded. "We might tease a little, but we're willing to treat you as well as you treat us."

Connor grinned as he held the digital recorder

close to his mouth. "The first commandment. Do unto others-" he broke off as Ashley dissolved in a fit of laughter at his pompous tone of voice.

Nicholas waited for the laughter to subside. "Let me get this straight. You're still willing to have me as your team leader if I follow yet more of your rules."

"We're not asking you to jump through hoops." Seth's voice was quiet, his tone serious. "All we really want to know is if we can trust you. We don't expect you to be calm all the time. Even my dad tends to yell at me sometimes and I bet Ashley's mum wants to pull her hair out some days. Don't lie to us. Don't sabotage us and don't treat us like idiots. Do you have kids?"

Nicholas looked momentarily startled then shook his head. "I haven't had anything to do with kids since I was one myself. I usually make it a policy never to work with them."

"Well there's your problem," Connor said. "Don't think of us as kids. Think of us as young looking adults. Not to mention good looking, brilliant-"

"What mirror have you been looking in lately?" Ashley grinned at Connor.

"The wicked witch's. So I have it on the best authority that I'm the most handsome one of all," Connor said.

"Okay, so maybe some of us are a little immature at times, but that doesn't mean we're idiots," Seth said. "What's your answer?"

"Can we trust you?" Gina asked. Silence filled the kitchen and she listened to the sound of Nicholas' heartbeat. His breathing was even, his pulse normal. A frown formed and it looked like he was thinking about his answer. Finally he nodded. "I need more than a nod. And more than one word." She hoped everything she'd learned about polygraphs would help her read Nicholas.

"You can trust me." He relaxed enough to smile slightly. "And if you help me get level one clearance I'll even consider naming my firstborn after you."

"Are you planning on having kids?" Seth asked.

Nicholas' smile became a fleeting grin and he suddenly looked very young. "No."

Connor sighed dramatically. "That's a relief. Who knows what name the poor little bugger might have ended up being called. Connor Senior is taken, which makes me Connor Junior. What's left for him? Connor Junior, Junior?"

"Nope, we'd just call him Connor the turd." Ashley grinned. "I mean the third. Really, it was an honest slip."

Seth held out his hand to Nicholas. "I guess it's time to go sign that contract, Nick."

"Do you really have to keep shortening my name?"

Connor rose to his feet. "You think you've got problems." He gestured towards Seth. "He calls me Connie."

Seth grinned as he rose from the table. "What are friends for?"

"To help keep your ego under control." Ashley draped an arm around Seth's shoulders. "And you do such a wonderful job of it."

Seth's phone rang and he glanced at the display. He slipped Ashley's arm off his shoulders. "I'll meet you in the dining room. I've got to take this call."

Ashley linked her arm through Nicholas'. "Come on, Nicky." She looked him up and down. "So who does choose your wardrobe?"

Gina laughed as she and Connor followed and she heard the slight sigh Nicholas made. "Don't let her dress you. We looked like we were heading to a heavy metal concert one of the times she got her hands on us."

"Who's on the phone," Connor whispered.

"Anthony."

"What does he want?"

Gina shrugged. "We'll find out soon enough."

As they approached, the lawyer returned his own paperwork to his briefcase and went over the main points of the contract with them. Seth joined them as they were signing. One copy was given to Francis, they kept a copy and the other they handed to Nicholas.

Once the lawyer left, Nicholas said, "I'll collect my digital recorder and head back to the office. When do you think you'll be ready for your first job?"

"Second job. And no you can't have the digital recorder. It needs to be wiped," Seth said.

"I have notes on it I need."

"We'll email them to you. Leave your details," Seth said.

"Trust works both ways," Nicholas said.

"If we return it to you, what will you do with it?" Gina asked. She listened to him carefully.

"Remove my notes then wipe the device until there isn't even a shadow left on it that some IT expert could resurrect."

Gina stared at him, her eyes unfocused as she concentrated on tone and heart rate. She slowly nodded her head and Ashley collected the device before Nicholas even noticed she'd left. Gina took the digital recorder from Ashley and held it out to Nicholas. She continued to hold onto it even when he grasped it. "Don't let us regret trusting you. You are not to listen to it again. You will do exactly as you said."

"I'll deal with it the minute I return to the office." Nicholas pocketed the digital recorder when Gina let it go.

"Give us a week," Seth said.

Nicholas turned to him. "For?"

"Our second job. We'll need some help dealing with schools and parents." Seth grinned. "It will involve some lying so you should enjoy that."

"So I'm not allowed to lie to you, only for you?" Nicholas asked.

Ashley grinned. "Sounds good to me."

Nicholas pulled out a business card and handed it over. "My direct lines and email. Call me when you need me to lie for you."

Ashley linked her arm through Nicholas'. "That's the spirit, Nicky." She walked with him to the front door. "And thanks for the date last night. Next time how about you tell me where we're going. I felt a little overdressed."

"Is that your way of asking me to keep you in the loop?" Nicholas paused, his hand on the front door handle.

"And they say you can't teach an old dog new tricks," Ashley said.

"Just don't expect me to jump through hoops of fire. I have to draw the line somewhere."

Ashley laughed as Nicholas pulled away from her and stepped outside. She rested her hand against the doorframe as her friends came to stand around her. "You know, we might make something of him yet."

Gina watched Nicholas get in the car, the same woman driving. "That's probably what he's thinking."

Connor waited until the door was closed to speak. "What was the call about?"

"Can we wait a bit first? I want to listen in on Nick." Gina grinned with a shrug. "I probably have trust issues, but I like to find out first hand if we're right to trust him." She held up her hand as Seth nodded and started to speak.

"Did you get anything worth recording?" the woman driving Nicholas asked.

"They confiscated it from me so I couldn't use it," Nicholas said.

"Don't tell me they've got x-ray vision."

"No. They did a search."

"Maybe next time you should get something

smaller. Hide it in a hollow shoe heel or something like that."

"They signed the contract, Erika."

The woman sighed. "I guess we better not do anything to risk breaking it. Did you ask them how they managed to get the information?"

"No."

"You were in there a while."

"Francis was there."

Erika laughed. "I bet you loved that. Did he make you sweat as he went through every word?"

"You know what he's like."

"Yeah. Francis never changes." Silence filled the car.

Gina relayed the conversation, keeping part of her concentration on Nicholas, and asked about the phone call.

Seth grinned. "Dad has a location and confirmation from satellite imaging that Raymond is at their secondary lab."

"When do we go after him?" Connor asked.

"Four tomorrow morning is when the least amount of staff are on the premises. We need to be out of there before six." Seth looked around the group. "What do you think?"

"I'm in." Ashley grinned.

"Me too," Connor said.

Gina hesitated a moment before nodding. "Yeah. Let's get this done so I can eventually go home."

Chapter Twenty-Eight

The next morning they sat in the four-wheel-drive as they waited for the right time. Seth finished sending an email to Nicholas, giving him details of schools and parents that needed to be spoken to and what each should be told. He glanced up and did a scan of the area.

"See anything," Connor asked.

Seth shook his head as his gaze returned to his laptop.

Connor shifted in the driver's seat. "It's all right for you, Lilly. You've got something to do. The rest of us are sitting here bored."

"You wanna make out." Ashley grinned at Connor.

Seth glanced up. "Please. Spare us."

Ashley laughed. "I was just wondering if you were paying attention."

"Cruel and heartless to get my hopes up like that." Connor tried to look mortally wounded.

Ashley planted a kiss on his cheek. "I'll make it up to you later."

"I may survive." Connor's tone remained mournful.

Gina couldn't help smiling as she watched them. She looked over at Seth who momentarily rested his hand on hers before he returned to tapping on the keyboard. He glanced up when her gaze remained on him and smiled before he turned back to the laptop. She closed her eyes and did a sound scan of the area. Nothing seemed any different to when they'd arrived twenty minutes ago. She searched further afield to where she'd tracked Nicholas earlier. It was too far away and she could no longer find him. She wondered if he was still asleep, all alone in his apartment. No one else had been with him. Not even a pet. Gina wondered if he ever got lonely. Her home was regularly cluttered with family, but she liked it that way.

"Gina."

Seth speaking her name dragged her attention back. "What?"

"You ready?"

"Yeah."

"Who were you listening to?"

"No one. I was checking to see if Nick is still asleep, but he's too far from here."

"Does he snore?" Connor asked.

Gina laughed. "No."

Connor took an apple from the centre console. "If we're here much longer, I'm going to run out of food." He took a bite.

Seth's phone beeped and he checked the message. "Time to move. Gina, anything out of the ordinary?" He did a visual scan as he asked.

Gina shook her head. "Not that I'd really be able to tell. I hate the soundproofing these guys use."

"Better not mention it to Nicky. He might do his apartment and then you won't be able to eavesdrop on him." Ashley opened the door. "Let's pay Raymond a little visit. I wonder if he's missed us."

They all piled out of the four-wheel-drive and ran towards the fence as they pulled on small backpacks containing emergency gear. Gina gave a nod when the power was momentarily cut and they climbed over the fence in the space of a heartbeat. They ran through the grounds, avoiding security cameras Seth had spotted, and stopped at a door at the back of one of the buildings. A four storey building that their surveillance equipment had showed Raymond entering earlier. Gina breathed easier the moment the sounds of the building washed over her.

Connor paused, breathing deep as his head slowly turned. "I can smell Raymond. Let's get him." He pointed to a door to their right.

Seth led the way, opening the door to find it was a stairwell. At each landing, Connor pointed upwards and they ran up the stairs, their feet making hardly any sound. Connor nodded when they reached the top landing. Seth opened the door a crack and peered inside. He opened it wider and they entered a long corridor. Halfway down the corridor, Connor indicated right. Several doors down, he stopped and pointed, holding up two fingers. He pointed to himself then the door.

Ashley pointed to herself and then at the room and made the hand sign for R. When Seth nodded, she grinned and flung the door open. Nearly flying across the room, she pinned Raymond against the wall. Connor was on her heel, doing the same to the other man in the room. Ashley still grinned. "Miss me, Raymond?"

"How did you find me?" Raymond demanded.

Ashley laughed. "Don't play games. I followed the directions you left me."

"You're in on this with them?" the other man demanded as he struggled to escape Connor's grip.

Seth ignored the drama and went to the computer station. His fingers flew over the keyboard as he searched the data. He plugged in an external hard drive and turned to the laptop that sat near the desktop. Gina hovered just inside the door, wondering what she should do. Everything seemed under control.

"Of course I'm not with them, Milo. They're playing games," Raymond said.

Gina could hear the fear in his voice and his heartbeat was out of control. She heard another noise. A door opened at the end of the corridor. She glanced out to see what it was and swore at the rain of bullets that came her way. She ducked back inside as men ran down the corridor towards them.

"Lockdown," Milo screamed before Connor covered his mouth with his hand.

Connor snarled. "Bite me again and I'll break your bloody neck." He shook Milo whose head hit the wall hard.

Gina ran across the room to the computer station. It was made of solid metal and hopefully bullet proof. The other three dropped down beside her, their captives with them. Gunfire burst into the room and

Gina held her breath. The computer station protected them.

"Now what?" Ashley asked.

"I want to know who he is." Seth pointed to Milo. He wore a dark grey suit, his black hair showed strands of grey, he had a trimmed moustache and brown eyes that were dagger sharp.

Taking a guess, after the fear she'd heard in Raymond, Gina said, "His boss."

Milo growled and would have lunged at Raymond if Connor hadn't still held him. "Traitor. I'm going to kill your family before your eyes."

"I'm not. I don't know how they got their information." Raymond struggled against Ashley who shook him until he stopped.

She narrowed her eyes as she looked at Milo. "Isn't there a movie about Milo? A dog or something?"

"Milo was the cat. Otis was the dog," Connor said. At Ashley's expression, he demanded. "What? I was a little kid once."

"Great. But that still doesn't tell us what we're going to do." Gina's eyes widened as she looked towards Connor. "Behind you." She pointed to the gunman who moved across the floor.

Connor let go of Milo to grab a chair and throw it at the gunman. Milo threw himself at Raymond, shoving something down his throat. Raymond gagged on it and struggled to get away. Gina and Connor both tried to capture Milo, getting in each other's way. Milo called out to his people as he rounded the corner of the computer station. When Connor tried to follow him he had to dive for cover from the burst of gunfire.

"What did he give you," Seth demanded.

Raymond shoved his finger down his throat, gagging. He gasped, his hand clutching his stomach. "One of my own devices." He laughed, no humour in the tone. He looked around at the four of them, a calculated look in his eyes. "I've got ten minutes to live. Then my insides are going to be splattered all over my lab. Warn my wife to run and I'll give you want you want."

"Can't you ring her?" Ashley asked.

Raymond shook his head. "No outgoing lines and there's something to prevent mobile phones being used on the property." He laughed again. The same humourless laugh. "Another one of my devices. Ironic, isn't it?" A sudden indrawn breath left him speechless and he clutched at his stomach.

"Can't you take something to make you throw it up?" Gina asked.

"No. It buries into the body. See. I thought of

everything. Now make up your mind. We're running out of time," Raymond said.

"We'll warn her," Seth said.

Raymond stared at him a moment then nodded. He turned to point at the benches along the wall behind him. "Drawer third from that end. Bring it here."

Gina listened carefully. There were still men nearby. She started to mention them when Connor interrupted.

"I'll take care of the men." He grinned. "Be back in a minute." Before any of them could argue, he dashed from behind the computer station and a burst of gunfire filled the air.

Gina listened to them follow him, some of the men hitting the wall with a great deal of force. She winced at the sound. "Room's clear." She stood up and looked around to confirm what her ears had heard.

Ashley ran to the door and peered out. She jumped back at the gunfire. "Corridor isn't. Is Connor okay? I can't see him."

Gina nodded. "He's on the ground floor. Some of them followed him." She turned to see Raymond rummage in the drawer. He pulled out a slim box and opened it to reveal buttons.

Chapter Twenty-Nine

Delight lit Raymond's face as he keyed in a sequence. His finger jabbed the final button with a smile. He grabbed the bench in front of him as an explosion rocked the building.

"What did you do?" Seth grabbed Raymond by the front of his lab coat, his face centimetres away from the man who still smiled.

"Took care of one of your problems. Milo's helicopter exploded. And from how far away the sound of the explosion was, I'd say he was in it."

Gina searched for Milo's heartbeat. She couldn't find it. "He's dead."

Seth swore and let Raymond go. "We didn't want you to kill him."

"There are two other scientists in the ground floor lab. All the notes are in this building and my wife has the rest of the details. Give her a secure address to send them to. Tell her to send the flare. That's the key phrase." Raymond pulled his phone out and handed it over. "Contact details, passwords. Everything you'll need to access the data she sends is in here."

"Milo's dead. He can't kill your family now," Gina said.

Raymond shook his head. "His death will trigger an assassin."

Connor burst into the room, gunfire coming from the corridor behind him. "There's people dead in a sealed room downstairs. And whatever it is, it's leaking into the corridor. One of the guards died in seconds. And it gave me a nosebleed. It's stopped now."

Seth glanced at his watch. "Raymond has four minutes ten seconds."

"They must have initiated lockdown," Raymond said. "You need to get out. Use the far exit. It'll take you to the roof. Jump." He tapped his stomach. "This isn't going to be a little explosion."

"Jump! We'll break our necks," Ashley exclaimed.

"Possibly, but that's not as bad as exploding into little pieces." Raymond pointed to his phone. "Ring my wife the moment you get off the premises."

Seth grabbed the external hard drive and laptop. He slid them into a padded bag before he put them inside his backpack. "We won't be able to do that if we're dead."

"I said you'd probably break your necks. I didn't say you'd die. Don't let them bury you unless they're one hundred percent positive cell regeneration has stopped," Raymond said.

Gina's mouth dropped open. "We can come back from the dead?"

"Maybe." Raymond shrugged. "Theoretically, but it needs to be tested. I would have loved to have done those tests." His eyes lit up.

"How would you test that theory?" Seth asked.

"Kill you," Raymond said.

"Ahh, great." Gina took a step backwards. He'd said the words as simply as if he'd said blood tests were needed. She much preferred Seth and Anthony's methods even though they involved needles.

Seth glanced at his watch. "We've got to go."

Raymond nodded. "Warn my wife. Tell her," he clutched at his stomach and breathed shallow. "Tell her to look after our son."

Seth nodded and then turned to Gina. "Is it clear?"

She shook her head. "There's five of them."

"Tackle them." Connor ran to the door. "I bet I get the most."

"You wanna bet?" Ashley ran through the door as he opened it. A burst of gunfire greeted her.

Seth turned to Gina. "Time to go. Now."

She heard the urgency in his voice and didn't hesitate. She ran into the corridor, past the unconscious guards. When she would have stopped to grab one, Seth's hand wrapped around her wrist and dragged her with him. They entered the open door and took the steps two at a time, bursting into the morning sunlight. Ashley and Connor stood at the edge of the building, tying off four ropes they'd taken from their backpacks.

Ashley grinned at them. "They won't get us to the ground, but hopefully we won't break our necks when we drop the rest of the way." She grabbed the end of one of the ropes and stepped off the edge of the building with a yell. Connor followed, echoing her yell of exhilaration.

Seth made sure his backpack was secure before he took hold of one of the ropes. "Meet you on the ground." With a quick smile, he jumped.

Gina felt her stomach plummet with him. She didn't have time to think. She grabbed the last rope and stepped over the edge. She closed her eyes as she screamed. Air left her lungs as she collided with the building. The impact caused her to lose her grip on the rope and she dropped rapidly. The ground met her with a solid impact and she struggled to breathe. When someone started to drag her across the ground, her eyes flew open and she saw Seth limping beside her. She tried to get to her feet.

An explosion filled the air, causing the ground to tremble beneath her. Seth threw himself on top of her, knocking the breath from her, after she'd finally managed to take one. Debris rained down around them, dust filling the air. Alarms shrilled and she heard the sounds of people calling in panic followed by others shouting orders. She listened for her companions, relieved when she heard each of their heartbeats. She struggled to sit up, pushing Seth off her.

"Seth?" Panic bloomed in her when he remained still. "Seth." She shook him and was relieved when he groaned.

"Gina? You okay?" Ashley staggered over to her, covered in dust and dirt, blood forming along several cuts.

Connor joined them. He looked as bad as Ashley. "We have to get out of here before they get organised."

Seth groaned again and his eyes opened. He glanced around and relief filled his expression when he saw all of them. He took the hand Connor offered him and staggered to his feet. "Let's get out of here." As they ran for the fence, he pulled out Raymond's phone. As soon as they were on the other side, he dialled Raymond's wife.

Gina couldn't resist a glance at the building that was now a jagged pile of rubble, having caused a lot of damage to the other buildings around it. Hopefully that was all the experiment data destroyed.

Connor grimaced as they climbed into the four-wheel-drive. "Do you think Todd does car detailing too?" He grabbed an apple from the centre console and took a bite.

"Hello," Seth said when his call was answered, putting it on speakerphone. They all fell silent.

"Who is this? What are you doing with Raymond's phone?"

"He wants you to run. It's not safe. Milo killed him and Raymond said to tell you to send the flare."

There was an indrawn breath and when she spoke, her voice was unsteady. "Where do I send it to?"

Seth gave his father's postal address. "His last words were, 'look after our son.' I'm sorry to have to tell you this."

"He was on borrowed time. The moment he fell in with Milo."

"He took Milo out before he died."

Raymond's wife laughed bitterly. "That sounds like him. Thank you for calling. I'll send the flare the moment I can. You'll have it within the week." She disconnected.

The lengthy silence was broken by Ashley. "Now what do we do?"

"Use your spa?" Connor glanced towards her.

"No way. You can wash that filth off you first." Ashley grinned. "You know, apart from the building exploding around us, that was fun. I want to learn how to do that thing where they bounce down buildings with a rope."

"Abseil?" Seth asked absently as he checked the information on Raymond's phone.

Ashley turned in the seat to look at Gina and Seth. "Yeah. What do you say? Sound like fun?"

"No." Gina shook her head. Her stomach still felt like she'd left it behind on top of the building. And since the building had exploded that didn't say much for what kind of state her stomach must be in.

"Aw come on, Gina. What about a little building?" Ashley asked.

Seth looked up from the phone. "You know a bit more training probably wouldn't hurt. We might be less likely to break our necks."

Ashley shuddered. "I seriously don't want to find out if we can come back from the dead. That's just creepy. It makes me think of zombie movies."

"I thought you liked horror," Gina said.

"Not if it's real and I'm the star." Ashley opened up the centre console and, after she took a look in it, glared at Connor. "You ate all the apples."

Connor grinned. "Probably karma from your earlier cruelty."

Ashley hit him. "I'll give you karma."

"Can you at least wait until he's not behind the wheel?" Seth asked. "I'd rather not test the zombie theory."

"I can't believe he would have killed us to see if we'd come back from the dead," Ashley said.

"I can't believe we left all those guards there to die." Gina's words were a whisper.

Seth reached out and took her hand. "Dad's organised debriefing for us. After lunch."

"What for?" Ashley asked.

Seth glanced over at her. "Standard operating procedure."

"Who will debrief us?" Ashley asked.

"A psychologist," Seth said.

Connor laughed. "A shrink. That'll impress my parents."

Seth smiled. "Afterwards, we can all go home."

"Home?" Gina stared at him. "Today?"

Seth nodded. "Today."

Gina grinned and threw her arms around him, stopped from getting as close as she would have liked by the seat belt. "Today." She laughed. "I can't wait. Do they know? Has someone told them?"

Seth laughed softly. "Not yet. Don't you want to do it yourself?" He pulled away to hand her his phone.

"But what about the people watching our parents?" She stared down at the phone, unable to take it.

"I sent a message to Dad. There were teams on standby waiting to pick them up the moment I gave the all clear. Initial questioning gives Raymond as their boss. They're shocked to hear he's dead." Seth continued to hold the phone out.

Gina took it and stared down at it. Her hand tightened on the phone and she heard the case protest. She loosened her grip. Her gaze met Seth's. "I can go home. This arve." When he nodded, she grinned and dialled her home phone number. "Mama!" Tears ran down her cheeks as she heard her mum speak.

Chapter Thirty

Gina rolled over in her bed. The same bed she'd slept in for years. She was surrounded by familiar smells and sounds, yet everything felt alien. Sitting up, she swung her feet to the floor. No. Everything didn't feel alien. It was her that was alien. She crossed the room, not needing a light to find her way. Silently she made her way through the house to the kitchen. She took leftover apple pie from the fridge and stepped out the back door onto the deck. She perched on the rail as she ate. Behind her she heard her grandfather come outside.

"Did you feel like an alien when you went back home after being here for so many years, Nonno?"

He stopped beside her, his arm going around her shoulders. "No one can go backwards. Only forwards."

"What if I wasn't ready to go forward?"

He dropped a kiss on her forehead. "You go anyway. But we will walk with you, bambina. We're family. We stick together." He wrapped his other arm around her and Gina rested her head on his shoulder.

"I missed you, Nonno." Gina tightened her arms around him. "Tell me about when you first came here?"

He chuckled. "You humour an old man I think. No one wants to hear those stories."

She smiled. He always protested. She slid off the rail. "Come on, Nonno. Let's get comfortable." She drew him to the bench seat at the back of the deck and leaned against the wall. As her grandfather started to speak, she closed her eyes, listening to the familiar sound of his voice. She didn't realise she'd drifted off to sleep until he patted her gently on her shoulder.

"I'm too old to carry you to bed, bambina. And these bones are too old to sit out in the night air till dawn."

Gina sat up and smiled. "You're not old. Your heartbeat is strong and your breathing is good."

"What an odd thing to say."

"I can hear them." She grinned. "So you better watch what secrets you spill around here."

"Your Nonna will take the wooden spoon to you if you go listening to things you shouldn't."

Gina laughed. It was an old threat. One she'd never seen carried out. She dropped a kiss on his weathered cheek. "Love you, Nonno."

"Love you too, Gina." He patted her on the shoulder. "You remember what we've taught you. You come to your family when you need help. We stick together."

"I know." She rose to her feet and after a long look at him in the shadowy night, returned to her room. She was so tired that being an alien in a familiar world couldn't keep her awake and she slept until she heard her name spoken.

"No, it's too soon. She can't go back to school today. We just got her back, Tommaso." Gina smiled as she listened to her mum's voice. It took her only seconds to realise she was in the kitchen.

"Tommy is right, Ari," Nonna said.

"No." Ariana's voice was filled with anger, but under it was fear.

Gina rose from bed. She readied herself for school in seconds, wanting to prevent a full-scale war between her mum and Nonna. She slid the mobile phone, Nicholas had sent her yesterday, into her pocket. "What's for breakfast?" Five startled faces stared at Gina, who stood in the kitchen doorway. Her parents, her grandparents and her sister Renata.

"You're in your uniform." Ariana's voice held a hint of tears.

Gina shrugged. "I've got to go back there some time. No point putting it off. I'll already have enough work to catch up on." She stepped forward and held out her mum's necklace. "Thanks for letting me borrow this."

Ariana shook her head and pushed Gina's hand back towards her chest. "You keep it. You need it, bambina."

"No. It's odd to see you without it. I want you to wear it, Mum." When Ariana continued to shake her head, Gina said, "I need you to wear it. There's already been enough changes."

Ariana reluctantly took the necklace. Tommaso came to stand beside her. He took the necklace and smiled at his wife. "Let me put it on you, Ari."

Gina's phone beeped and she pulled it out to read the message. It was from Connor. *Do you want a lift to school?*

"Where did you get that from?" Ariana asked. "Mobile phones are expensive to run."

Gina hated to lie to her parents but she could see her mum was barely coping. "It's so I can get in touch with my shrink if I need to. Didn't Nicholas tell you?"

"He's not our kind of people. Don't trust him," Ariana said.

Nonno rose to his feet. "Leave the girl be, Ari. She knows what she's doing." He met Gina's gaze. "She's moving forward."

Gina nodded. "I'm going to get a lift with Connor."

"We don't know him. I don't want you getting into a car with a stranger," Ariana said.

"You'll like him," Gina said. "We all took care of each other. Just like family does." Silence filled the room

Tommaso was the one to break it. "Tell him to come to dinner one night."

"I will cook," Nonna said.

"It's my kitchen," Ariana argued.

Gina smiled and shared a look with her dad. She mouthed the words thank you and grinned when he winked at her. She helped herself to cereal and sent Connor a text while she ate. Ariana and Nonna were still arguing when she kissed each of them on the cheek and headed outside before Connor could turn off the engine. Gina examined Connor as she closed the door of the four-wheel-drive.

"Are you sure you don't want a pic? You do have a mobile phone you can use now."

Gina grinned. "How was your night at your parent's place?"

Connor rolled his eyes. "World war three. They've forbidden me to move out of home. Nick has arranged for some guys to help me move out my personal stuff after school today. It should be interesting." He grinned. "You want to come and see the fireworks? Although they'll probably be pretty mellow since they'll be in the public eye."

"I'll be right." She took out her phone again when it beeped. She smiled when she saw it was a message from Seth. *Have fun your first day back at school. Make sure Connor brought lunch. The tuckshop won't have enough food for everyone if Connor buys.*

Connor pulled up at school and turned the engine off. "What's the plan?"

She ignored all the whispered conversations as people started to realise who had arrived. "Plan for what?"

"Well, for here." Connor gestured towards their school. "You know. Will it be like before?"

Gina felt completely confused. "Connor, pretend I'm super simple and spell it out real clear for me. What plan and what about before?" She could hear the stress in his voice and his vital signs showed clear signs of discomfort. She nearly grinned at that thought. Obviously Seth was rubbing off on her.

Connor sighed. "Do you want me to stay clear of you at school?"

"What for?"

"We don't really hang with the same crowd."

Gina finally realised what Connor was asking and reached out to rest her hand on his arm. "If you talk to me at school I'm not going to ignore you. But I also won't let your mates hassle mine. We'll figure it out somehow, but whatever the answer turns out to be, we're friends. I don't turn my back on my friends. Even if it means facing a pack of wolves."

Connor smiled. "So if I ditched the pack of wolves and sat with you at lunch you wouldn't ignore me?"

"I know what this is about now. You can smell the food Nonna made for my lunch. Don't go thinking you're getting any of it." Gina waved a finger at him. She listened as his vitals signs started to return to normal.

Connor laughed. "You found me out." He glanced out the window. "Where do you sit for lunch?"

Gina described the area where she sat. "Mary sits with me. I can't promise she'll be nice, but I'll ask her to try. And if you need me today, you might want to say my full name. I'm guessing I'm going to be hearing both our first names spoken a lot today." She frowned. "Nicholas?"

Connor said at the same time. "What's Nick doing here?"

Gina laughed. "Come on, super freak. Let's go find out what he wants."

It didn't take them long to track him down in an empty classroom. It was one of the lower level art rooms. The room smelled heavily of chalk, paint and dust. Connor's breathing became shallow and Gina sympathised. If the smells were overpowering for her, they must be a lot worse for Connor. Nicholas sat on the teacher's stool looking completely out of place.

Gina wrinkled her nose. "Next time can we meet somewhere less smelly?"

Nicholas rose to his feet. "I've arranged for you to leave your classroom if you find it necessary. The principal has also been informed that there will be regular counselling sessions that sometimes will occur during school hours and you have permission to have your mobile phones turned on in case you need to ring your psychologist and talk to him." Nicholas came to a stop in front of them. "Next time you decide to blow something up, give me a warning so I can have a suitable story for the media."

"Those explosions weren't our fault," Connor said.

Gina grinned. "Yeah, it was Milo and Otis."

Nicholas stared at them a moment. "Why do those names sound familiar?"

Connor laughed, stopping mid sound when Nicholas turned to look at him.

"Anything you wish to share with me?"

"Thanks, Nick. Do we also have permission to leave school grounds? Like at lunchtime?" Connor grinned. "There's an all-you-can-eat place just up the road."

"No. You only have permission to leave for appointments with your psychologist."

Connor groaned. "How long have we got to keep seeing him? I thought it was only for debriefing."

"It's your cover for when I need you to do a job that occurs during school hours," Nicholas said.

"Oh."

Gina could hear Connor's embarrassment. "That excuse will be pretty tough for Connor."

Nicholas turned to Gina. "Why?"

"Because when you have to see a shrink you shouldn't look excited. Connor and Ashley are adrenaline junkies," Gina said.

"He'll have to take acting lessons from Ashley." Nicholas strode to the door, his phone in his hand. He paused at the door and turned to face them. "Milo and Otis. I am not amused." He tucked the phone in his pocket, spun on his heels and strode down the corridor.

Chapter Thirty-One

"What's got him all bent out of shape?" Connor demanded as soon as Nicholas was out of hearing.

Gina shrugged, held up her hand in a gesture of wait and listened as Nicholas left the school grounds. It was several minutes before Nicholas spoke. "Back to the office."

"The boss did have some concerns about your suitability for this task. You know nothing about children," Erika said.

"They're not children. They're young adults," Nicholas said. "I am perfectly capable of being their team leader."

"And that's why you knew all about what they'd planned and was scrambling to put out media fires since yesterday," Erika said. "Face it, Nicholas. Those young adults," she stressed the word, "are going to run rings around you. And if you're not careful, you'll be demoted or even lose your job."

"I will not lose my job."

"You better start looking around for a hobby. When they take away your job, or should I say entire world, you're going to want something left in it." Silence met Erika's words and Gina's hands clenched into fists. No wonder Nicholas had been worried about getting them to join his team.

"Bitch," Connor said when Gina relayed the conversation. "Great, now I feel sorry for him."

Gina pulled out her phone. "I'll fix this."

"What are you doing?"

She typed in a message and showed Connor before she sent it. *Sorry. We'll keep you in the loop in future. It was unexpected. Next time we'll tell you.* When Connor nodded, she sent the message and listened as Nicholas' phone vibrated.

"I guess I do know what I'm doing," Nicholas said.

"You don't have kids. I do. That means they're sorry they were caught out."

"We'll see," Nicholas said.

Connor shook his head when Gina told him what had been said. "We're going to have to watch that bitch."

"Yeah." The bell rang and Gina waited for it to stop. "See you for morning tea?"

Connor nodded then smiled. "Are you sure you're not going to share that food with me?"

"They've barely packed enough for me." Gina managed to keep a smile from forming when she saw the disappointment on Connor's face. "But they did tell me to invite you to dinner. How about tomorrow night?"

"Sounds good." Connor walked beside her to the door and stopped to let her pass. Eventually they reached a hallway where they needed to go in different directions. "Later." Connor started to move away.

Gina took a snap lock bag of homemade Anzac biscuits from her backpack. "Hey, Connor." When he spun to face her, she threw them towards him and grinned when he caught the packet. He laughed when he saw what was in his hand and turned away, already opening the bag. She heard his whisper come back to her through the crowd.

"I don't know who cooks better. Todd or your family."

"Gina!"

She spun to see Mary further along the hallway, waving wildly. Making her way slowly towards her friend, she hoped Mary wasn't going to interrogate her. There were far too many secrets she needed to keep. Why on earth had she thought it would be a good idea to go to school today? She pasted on a smile as she reached Mary's side. "We haven't even checked to see if we have any classes together." It was something they did at the start of every school year.

Mary waved the comment aside. "Forget about that. What were you doing talking to Connor? I know you were stuck together because you were kidnapped, but in case you didn't realise, you're free now. And he's an arsehole."

"He's sitting with us for morning tea and lunch today." Gina thought it would be a good idea to get the drama over immediately.

"You've got to be kidding. And those bastards he hangs out with? Them too?"

Gina shook her head and stopped at the door of her classroom when they reached it. "No. Just Connor. Do you think you can give him a chance? Please?"

Mary pointed a warning finger at her. "If he says one thing wrong I swear I'll deck him. And I don't care what they said about giving you two special care after what you've been through."

"They what?" Gina stared at Mary.

"They had a special assembly and gave us this big

spiel about how we should act around you. I really hope you weren't expecting me to follow through with it. The specialist who gave the speech put me to sleep. And I don't mean metaphorically either. I just about fell off my chair." Mary glanced behind Gina. "Oops. Just got an evil stare from your teacher. I'll see you later." Mary waved over her shoulder as she hurried away.

Gina turned to face her classroom and wanted to sink through the floor when she realised they all waited for her. What made it even worse was she could hear the whispered conversations. She forced herself to enter the classroom. Yesterday she'd jumped off an exploding building. Getting through a day of school should be a breeze. By morning tea, Gina was beginning to wonder. She sat on a bench seat under a jacaranda tree, the purple flowers having died off and fallen away months ago. Connor sat beside her and Mary strode towards them.

"Next time I complain about jumping off an exploding building, tell me to think about the first day of school," Gina muttered.

"I googled it during maths earlier. There's forty one weeks in the school year when you take out holidays," Connor said.

Mary dropped onto the bench beside Gina and

looked past her to Connor. "Did you take into account year twelve finishes earlier than all the other grades?"

Gina sighed as Connor shook his head, his mouth full. "It doesn't matter. It's still far too many days to be stuck at school." She held a biscuit out to Mary. "Want one?"

Mary grinned. "This is the only reason I come to school. Your mum and grandma's cooking. Do you know how lucky you are?"

Gina nodded and handed Connor another biscuit. She was going to have to ask for more food. Especially if Connor continued to hang around her.

Mary leaned forward again to talk to Connor. "I've always wanted to know. Do you take steroids?"

Connor nearly choked on his biscuit. He glared at Gina. "You better–"

Gina interrupted. "It's a question. Not an insult. Mary speaks as she thinks. Or maybe that should be she speaks before she thinks."

Connor stared at her a moment longer before he glanced at Mary. "No." His tone was terse.

"Damn. Lucky I didn't make that bet with Simone." Mary turned to Gina. "But his dad is a doctor, so you have to admit it was always a possibility."

"I'm sitting right here," Connor growled.

"Of course I know that. Didn't I just ask you a question?" Mary shook her head, her dreads moving in time with the motion.

Gina hid her smile with a bite of cake when she heard Connor mutter too low for anyone else to hear. "Shoot me now and put me out of my misery." The bell rang and Gina groaned. She hadn't had time to eat all her food. She glared at Connor as he snatched half her slice of cake. This time his words were at normal volume. "Morning tea's over. Just trying to help you get to class on time."

Mary looked between each of them. "Comfort eating isn't a good idea. You'll both end up obese."

Gina shared a look with Connor before she turned back to Mary. "I'm sure we'll slow down once the novelty of regular meals is over."

Mary linked arms with her and Gina gave Connor a wave as they wandered off. If Mary hadn't been guiding her, Gina would have stopped. Towards the car park, she picked up the sound of Seth's heartbeat. She pulled away from Mary. "I remembered something I have to do. I'll see you at lunch." She hurried away before Mary could speak, barely controlling the urge to race through the school grounds. She stopped when she saw Seth leaning against his sedan. He straightened when he saw her and grinned.

All caution evaporated and she was in his arms seconds later, her lips meeting his. Minutes passed before he pulled back enough to look down at her. She stared at him. "Is everything okay?"

Seth nodded. "I missed you."

Gina grinned. "Me too." She made a mental note to see if Seth and Ashley could also join them for dinner tomorrow night. "I couldn't sleep last night."

Seth's hand ran across her cheek and rested against her neck. "You should have rung me."

"Nonno sat up with me." Gina rested her head against Seth's chest. She listened to his familiar heartbeat. "I don't belong there anymore."

"You need time to get used to being back home."

Gina tilted her head back. "I felt like an alien. I was so focused on getting home I didn't stop to think about what it would mean. They're my family and I love them. But it's not my home anymore."

Seth's hand ran slowly across her back. "Do you want to come back to our house?"

Gina smiled. "What about you?"

"Yeah. I'm staying there tonight. I'll probably still go home to Dad's place sometimes, but," he shrugged. "Things have changed. Probably not as much as it has for you, but they've changed. Will I see you this afternoon?"

Gina shrugged. "Mum has got a bit protective. You might have to visit me."

"I can do that."

Gina laughed. "You say that now, but wait until you've survived the interrogation. If you survive it." She frowned. "I've got to go. My teacher is asking if anyone has seen me."

"Don't run so fast this time." Seth kissed her lightly. "I'll be at your place around four."

Gina returned his smile before she ran to her classroom, keeping to a normal running pace. Almost normal. The teacher made no comment as she slipped into her seat and she ignored the whispers that filled the air around her. To take her mind off the whispers, she checked on Connor. He rapidly tapped a pencil on his desk and shifted regularly in his seat. He sighed a couple of times, but otherwise was quiet. Gina searched further afield, trying to find Nicholas. He was just in range.

Chapter Thirty-Two

Gina was surprised to find Nicholas at home. She heard the tap of keys as he worked at his computer and finding his lack of conversation boring, she checked to see which of his neighbours were home.

"I'm not. You're wrong, Nancy," a woman said.

"What's your definition of a stalker?"

"Some creepy guy with a pair of binoculars."

"Try again, Audrey." There was a flicker of paper. "Exhibit A. Do you recognise this? It's called a dictionary."

"I'm not stalking him," Audrey said. "I don't even own a pair of binoculars."

"You leave for work when you hear him leave his apartment. You've taken a split shift so you can be home during the day when he comes home for an hour or two. You leave again when he does even if it's not time for you to start work. That's stalking," Nancy said.

"No it's not. It's called working up the nerve to ask him out," Audrey said.

Nancy snorted. "He's probably gay. You've never seen him bring a chick home, he's always dressed perfectly and you don't even know his name."

"I do."

"Since when?" Nancy demanded.

"A few days ago. It's Nicholas."

Gina was so startled to hear that name, she knocked her book off the desk. She picked it up and, with an apology, returned to the conversation. It took her nearly a minute to locate them again. Surely Audrey wasn't talking about their Nicholas.

"Don't you dare. I'll never ask him if you're in the elevator too," Audrey said.

"At least I'll make a good excuse as to why you chickened out again," Nancy said.

"Please, Nancy."

"Oh all right. But you've either got to get up the nerve to ask him or quit stalking."

"Today. Well, as long as there's no one else in the elevator," Audrey said and Gina heard footsteps and a door open. A few seconds later, Audrey's voice changed to an uncertain whisper. "Hello."

"Hello," Nicholas said. There was silence to Gina's annoyance. The silence was followed by the sound of the elevator as the doors whooshed open. "Ground floor?"

"Yes. Thank you." Again Audrey's voice was hesitant.

Gina wished she could tell Audrey to hurry up and ask. It wouldn't be long before they reached the ground floor. She thought of her phone with Nicholas' number stored in it. She rose to her feet. "Excuse me." Gathering her gear, she headed for the door. She rang Nicholas as she walked towards a secluded spot, relieved he was still in the elevator. It sounded like they were the only two people in it. "Hi, Nick."

"Is something wrong?"

"Is she pretty?"

"Who?"

"The woman in the elevator with you."

Nicholas sighed. "Is this going to be another one of those conversations where you'll eventually tell me the point of it and it'll be nothing like it started out to be?"

Gina laughed. "No. If you like her, you should ask her out to dinner."

"Are you embarking on a new career, Gina?"

"She really likes you."

"Where are you?"

"I'm sorry about the explosions. I thought I'd try and do something nice to make up for all the trouble we gave you." Not to mention the trouble they'd caused him over the contract. She hadn't known his job was at risk. Silence met her words. "Are you still there, Nick?"

"Yes."

"Is she absolutely hideous?"

"I wouldn't say that."

"What would you say?"

"Nothing right now. Can we have this conversation later?"

Gina heard the elevator doors open and they both stepped out. She wondered what Audrey was doing to find a reason to stay nearby. She decided to ask. "What's Audrey doing?"

"Who?"

"The lady who wants you to ask her out."

"I'm going now, Gina."

"Don't hang up. I'll just ring back." Nicholas started to use his calming technique and Gina grinned.

"What will it take for you to go back to class and leave me to return to work in peace?"

"Ask Audrey on a date."

"Are you serious?"

"If you met her in a bar, would you talk to her?"

"I don't go to bars, Gina. Now enough of this and go back to class."

"Ask Audrey on a date. She's waiting. Otherwise she wouldn't still be hanging around."

"How do you know this? Should I be looking for something? Maybe I should have put my own clause in the contract. What happened to trust?"

"I was worried about you. You won't lose your job over the explosion, will you?"

"I can take care of myself. Now go back to class." The annoyance left his voice to be replaced by weariness.

"Ask her. Please."

"When I'm told no you will drop the subject."

Gina grinned. "Sure, Nick. But if she says yes, you've got to tell me how your date went."

"I've got a feeling you won't need my help with that detail. Are you going to tell me why I'm right?"

That depended on where he took Audrey to dinner. There were limits to her ability. "Ask her before she runs out of reasons to stick around." She disconnected so Nicholas couldn't argue anymore and closed her eyes so she could focus on listening.

She heard Nicholas go through his calming routine twice before he moved closer to Audrey.

"Do you need any help? Have you lost something?"

Audrey dropped something heavy that made various noises. Gina guessed it was probably her handbag. "Oh. Ahh. No. That is, I was just checking. I should clean my bag out. It's-" Audrey drew in a shaky breath and laughed nervously. "Sorry. That's…" her voice trailed off.

"Here." There was the sound of items moving against each other and Gina wondered if Nicholas had picked up the handbag.

"Thank you. I… I guess I shouldn't hold you up. I mean… work. You probably have to get back to work," Audrey said.

"Yes. Actually, before I go, I was wondering if you wanted to go out to dinner this weekend."

"Really?"

Gina wanted to tell Audrey to breathe, that she needed oxygen or she was likely to pass out.

"I know it's short notice-"

"Yes. I mean no. That is. It's not short notice and I would love to go to dinner."

There was a scratch of pen against paper then of paper being torn from a spiral notebook. "Ring me to arrange a time." There was a moment of silence.

"I'll wait to hear from you, Audrey." Nicholas headed outside and Gina was torn between who to listen to. She tried to focus on both, but she was already monitoring the area around her. Three places were too much and Nicholas was starting to move out of her range. She stayed with Audrey.

"Oh my, oh my." Something fell. "Damn." Silence. Gina was about to leave when Audrey spoke again. "Nancy. He knows my name." Another moment of silence. "We're going to dinner this weekend. I've got his number. I have to ring him to sort out a time. Okay. I'll wait here for you." Audrey squealed slightly. And Gina wondered if the sound she was making was her dancing. She grinned and was distracted by her phone ringing.

"Hey, Nick."

"She said yes."

"Congratulations."

"Where the hell am I meant to take her?"

"Ashley would know."

"Do you really think I'm going to ask a kid about dating?"

Gina frowned as she heard Connor move closer to her. She wanted to ring him and ask if he was okay, but she was already on the phone.

"Are you still there, Gina?"

"Yeah. Ask Ashley where to go, just don't let her choose your clothes. And don't wear your work clothes."

"I cannot believe I'm having this conversation. What else can I wear? I only own suits."

Gina thought of Erika's comment that his job was his life. A wave of sadness washed through her. "Actually, I think you could wear a clown suit and Audrey would still be happy to go out with you." Gina nearly dropped the phone when she heard Nicholas laugh.

"Now that I do have access to."

"You're not going to wear it, are you?"

"I'm not an idiot, Gina."

Gina glanced up as Connor stopped in front of her, a question in his eyes. She patted the bench seat beside her and he sat down. "I know."

"This conversation has made me think there's a job you can help me with. We're having trouble bugging a place."

"We can't make recordings of our findings. It would be a verbal report. Or a written one."

"That will be fine. What information do you need about the location?"

"The address. Maybe some names."

"I'll text the information."

"Okay."

"And Gina?"

"Yeah?"

"Quit spying on me."

She laughed as he hung up then turned to Connor who'd draped his arm around her shoulders.

Chapter Thirty-Three

Gina checked Connor over carefully. He seemed fine. "Are you okay?"

"I was going to ask you that. Why aren't you in class?"

"I was busy interfering in Nick's life." She filled Connor in and he grinned.

"I'm having a little trouble picturing him in a clown suit. Do you really think he owns one?"

"He didn't say he owned it, just that he had access to it." She glanced down when her phone beeped and turned it so Connor could see the address and names listed. "You know, this is going to be harder than I expected."

"What?"

"Going to school and all the other stuff."

"What did Lilly want? Other than to make you smell like him?"

Gina laughed. "I'm surprised you didn't say mark his territory."

Connor sniffed. "He pretty much did. So what did he want?"

"Same as you. Checking up on me." The bell for the next class rang and Gina sighed. "You know I barely remember one thing from a single class today. There's hardly any point in being here."

"We'll get the hang of it. Only one year to get through."

Gina stared at him. "We?"

"You think you're the only one?"

Gina slid her arm around Connor's waist and leaned her head on his shoulder. "Only one more class till lunch. Surely we can last that long." Connor's answer was a shrug as he pulled away from Gina and stood up.

Taking the hand he held out, she rose to her feet and walked beside him to her classroom, a fleeting smile in thanks when they reached the door. He nodded in understanding before he headed to his next class.

Gina ignored the whispers and sat down. This time she tried to concentrate. As Connor had said, it was their last year of school. Less than forty weeks. She sighed. It felt like a life sentence. Maybe she should have waited for Monday. No, she probably would have found another excuse to postpone returning. Her mind wandered. She listened in at the staff room and the school office. Finding nothing of interest she went further, listening through random streets and homes. When the bell rang, she bolted from her seat, her still closed books clutched in her hands.

She was the first one at the bench seat under the jacaranda tree. Connor arrived not long after her. Both of them began to eat, no conversation starting until Mary arrived with a shocked, "You can't eat all that. You'll make yourselves sick."

Gina swallowed her mouthful, glad some of their food had been eaten before Mary arrived. "Who?"

"Both of you. What's going on, Gina? Please tell me you haven't ended up with bulimia or something like that."

"You should have seen us when we first got out of hospital. We're slowing down. We'll be back to normal before you know it," Connor said when Gina didn't answer straight away. "Apparently it's a normal response."

Gina could only nod.

Mary sat down. "I hope you get over it pretty quick. The thought of that amount of food is enough to make me feel sick. Especially since I can still remember overeating on Christmas Day. Remind me to put a note on my calendar not to overeat this year. It's so far away I'll have forgotten all about it by then."

Gina looked up to see why Connor swore, his words so soft Mary didn't hear them as she continued to talk about her Christmas. Gina felt like echoing Connor when she saw his old pack. She glanced at Connor when she realised Will, David, Marcus and Neil walked straight towards them. She examined Neil and saw he looked a lot better than the last time she'd seen him, bleeding on the footpath.

Mary broke off in mid sentence, her gaze drawn to the boys that had almost reached them. "I thought you said they weren't joining us for lunch."

"They weren't invited," Connor muttered.

"What are you doing sitting with the freak?" Neil stared at Connor, with a single glance towards Mary.

"Did you faint when the guy pulled a gun on you?" Marcus grinned. "People are talking, Connor."

"People are clueless," Connor said.

"So are you if you're going to keep sitting here." Neil gestured towards Gina and Mary. "With them. Come on, man. Let's go. You've had your joke."

Gina watched Connor as she kept an eye on his old pack in her peripheral vision. She didn't trust them. When Connor turned to look at her, she gave him a reassuring smile. She wished she could tell him it was his choice, but didn't want to say anything in front of the idiots who stood around waiting for Connor's answer. Connor rose to his feet and she heard his pulse increase slightly. Not enough for it to be fear. She guessed that maybe it was anticipation.

"I'm comfortable here," Connor said.

"Don't do anything stupid." There was a definite warning in Neil's tone.

Connor smiled slightly. "I'm doing the exact opposite."

"If you're not with us…" Neil's voice trailed off and his fists clenched.

Connor shrugged. "I guess I'm against you." He stepped to the side as Neil swung at him. He grabbed Neil's arm and twisted it up behind him so he couldn't move. "Don't ever try that again." His mouth was beside Neil's ear, his voice low.

Marcus and Will stared, their mouths open. David took a step back. No one else spoke for nearly a minute. It was Mary who broke the silence.

She rose to her feet and stepped around Connor and Neil, her gaze sweeping between all the boys. "What about them? Do they take steroids?"

Gina laughed. "What's with your obsession over steroids?"

"I read this article that said it's getting worse in high school kids. Yet I haven't found a single person who takes them. Maybe I'm asking the wrong people," Mary said.

"You can't want to spend time with these freaks." Neil howled in pain when Connor pulled his arm further up his back.

"Time to let him go, Connor. We really don't want to end up at the office on our first day back." Gina could hear a teacher headed their way and wondered who'd squealed.

"This isn't over." Neil glared at Connor when he let him go. "I won't forget this."

Gina stood beside Connor. "I'd suggest you do forget."

Connor draped an arm around Gina's shoulders. "Although it'd be much more fun if he didn't." He grinned. "You can take him and I'll take the rest of them."

"Teacher alert," Mary said from behind them.

"Watch your backs." Neil spun on his heels and strode off, his pack with him. The teacher stopped and watched as the crowd broke up.

Connor looked at the time on his phone. He swore. "Look how much of my eating time they wasted. How am I meant to finish my food now?"

Gina grinned. "By shutting up and eating." The rest of lunch passed in silence. At least between the three of them. Gina heard the rumours. People talked about them in the same tone of voice used to discuss a rabid dog. She closed her lunchbox and wondered what the next school day would be like. Surely it couldn't be as bad as today. When the bell rang for the next class, she rose to her feet, Connor beside her.

"Connor." Mary waited until he turned to face her. "You're all right." She rose to her feet. "But I'd get a different haircut. You're too perfect looking. It makes people wonder if you're real."

"Ahh… thanks?"

Mary laughed at Connor's uncertainty. "You're welcome." She strode off, a cheerful wave over her shoulder. "See you Monday."

"Is she always like that?" Connor walked beside Gina as they headed for their next class, which they had together.

Gina laughed. "Isn't she great? You could never get bored with her."

"That's one way of putting it."

Gina hit Connor on the arm with the back of her hand. "That better have been a compliment."

Connor grinned. "If you want it to be."

Gina couldn't resist returning his grin and they

walked in silence to their class. They sat beside each other and the class was made a little less boring by passing notes. By the time Gina got through her final class, she was ready to scream.

When she climbed into Connor's four-wheel-drive she buckled up and closed her eyes. "Tell me the term has nearly ended."

"We'll get the hang of it." Connor sounded like he was trying to convince himself too.

"Do you want to come in and meet my family?" She opened her eyes and grinned at him. "They'll have afternoon tea ready."

"Why does that sound like a bribe? The kind you offer to someone when you want them to take really bad medicine."

Gina laughed. "Maybe because it is. Mum is going to interrogate you. But I thought it'd be better to get it out of the way now. Before you come to dinner."

"Can you call for reinforcements?"

"Seth will be there at four. I'll tell him to bring Ashley."

"Okay. But I have to leave at a quarter to five. I need to go and upset my parents. I wonder if Ashley would like to help me."

Gina sent a text to Seth and he soon replied that Ashley would join them. The moment Connor pulled up Gina hopped out of the vehicle and headed inside, Connor hesitantly followed. As soon as introductions were made, they were ushered onto the deck.

Gina's parents and grandparents joined them at the table on the deck for afternoon tea and her mum fussed over her while she interrogated Connor. When Seth and Ashley arrived, the gentle interrogation continued until Ariana went inside to start dinner when Nonna offered to cook. Nonna followed her, offering unwanted advice. Tommaso and Nonno retreated, leaving them alone. Gina told them about their visit from Nicholas and learned he'd spoken to them too. She made a mention of Erika's attitude.

"Bitch," Ashley growled. "The only person allowed to torture Nicky is us."

"We don't own him," Seth said.

Ashley gave him a look that plainly said he didn't know what he was talking about. "Yep. We do."

Gina continued her story and mentioned introducing Nicholas to Audrey and the job he had for them.

Ashley pointed at Seth. "See, he is ours. We even got him a girlfriend."

"She's a stalker," Seth said. "What will you do when she takes over his life and locks him away?"

"Kick her arse," Ashley said.

"She's nice," Gina said. "Voices and vitals don't lie. I can even pick up the lack of sincerity in actors. It kinda spoils TV for me now."

The conversation moved onto the surveillance job and Gina talked her mum into letting her go out for an hour with Seth while Ashley went with Connor. It didn't take her long to locate the people she needed to listen to and she started jotting notes in the spiral notebook Seth gave her. When they returned to her parents' house she'd covered several pages with her messy scrawl. They sat out the front in Seth's car while he flicked through the pages.

Gina watched him. "This job mightn't be as boring as I thought it'd be."

"Stalker."

She laughed. "It doesn't count if it's work related."

Seth reached out and unbuckled her seat belt so he could draw her close. He stared down at her, his lips a breath away. "I missed you today."

Gina slid her hand across his chest and over his shoulder to twine her fingers through his hair. "I don't know how long it'll take to convince Mum, but I'm moving in with the three of you. I was never in a hurry to leave home. Now I want to move out this minute." She wasn't quite sure how she felt about that yet. Other than confused.

Seth ran his finger across her bottom lip. "Good." His lips replaced his finger, his hands splayed across her back as he held her tight.

Gina returned his kiss, heat rushing through her as seconds turned into minutes. She reluctantly pulled away from him when she heard her dad walking towards the front door. She smiled up at Seth. "My dad will be out here in a second. I don't think this is the way to convince them to let me move."

Seth laughed softly. "I'll see you tomorrow."

Gina nodded and opened the car door. Still seated with one foot on the edge of the gutter, she turned back towards him. "We're going to spend the entire weekend together soon. No work. No school. Just you and me."

"It's a date."

Gina heard her dad open the front door and she slid out of the car, smiling. She turned and waved as Seth drove away. She listened to the sound of his heartbeat, his breath still not quite even. Her smile became a grin when she heard Seth ask, "Are you listening, Gina?"

Taking out her phone, she sent him a message. *Yes.*

Chapter Thirty-Four

It took four days to convince her family. Nothing she said made a difference. It wasn't until Nicholas had a talk to them that they agreed it might be best. They'd sent her from the room, Ariana warning her not to listen in. She hadn't been able to resist. Not with how noisy and argumentative they'd been. What had they expected?

So she'd sat in her room and given up on trying not to listen as Nicholas told her family she needed to learn how to look after herself. That there were others who'd try and use her for their own purposes. Ariana had been the hardest to convince. Finally agreeing, but saying she needed another week with Gina. When they called Gina in, she'd managed to get that week back to a day, with Nicholas' help.

Wednesday night the house was crowded by family who'd been called in for an impromptu dinner party. Gina guessed her mum was trying to point out what she'd miss. She knew she'd miss her family, but things were different now. She wasn't the same person she'd been before Douglas had burst into her life.

Thursday after school Connor drove her home. To their home. It felt odd. She stayed in the vehicle when he parked, letting the sensation sink in.

"Are you okay?" Connor had his door half open.

She thought about his words a moment before she answered. "Yeah, I think I am. It just feels weird. I didn't expect to leave home until after I'd finished uni. Well, if I could ever figure out what to do at uni."

Connor laughed, a grin remaining. "I couldn't think about anything other than moving out of home and how quickly I could manage it."

She smiled slightly. "Life is so odd." Her smile became a grin when she heard Seth say her name.

"Gina? Where are you? Didn't I hear Connie's car before? I wouldn't take much longer to get inside if I was you. Ashley might eat all your afternoon tea."

"Seth is looking for me. He said Ashley's working on eating our afternoon tea." She opened her door. "At least now I don't have to worry about sending my parents bankrupt with how much I eat."

"Ashley better not eat it all." Connor strode inside.

Gina followed more slowly. She heard Seth coming towards her before she reached the door. She waited in the doorway for him, wrapping her arms around him when he reached her.

"Are you okay?"

"I will be." Once she got used to moving out of home.

"Come on then." Seth pulled away, linking his fingers through hers. "We better get inside before Ashley eats everything."

"And Connor."

During afternoon tea, Ashley and Connor argued about having a party at the house. Connor thought that they should at least have a housewarming party and Ashley didn't want any of his mates there, even ones he said didn't go to his school and were no where near as bad as the wolf pack.

After she'd eaten, Gina escaped to the study to do her homework. The rest of the afternoon dragged and she kept wondering why she was even bothering with school. It looked like they had a job. At least for the next two years.

Giving up partway through her homework, she went to find Seth. She'd finish it later. She smiled when she heard Connor grumbling in his own room about homework and talking about asking Nicholas if he could get them out of doing it.

"What are you smiling about?" Seth asked.

She shook her head.

"Who are you listening in on?"

Laughter bubbled up. He was beginning to know her so well.

She didn't get back to her homework until well after dinner. Seth was using the study too so she found herself more often checking what he was doing and listening to what was happening in the neighbourhood than working. Hopefully Connor was right and she'd get used to school again, but it was probably going to take a while.

By the time she headed to bed she'd only done half of her homework. That would have to do. It seemed like she'd no sooner fallen asleep, snuggled up to Seth, than his phone rang.

Peering at the time on the alarm clock, she wondered who was ringing at one a.m.

Seth groaned, reaching for his phone. "Hello?"

"I'm on the way to your place. Wake the others. You've got a job," Nick said.

Gina wanted to roll back over and go to sleep. She had school today. Couldn't he have waited until the weekend?

"What sort of job?" Seth reached out and turned on the bedside light.

"I'll be there in about ten. I'll explain everything then." Nick disconnected.

Seth threw back the bed covers. "You wake Connie and Ashley. I'll organise a snack."

"What if we don't agree to do the job? Not because it's morally wrong, but because we want to sleep?"

Seth shrugged. "I guess we have no choice. Maybe we'll have to add something like that in our next contract."

Gina slowly forced herself out of bed. "You better make coffee to go with that snack. Otherwise I might fall asleep on the job."

They were still eating when Nicholas arrived, handing a set of black clothes to each of them.

"What are these for?" Ashley set the clothes on the table beside her.

"We don't want your identity discovered. You'll be working with other people tonight." Nicholas placed a manila folder on the table.

Seth reached for it, flicking through the loose pages. "What people?"

Nicholas reached out and stopped Seth from going to the next page. "This man, Carl," he tapped the picture, "escaped tonight. His wife's testimony put him away. They have three children under the age of five. The police have moved them somewhere safe, but they have a right to live their lives, not hide in fear."

"What did he do?" Ashley asked.

"He was one of a team of hitmen. We believe they're the ones responsible for helping him escape when he was being moved to a more secure location." Nicholas withdrew his hand.

"We have hitmen in our country?" Connor took the mugshot and stared at the photo for a moment.

Nicholas nodded. "There's a chopper waiting to take you close to where we lost him. He's trying to head west and lose himself in the outback. They escaped by car and we tracked them to the edge of dense bushland where his accomplices had stashed motorbikes. By the time we brought in our own motorbikes we'd lost them. We found the motorbikes where the bushland thinned, but that doesn't mean they're on foot. They could have had other transport."

Accomplices. That didn't sound good. Gina thought of the small army they'd recently faced. "How many accomplices?"

"Five."

"What do you want us to do?" Seth held up a

picture of a woman and three young children. "You didn't need to put this in."

"I wanted to make sure you knew who you were protecting," Nicholas said.

Seth shook his head. "No, he's a hitman. We're protecting far more than four people." He rose from the table, letting the page fall back onto the table top. "Give us a few minutes to get ready." He took his pile of clothes and, with a glance around the table, headed towards the bedroom.

After staring at the family photo for a moment, Gina followed him, taking her own pile of clothes. She waited until she'd shut the bedroom door before she spoke. "How do we know everything Nicholas said was true?"

"I saw it on the news about a year and a half ago. It was on every station. I'm surprised you didn't see it."

Gina shook out the clothes, laying them on the bed. "We don't watch much TV at our place." She eyed the garments. "It looks like he's trying to turn us into ninjas."

Seth laughed, pulling his shirt over his head. "I think he wants something much better than ninjas."

She started to comment when she heard Connor ask Nicholas if he had something worn by Carl. She guessed he must have answered with a nod or shake of his head since she didn't hear his reply. "Connor's ready." She heard Ashley walk towards Connor and Nicholas. "And Ashley."

"Better hurry up before they're hassling us."

She smiled as she started to change her clothes. "Too late. Ashley is already telling me to hurry up."

As soon as they were both dressed they joined Nicholas who ushered them out to his vehicle. He took a plastic bag that contained prison clothes from the car boot and gave it to Connor.

Gina got in the vehicle and listened to Connor breathe in deep as soon as he was seated beside her, the plastic bag on his lap. The trip to the chopper was made in silence and when they pulled up, Nicholas told them to put on their balaclavas. Once in the chopper, Gina reached for Seth's hand. He squeezed her hand lightly and she met his gaze, seeing the edge of his eyes crinkle. She guessed he was smiling at her.

"Are you okay?" His words were little more than a breath of air.

She nodded, slipping on the headset Nicholas handed her.

When they rose into the air, Ashley said, "Now this is cool."

"No wonder school is so boring." Connor peered out the window.

"This isn't a game," Nicholas said. "These men will kill."

Ashley reached out and patted his knee. "Are you worried about us, Nicky? Don't be."

Nicholas brushed her hand away. "I don't know why I bother," he muttered.

Gina grinned as she listened to him. They were definitely rubbing off on him. She couldn't hear him doing his calming exercises. In fact, she didn't hear him do them once during the entire trip. Not even when Seth asked him more questions about Carl and the area they were going to and Ashley kept interrupting to point out something that had caught her attention.

When the chopper landed, they piled out, Nicholas joining them. "Be careful."

"We'll be back before you have time to miss us, Nicky."

Nicholas slowly shook his head at Ashley's words, not bothering to comment.

"Which direction, Connie?"

Connor slid the lower half of his balaclava down far enough to expose his nose and slowly turned, shrugging his shoulders. "There's too many people. And dogs."

Gina listened. "Yeah, he's right." She turned to

Nicholas. "Can't you send them all home?" There was a constant noise of people and animals. How were they meant to find someone hiding in all that racket?

"No. We need this man found. Now. And his accomplices. They're not about to pull everyone in and leave only a handful to find him."

"If you really wanted us to find him, you'd get it sorted." Connor glanced towards Nicholas before he returned to breathing in deeply as he slowly turned around.

"I'll see what I can do." He held out four earpieces. "You're on a separate channel." When they took them from him, he removed another from his pocket and slipped it on. "Only I can hear you."

Gina met Seth's gaze before he looked at each of them. She could almost hear his warning to watch what she said. She slipped the earpiece on. It was awkward with the balaclava.

Chapter Thirty-Five

"Can you all hear me?" Ashley asked the moment her earpiece was in place.

Connor rolled his eyes. "I'm standing right next to you, Ash. What do you think?"

Ashley gave him a look. "You know exactly what I mean."

"We can hear you." Seth looked around. "Any ideas on directions?"

Connor shrugged and Gina mimicked his action. In every direction she listened she heard movements, heartbeats and conversations.

"Okay, let's split into teams," Seth said. "Gina and I will head north west, you two can head south west."

"What if he's trying to make us think he's headed west and is actually heading east?" Ashley asked.

"Then we'll try that direction next." Seth turned

to Nicholas. "Try and clear out the area for us." He strode north west before Nicholas could reply.

Gina followed him. "What if Ashley's right?" Above her she could hear a couple of choppers. They certainly weren't trying to make it easy for them.

"Of course I'm right," Ashley said.

For a moment she'd forgotten the others could hear them. "Well?"

"Let's move it. Time's wasting." Seth sped up, running through the shadowy bushland.

She kept behind him, stepping where he did since he had better eyesight. All around her she could hear people searching. Not a single heartbeat remained in one place. An hour later, Seth had them change directions.

"This is so boring. And I'm getting hungry," Ashley said.

"I can smell a snake not far from us. I hear they're good eating," Connor said.

"I'm not trying it. How about you have it and tell me what it's like," Ashley said.

"You were the-" Connor stopped abruptly.

"Watch what you're doing. Give me a warning next time you want to stop suddenly," Ashley said.

Gina was tempted to say the same to Seth when he also stopped.

"What's wrong?" Seth asked.

"We might be heading in the right direction," Connor said.

"Might or are?" Seth asked.

"I don't know. This place has been trampled by a million people."

Gina listened for Connor's voice and the direction he was in. "Should we join you."

There was a moment of silence before Connor answered. "Yeah."

"Give me your location," Nicholas said.

"Not bloody likely," Connor muttered.

"Do I have to remind you how important this is?" Nicholas demanded.

Gina pointed out the direction to Seth as she thought of the photo Nicholas had put in the file. And about all the people Carl would have murdered to earn the title of hitman. "No. Which is why we're not telling you the direction." She ran behind Seth, the trees and scrub rushing past her.

When they reached Connor and Ashley, Seth removed his earpiece and fiddled with it for a moment. He stepped away from them and returned it to his ear. "Testing."

Connor grinned, his teeth unnaturally white in the

near darkness. "Looks like we're going silent for a bit, Nick."

"Don't you dare turn those earpieces off," Nicholas said.

"We'll talk to you later, Nicky." Ashley handed her earpiece to Seth.

When Connor did the same, Gina handed hers over, ignoring Nicholas' warnings and demands to know if any of them were still there. "Now what?"

"Now we can talk without anyone listening. But I do think we need our own set of these." Seth patted the pocket he'd slipped the earpieces into. "Ones that no one else can listen in to." His phone started to ring and he checked it before turning it off. "You have to give Nick points for persistence. The rest of you might want to turn your phones off."

Once all the phones were off, Gina listened to what was in the area. "I actually think Ashley is right."

"About?" Ashley asked.

"I can hear six heartbeats, in groups of two, headed east. Everyone else is working their way west."

"How far apart are each of the three groups?" Seth asked.

Gina shrugged. "I'm not sure. Maybe fifty metres. I'm not very good at distances."

"That's something we can work on." Seth turned to Connor. "Can you smell him?"

Connor shook his head. "I thought I could for a moment, but I lost it again."

"Water. I can hear water. Do you think he's trying to throw the dogs off the scent?" Gina asked.

"Might be what's throwing me off the scent." Connor raised his head and breathed in deeply again. "It smells a lot better in the bush. You can't imagine how many smells a city has. Most of them not very nice."

"Are we going after them?" Ashley asked. "I'm getting bored standing around."

Seth nodded slowly. "We'll take them out one group at a time. Which is the group furthest away from the others?"

Gina frowned as she tried to figure it out. She pointed south east. "That way."

"Come on then." Seth led the way, running through the scrub with Gina behind him, the other two following her.

"It's much easier following Lilly. Why couldn't we all have had each ability?" Connor muttered.

"I'd like to know that too. We should do some testing," Seth said over his shoulder.

Gina shuddered. "Not if it involves needles."

Seth chuckled softly.

She heard the heartbeats closer. "We're nearly there. It sounds like they've veered away from the water."

Seth slowed to a walk. "How close?"

"Really close." Connor sniffed the air. "Their sweat stinks of fear."

"We need to keep them quiet. Take them out before they can alert their friends," Seth said.

"There's only two of them and four of us. Who misses out?" Ashley asked.

"Better not be me," Connor said.

"I'm the only one who can see in the dark. Sort it out. Who's following me?" Seth asked.

"Me," Connor and Ashley said at the same time.

"There's more than just these two. You can all have a turn eventually," Seth said.

"I'm going first," Ashley said.

"Why should you get to go first?" Connor demanded.

"Quiet." Gina listened carefully. "One of them asked if his companion heard something. We can't stand around here all night arguing."

"It's way past midnight so it's not night. It's morning. And I'm going first," Ashley said.

Connor sighed heavily. "Fine, but I'm second."

"You two wait here. Only come if I call you. Once we capture them, Ashley and I will take them to the closest people searching. Which direction is that, Gina?"

She listened, searching the area, pointing in the direction as soon as she found it. "About four, maybe five kilometres that way."

"Thanks." Seth reached for her, pulling the lower half of both their balaclavas down enough to kiss her.

When he started to pull away, Gina held him close a moment longer. "Be careful."

"You too." He pulled his balaclava back into place.

She fixed her own as she listened to them race off.

"What's happening?"

"Shh. How can I hear if you keep talking?" She went back to listening. A word was cut off by a scuffle, rapidly followed by another one. When Seth said they were subdued, she turned to Connor. "They've captured them. Both the men are alive."

"How do we know we've got the right people? We don't even know what Carl's mates look like."

Gina shrugged. "I wouldn't have a clue, but you did catch his scent in this direction and no one else is searching over here." She listened as Seth and Ashley ran towards the searchers, their footsteps sounding heavier. "They're taking the men to the searchers."

"I hate standing around waiting. We should have taken on the next two. We don't need Lilly to hold our hands."

Gina opened her mouth to reply, then stopped. She frowned, trying to figure out what the noise was. It didn't make sense. "Come on."

"You agree?" Connor's tone was filled with surprise.

She struggled to figure out what he meant. "About what?"

"Taking the next two out ourselves." Connor walked beside her.

It was harder trying to figure out where to step without Seth to follow. "No. I can hear something." She reached the sound and looked down at the handheld radio that was emitting a tapping sound.

"I think it could be Morse Code."

"Do you know it?"

Connor shook his head.

Gina picked up the radio. "Maybe Seth or Ashley does." She listened for them. They'd just reached the searchers. "Come on."

Connor ran beside her. "Lilly better not bitch about us not following orders."

Gina swore, coming to a stop. "They're moving.

As soon as they stopped trying to communicate they started running."

"We might lose them."

Gina looked in the direction Seth and Ashley were in before turning her back on it. "We can't let them get away. Come on."

"They won't be able to find us," Connor said.

Gina headed to where Seth had left them. "We'll leave them a message." When they reached the spot, she cleared some leaf litter from the ground to write a message, leaving the radio beside it. 'They're on the move. Using Morse Code. Don't know what they said. Turning my phone on.' Next to the message, she drew an arrow. She turned her phone on, putting it on silent and ignoring the missed calls messages.

"Don't get me wrong, I want to go after them, but there are four of them and two of us. Are you sure you're up to this?"

The family photo came to mind and she could have almost hated Nicholas for adding it to the file. "I'll have to be."

Connor nodded once before breathing in deeply. "I can smell him. He's surrounded by the scent of others, but I can smell him now."

"I can hear them. One of them said shoot first."

"Okay. Let's go."

Chapter Thirty-Six

As they ran towards Carl and his friends, Gina heard
Seth and Ashley start running towards them. They
didn't have time to wait. One of the men said they
were getting close to the vehicle that was waiting for
them. She searched the direction they were headed,
finding another person.

"What's happening?"

She told Connor, keeping her voice low.

"Okay. We don't let them get to the car. We each
take a different one down."

"Nearly there."

"I know. I can smell them."

"They heard us." There was no time to warn him.
Hearing an object whistle towards them, she pushed
Connor to the ground, landing sprawled in the dirt
and clumps of long grass.

Connor pushed himself off the ground, remaining

crouched. "We'll split up. I'll come in from the right. Stay low. Don't get shot."

"Okay." As if she wanted to get shot. She came up into a crouch, heading to the left.

Well behind her she heard Seth swear, warning her they'd talk later and that he was turning his phone on. Hopefully the talk was going to be about getting their own earpieces, but she doubted it.

Again the men fired, the bullets missing her by a metre. The guns made very little noise and if it hadn't been for her ability she wouldn't have heard them. Her phone vibrated and she kept moving as she answered it. "Keep heading in the direction you're moving in. I think you're about a kilometre away."

"We are definitely going to work on distance," Seth said.

"Be careful. They're firing at us. And I guess they're using silencers or at least that's what they're called in the movies."

"You be careful too."

She started to tell him she would, when one of the men ran in her direction. "Got to go." She disconnected the phone, returning it to her pocket before she leapt forward. Tackling the man to the ground, she grabbed his hand when he tried to shove a gun in her face. It went off before she could force him to drop it. About to render him unconscious, she let him go and spun away when she heard another body come towards her.

She was on her feet and attacking the second man before he had a chance to recover from her move. Her phone vibrated and she ignored it. There was no time to answer. She heard Seth quietly call her name.

There wasn't any reason to be quiet. Carl and his mates obviously knew they were here. "Seth! Over here." She ducked the man's fist, sidestepping and coming up behind him. Hitting him in the back of the head, she winced as he crumpled to the ground, hoping she hadn't caused permanent damage. The second man came for her, a gun aimed at her.

"I've got Carl," Connor called out.

As she dodged the bullet she heard a car start and guessed it was the one waiting for Carl. For a split second she was torn, then Seth and Ashley came out of the scrub behind the man. "Take care of him." She shoved him towards Ashley, running in the direction of the car. It was still in the same place, the engine idling. But that didn't mean it would stay there.

"What's going on?" Seth ran after her.

"What about the men?"

"Ashley and Connor can take care of them. What are you doing?"

"The getaway vehicle started its engine."

"Where is it?"

"Straight ahead of us. It hasn't moved yet."

Seth pointed to the right. "You go that way and I'll head to the left. We'll cut it off so it can't get away."

"Okay." She veered to the right hearing a familiar tapping sound. When the tapping went unanswered, the man in the vehicle swore. With a burst of speed, she came out onto the road in front of the vehicle, drawing to a stumbling stop.

The man floored it and the vehicle came straight towards her, Seth coming out onto the road behind it. The man was going to escape. Again she thought of the picture Nicholas had added to the file. She was definitely going to say something to him about that.

Running towards the car, she jumped onto the bonnet and smashed her fist through the windscreen. The man reached for the gun on the seat beside him. Grabbing the steering wheel, she gave it a sharp turn. There was a crunching sound as the car hit a tree and she was thrown through the air, the breath knocked from her when she collided with the road.

Seth crouched over her. "Are you okay?"

She nodded, struggling to sit up. "He's still alive. The man in the car. He's trying to get out."

"I'll take care of him."

Her phone vibrated and she checked the screen once she was on her feet. It was Connor. "What's wrong?"

"I can smell blood on the breeze."

She looked down at herself. She was fine. Probably had a few bruises, but there was certainly no blood. Which surprised her since she'd smashed the windscreen. "I'm okay. I'm not so sure about the driver though." She watched as Seth pulled him out the side window he'd smashed. The front end of the car was crumpled and the door didn't look like it could open.

"You got him?"

She thought of the moment when she'd jumped onto the bonnet. "Yeah." She still found it hard to believe she'd actually done that.

"So what do we do with these guys?"

"I don't know. I'll ask Seth." She strode to where he'd dumped the man on the road, pointing his own gun at him. He looked up at her approach. "What should Connor and Ashley do with the four guys they've got?"

"Tell them to bring them here. I'll get in touch with Nicholas." Seth took one of the earpieces from his pocket and turned it on.

She relayed his message, disconnecting when

Connor said he'd be with them shortly. She took the gun Seth handed her and kept it trained on the man.

"Are you there, Nick?" Seth took out his phone and opened an app to find out the GPS coordinates.

"Don't you ever do that to me again. I'm meant to be your team leader. I've spent the past hour lying to everyone on your behalf."

Seth glanced towards Connor who came out of the bush and dumped an unconscious man at his feet before disappearing back into the bush. "We're waiting for you to collect the rest of these men." He read off the coordinates.

Gina kept her gaze on their prisoner as she waited for Nicholas' reply. There was a lengthy silence before it came.

"You have Carl?"

"Yes."

"He's alive?"

"All seven of them are alive. Two of them are already with the searchers."

"I know about those two. It went out over all the channels." Again there was a lengthy silence before Nicholas spoke. "You caught the rest of them?"

"Isn't that what you wanted us to do?"

This time it was Ashley who came out of the bush. She dropped an unconscious man next to the first one. "You talking to Nicky? Tell him I said hi." She waved to them before she ran back into the bush.

"We'll be there shortly." There was a pause before Nicholas continued. "Do not turn off the earpiece."

Gina couldn't help laughing. The man she held the gun on launched himself from the ground at her. Not expecting the move, the gun was knocked from her hand. He tried to reach the gun first. She tackled him before he managed, his head connecting hard with the road. He lay there unmoving. Scrambling to her feet, she listened for his heart beat. Relief rushed through her when she heard it.

Seth picked up the gun. "Sorry. I guess I should have rendered him unconscious."

"I don't know, it seems kind of wrong doing that to everyone."

"It's got to be better than killing them. And safer than knocking them out."

Ashley and Connor came out of the bush with the last two men. Dropping her man with the rest of them, Ashley dusted off her hands and surveyed the scene. "You know, I think we need handcuffs."

Before Gina could ask what had happened to Douglas' handcuffs, the chopper she'd been listening to as it came closer, landed on the road, a searchlight turned in their direction. Nicholas climbed out and strode towards them.

Ashley laughed when he reached them. "You know, Nicky, you shouldn't make faces. The wind might change and you'll be stuck looking like that."

Seth held out the four earpieces. "We won't be needing these again. No spying on us, remember?"

Nicholas jammed them in his pocket. "You need to learn how to work as part of a team."

Gina was surprised at the amount of anger in his voice. She frowned as she tried to figure out what his vital signs were telling her. His tone of voice, his heartbeat and his breathing all reminded her of something.

"We already know how to work as a team." Seth made a gesture that encompassed the four of them. "We are a team."

Nicholas pointed towards the unconscious men lying on the road around them. "These are professional killers. You lot are children. Were you trying to get yourselves killed taking off alone like that?"

Gina finally figured it out, crossing the distance between her and Nicholas. "We're a lot less fragile than you think. You didn't have to worry about us." He had reminded her of her mum.

"I wasn't worried about you. If you get yourselves killed, my job is on the line."

Gina smiled, glad he couldn't see it. She decided not to call him on his lie. He'd been worried. But she doubted he was going to admit it. Besides, she could hear vehicles coming closer and one of the prisoners was starting to regain consciousness. "If you say so. Nicky."

Ashley smothered a laugh.

"Carl is starting to stir," Seth said.

Ashley's hand curled into a fist. "Want me to knock him out?"

"No." Nicholas drew a gun and took a step away from Gina to point it towards Carl. "That won't be necessary."

"Do you think we can call in somewhere on the way home and grab something to eat?" Connor asked.

"I doubt we'd find parking for the chopper," Nicholas said dryly.

"I'm starved too," Ashley said. "You know you could hover above a takeaway joint and throw out some ropes. We can climb down, grab food and climb back up."

Nicholas stared at her a moment.

"You're making one of those faces again. Although not as bad as the last one," Ashley said.

Nicholas shook his head several times before he turned his attention back to Carl who was now sitting up. "On your feet."

Carl made a production of rising to his feet as several dark coloured vehicles pulled up nearby.

"Knife!" Seth shouted.

Hearing the blade whiz through the air towards Nicholas, Gina rushed forward to grab the blade. Her hand wrapped around it just before it reached his chest. She heard Connor crash into Carl and behind her was the sound of running feet. Her gaze met Nicholas'. His heart raced along with his breath and he held himself still. Unnaturally still.

It was Connor who spoke first. "Now who's bleeding?"

Nicholas reached out and wrapped his hand around her wrist, turning it before he removed the knife from her hand. "Not fragile?"

She wanted to argue his words, but pain hit her as the night air touched the wound. It was all she could do to remain standing and keep her breath and gaze steady.

Seth took the knife from Nicholas as the prisoners were rounded up. "I believe this is ours." He handed it over to Connor before he pulled Gina's hand from Nicholas' grip, closing it. "There's barely a scratch."

Nicholas remained silent a moment before he nodded. "All of you in the chopper. I'll wrap things up here and get you home."

"Does that mean no takeaway?" Ashley asked. She and Connor grumbled good naturedly as they got in the chopper.

It was a silent trip back to Nicholas' car. Gina kept her hand closed. The pain ebbed and the skin around the wound started to tighten as it healed. By the time Nicholas had driven them home, Seth's earlier words were now true.

Nicholas pulled up at the front door and got out of the car with them. "Gina, do you have a moment?"

She stopped at the front door. The sun had risen, clearly showing her Nicholas' expression. She tried to figure it out and wished she had Seth's ability to zoom in on things. "Yeah." She handed her balaclava to Seth. They'd all removed them once they were in the car.

"You want me to stick around?" Seth's voice was a whisper meant for her ears only.

She shook her head slightly and listened as the three of them went inside. "What's wrong?"

Nicholas crossed the distance between them.

"Thank you. I didn't expect that. Not after you'd finished telling me you're a team. Just the four of you."

She struggled to think of something to say.

He reached for her hand and opened it up to stare at her bloodstained palm. "I thought it was worse. Especially with all that blood."

Tempted to tell him the truth, she drew her hand away. "We're not as fragile as you think."

He stared at her a moment longer before he nodded. He started to turn away, then faced her again. "I won't put it in the report." His gaze dropped briefly to her hand before meeting her gaze.

"Thank you." She watched as he walked to his car. When he'd driven away, she went inside to find Seth waiting for her.

"Is everything okay?"

She nodded, wrapping her arms around him and resting her head on his shoulder.

"In that case, how about we talk about the fact you took off when you were meant to wait for me."

Gina pulled away from him, grinning. "How about we discuss getting our own earpieces instead. But not here. Connor and Ashley have food ready for us."

Chapter Thirty-Seven

Gina heard her name spoken at the front of the school. She glanced towards her teacher and began to carefully pack up her gear, not wanting to draw her attention. The PA system crackled and she paused to listen to the expected message. "Gina Lancione. Report to the office please."

She gathered the rest of her gear together and at a nod from the teacher rose to her feet, heading for the door. She ignored the whispered speculations as she walked through her classmates. It was normal now. During the three weeks she'd been back at school, people had been uncertain how to treat her. They whispered and gossiped, trying to understand and coming nowhere near the truth. In fact, some of the rumours were so far from any possible truth they were laughable.

Gina grinned as she turned a corner to see Connor

push away from the wall he leaned against. "You waiting for me?"

"I could smell you coming."

"You do realise most people would take that as an insult."

Connor laughed. "Good thing you're not most people." He draped his arm around her shoulders as they walked towards the office together. "There's a party this weekend. You want to go to it with me?"

"I thought you'd be taking Ashley."

"I can take both of you, can't I?" He eyed her up and down with an exaggerated leer.

With a grin, Gina shoved Connor away from her. "Sleaze."

"I'm gonna invite Lilly too. So… do you want to come?"

Gina shook her head. "Nah. Not my scene. Too many drunken idiots."

"I'll convince you one day." He stopped at the office door and pulled it open, stepping back to let her enter first.

The woman behind the counter rose as she saw them. "You both made good time. Someone is here to take you for another therapy session." She gestured towards Nicholas who stood off to one side. He wore his usual black suit and Ashley still hadn't managed to convince him to add dark sunglasses to the outfit.

Gina nodded. "Did we have a session planned? I can't recall one." She knew they didn't.

Nicholas smiled easily. "No. One of your friends is having coping issues today. We thought it would be best to make it a group session. Your principal has excused you for the rest of the day and your parents have been informed."

It was only that she knew him so well that she could pick up that nearly every word was a lie. "I've got to get some stuff from my locker first," Gina said.

Nicholas nodded. "I'll meet both of you out the front."

Connor and Gina walked quietly to their lockers, which weren't far from each other. When she had her gear, she leaned back against her locker and stared at Connor. "I hate it when we get no notice."

"You hate it when you do get notice," Connor said.

Gina smiled reluctantly. "Okay. Fine. But it annoys me. I always worry about what they're going to expect of us."

"Come on. Or we'll all get another lecture from Nick's boss about how long it takes us to get to the office. And quit worrying. Nick's doing okay by us."

Connor grinned. "I bet it's because he's grateful you saved his life. Or it might be because you helped him hook up with Audrey."

Gina couldn't resist returning his grin. Ashley had tried convincing her to start up a dating agency. She said they'd make a killing because they'd always get it right. Gina was happy to stick with her one success. Twice might be pushing it.

A dark four-wheel-drive was parked at the front gates and they climbed in the back. Ashley was in the front next to Nicholas. Gina smiled at Seth in greeting as she buckled up. He shrugged at the question in her eyes and she faced forward, wondering what would be asked of them this time.

Nicholas pulled out onto the road. "Ashley, there's a folder at your feet. We need help to find a child that was kidnapped."

"Isn't that usually a police matter?" Ashley opened up the folder.

Gina leaned forward to see the glossy photo at the front of the paperwork. She stared at a girl of about eight with large blue eyes, plaited brown hair and a lopsided grin. Her arm was wrapped around the neck of a shaggy white dog with a tongue hanging out of its mouth. "Why us?"

"Because they're not looking for a monetary ransom. Her father is in a military research facility."

Gina took the photo Ashley handed her, glancing at the page of information Ashley held in her other hand. She stared at the innocent, happy face. This was something she could do. She looked over to Seth, when he took one of her hands, and smiled back at him.

"Defender." The word was a whisper for Gina's ears only.

She nodded, her gaze meeting Seth's. So far they'd been used for surveillance, tracking and a few more captures. Maybe she could stop worrying about what would be expected of them and start enjoying her new life. And it was a new life. Her mum had finally stopped wanting to visit every other day and was starting to accept the fact she and Seth were dating.

Todd was teaching them how to fight and each weekend he dragged them away for an afternoon to teach them something else. Evasive driving, abseiling and diving had been introduced. Eventually they'd learn more about each of those techniques, but he wanted to cover the basics in a lot more things first. He'd mentioned something about parachutes yesterday. Gina wasn't sure she was ready for that step.

Nicholas interrupted her thoughts. "We'll need an answer within the hour. We have to move on this fast. Her father has forty-eight hours to hand over his research notes."

Ashley gave Gina the pages she was finished with. "Poor kid."

Gina glanced through the overview of the case. She turned to Seth who nodded and then Connor who watched them. He gave a nod too. "Ashley?"

Ashley turned in the seat to look at them. She grinned. "Could be fun."

Connor laughed. "You say that about any possible fight."

Ashley made a face at him. "So do you. Anything's got to be better than surveillance. Not that we can help much with that."

"We'll get her back," Gina said quietly.

"Yeah." Ashley's fist punched the air. "Let's go beat up the bad guys."

Gina grinned as Ashley and Connor started to talk rapidly, discussing fighting techniques. She looked over to Seth and laughed as she noticed he had his smart phone out and was looking between it and the case notes. He glanced up at her and smiled before he returned his attention to the phone.

Gina linked her arm through his, so he had his

hands free, and leaned against him. She looked past him out the window and noticed they were nearly at the local headquarters. Weeks ago she'd worried about what she'd do with her future, or even if she had a future. Now her future surrounded her with possibilities. She stared at each of her companions. Friends and possibilities. Maybe she owed Douglas a thank you for bringing them all together. She should ask Nicholas if he had a grave or a wall niche somewhere. The least she could do was leave a flower for him. Her lips curved into a smile. Even if he probably would have taken it the wrong way.

Ashley glanced back at her. "What are you thinking of?"

"We owe Douglas a flower on his grave. If he has one."

Ashley laughed. "Why? So we can throw the flower at it and say, screw you, Douggie. We survived and you didn't."

Nicholas winced. "Must you mangle everyone's name?"

"Yep. But that's okay, Nicky. I know you really love it."

Gina listened, but didn't hear Nicholas start his calming routine. She smiled. Yeah, they were definitely growing on him.

"Heaven forbid," Nicholas muttered and for a moment Gina thought she'd spoken aloud until she realised he'd answered Ashley.

Yep, it was a fact. They were definitely growing on him.

Free Ebook

Subscribe to Avril's newsletter to receive a free ebook. This ebook is exclusive to those on her mailing list. To find out more about this offer visit: http://www.avrilsabine.com/free-ebook/

*

We value your privacy and will not sell, rent, exchange or loan your email address to third parties. Your information is confidential and you are under no obligation to remain on the mailing list and can unsubscribe at any time.

Acknowledgements

Thanks to the usual crew, especially Mum, Cat and Lloyd. You lot are amazing.

To The Reader

If you enjoyed this book, why not consider leaving a review to help other readers discover it too? Reader engagement is one of the few ways that lets an author know readers want more books in a particular series or genre. So leave a review and tell friends, not only about this book but also about other ones you've enjoyed, so you can continue to enjoy books by your favourite authors for years to come.

Dreams are meant to be lived,

Avril.

About The Author

Avril is an Australian author who lives with her family on acreage in South East Queensland. She writes mostly young adult speculative fiction, but has been known to dabble in other genres. You can find more information about her at her website www.avrilsabine.com where you can also subscribe to her newsletter to be kept informed about new releases, current projects, blog posts and exclusive news.

Titles By Avril Sabine

Stories about strong characters and characters who discover their strengths.

SERIES

Assassins Of The Dead- Young Adult Fantasy/ Paranormal

Book 1: Dark Blade

Book 2: Dragon Touched

Book 3: Society Against Vampires

Book 4: King's Request

Book 5: Duke's Courier

Book 6: Necromancer Resistance

Dragon Blood- Young Adult Urban Fantasy Romance (5 book series)

Book 1: Pliethin

Book 2: Wyvern

Book 3: Surety

Book 4: Knight

Book 5: Mage

Dragon Mage- Young Adult Urban Fantasy Romance

(Series two of Dragon Blood series)

Book 1: Promise

Book 2: Betrayed

Dragon Blood Chronicles- Young Adult Urban Fantasy Romance

(Companion stand alone series to Dragon Blood)

Book 1: Oath

Book 2: Betrayed

Guardians Of The Round Table- Young Adult Fantasy LitRPG

(Co-written with Storm and Rhys Petersen)

Book 1: Dexterity Fail

Book 2: Goblin Boots

Book 3: Singed Feathers

Book 4: Frog Mage

Book 5: Crystal Mine

Book 6: Cursed Harp

Rosie's Rangers- Young Adult Western Steampunk

(6 book series)

Book 1: Justice

Book 2: Vengeance

Book 3: Treachery

Book 4: Accused

Book 5: Wanted

Book 6: Corruption

Mark Of Kings- Children's Fantasy

(Upper middle grade/preteen)

(4 book series)

Book 1: The Arena

Book 2: The Island

Book 3: The Assassin

Book 4: The King

STAND ALONE SERIES

***Demon Hunters- Young Adult Urban Fantasy/
Horror/Romance***

Book 1: Blood Sacrifice

Book 2: Retribution

Book 3: Tainted

Book 4: Premonition

Book 5: Cursed

Book 6: Feud

Book 7: Extrication

Plea Of The Damned- Young Adult Urban Fantasy/Paranormal

(6 book series)

Book 1: Forgive Me Lucy

Book 2: Forgive Me Aiden

Book 3: Forgive Me Jena

Book 4: Forgive Me Kobe

Book 5: Forgive Me Marti

Book 6: Forgive Me Dawson

Realms Of The Fae- Young Adult Urban Fantasy Romance

The Sword (short story)

Heart Of Stone

Book 1: A Debt Owed

Book 2: Marked By The Hunt

Book 3: The Magic Collector

Book 4: An Unexpected Betrayal

Book 5: Imprisoned By Iron

Fairytales Retold (Short Stories)

Snow-White And Rose-Red

The Twelve Brothers

The Light Princess

Beauty And The Beast

Sleeping Beauty

Aschenputtel

The Golden Bird

The Frog Prince

The Death Of Koshchei The Deathless

Myths And Legends Retold (Short Stories)

Ion, Son Of Apollo

Sir Gawain And The Maid With The Narrow Sleeves

Princess Ilse, The Giant's Daughter

YOUNG ADULT NOVELS

Young Adult Fantasy Romance

Elf Sight

Earth Bound

Young Adult Urban Fantasy

Stone Warrior (with elements of romance)

The Jungle Inside

Young Adult Contemporary Romance

Through Your Eyes

The Ugly Stepsister

Perfect Little Princess

Young Adult Contemporary/Paranormal

Whispers In The Dark (with elements of romance and same sex relationships)

Over Too Soon (with elements of romance)

Young Adult Sci-Fi

Experiment X-One-Six (Urban Sci-Fi/Superheroes)

An Endless Dawn (Post Apocalyptic Sci-Fi)

CHILDREN'S BOOKS

Dragon Lord (Preteen/early teens) (Fantasy)

The Irish Wizard (Upper middle grade) (Urban Fantasy)

SHORT STORIES

Urban Fantasy

Eternally Late

Dealings With Joe

Glimpses (short story in That Moment When Anthology)

Contemporary

The Brat Next Door

Fantasy LitRPG

(Set in the same world as Guardians Of The Round Table Series)

Tales Of Inadon 1: The Disc (Co-written with Storm and Rhys Petersen) (short story in Game On! Anthology)

Post Apocalyptic Sci-Fi

Compulsive Directive

NONFICTION

A Year Of Weekly Writing Exercises (Creative Writing)

Cooking For Families With Allergies (Cooking) (Co-written with Storm Petersen)

Tell Me A Story, Grandma (Memoir)

Overview Of Independently Publishing A Book (How To)

For the most up to date details on available titles visit:

www.avrilsabine.com/books/bibliography

Disclaimer

This is a work of fiction. Names, characters, businesses, places, events and incidents are either the products of the author's imagination or used in a fictitious manner. Any resemblance to actual persons, living or dead, or actual events is purely coincidental. The opinions expressed or beliefs held are those of the characters and should not be assumed to be the opinions or beliefs of the author.